THE **Vicious Circle**

THE **Vicious Circle**

KERWIN MCLAUGHLIN

XULON PRESS

Xulon Press
2301 Lucien Way #415
Maitland, FL 32751
407.339.4217
www.xulonpress.com

Paperback ISBN-13: 978-1-6628-3240-6
eBook ISBN-13: 978-1-6628-3241-3

TABLE OF CONTENTS

A SPECIAL PLACE IN HELL

———————◆———————

The hundreds of angry voices lose their individuality and trans-morph into a roar of an angry mob that reverberates off the buildings and sounds like a giant lion getting closer. JERRY KEENE could hear that angry mob well before he got to the Federal building and when he saw the mob of screaming people getting pushed back by a phalanx of armed soldiers he realized he wasn't the only one who was unhappy.

Jerry had to be careful, he had just bought new tennis shoes with velcro straps instead of laces, and they weren't broken in yet. He could only shuffle his feet so a crack or uneven pavement might cause him to fall and at his age that would definitely lead to broken bones. Nonetheless, he had to get to the front of the line to speak to a soldier. He was a special case. He had a letter to be there, not like these complainers looking for a handout. "Why weren't they at work?" he asked himself. They were all able bodied and young. He didn't know what countries they were all from but he could see he was the only one with ashes on his forehead and the only one with a letter. "I bet they never even had a hot dog at a baseball game or even a slice of apple pie." They certainly didn't grow up the way he did.

He fought his way to the front of the crowd. He was, by far, the oldest one there. You would think that would offer him some respect, but no. When he got to the front he tried talking to the SOLDIER but was met with a rifle pushed across his chest.

"But I got a letter!" He yelled while waving the paper.

The soldier snatched it out of Jerry's hand a held it straight up over his head. A nattily dressed EXPEDITER came running over and the Soldier handed it to him from behind. He unfolded the wrinkled paper and scanned it before waving Jerry through. He guided him through the glass doors and motioned him to go through without saying a word.

He was led into a room where the noise from outside was drowned out by the constant clattering of keyboards coming from an ocean of cubicles. When a hand raised up from one of those cubicles to waive him over he pounced on it, moving as fast as those new tennis shoes would take him.

The young clerk took the wrinkled paper from Jerry and did her best to straighten it out even dragging it over the edge of her desk with both hands. She read it thoroughly, never taking her eyes off of it, as Jerry pleaded his case in aggravating detail pointing out who he was, what he did for a living, and how he was wronged. Though she was doing her best to help him Jerry didn't feel he was getting the treatment or eye contact he deserved.

"I want to see the boss!" he blurted out.

She put down the paper and with a smile chuckled," Sir, you can't just 'see the boss,' besides the red flag was put on by the company that handles your pension, not us."

"Who the hell are they!?"

Jerry couldn't believe his eyes when he got there. Not because of the grandeur of the building that Architectural Digest called "The Ivory Tower" but that there was no angry crowd protesting or trying to get in or rows of soldiers ready to put someone down, just an immaculate lobby and classical music. "Here is where they should be protesting," he thought to himself.

Like Jerry, the man at the front desk was a retired cop. Though he was much younger and had never met this old man wearing velcro strap sneakers, a windbreaker over a rolled collar tee shirt, and khaki pants, he could tell he was once "on the job."

When Jerry told him he was there to "see the boss" the first words that popped into his head were, "You gotta be kidding me. But for a retired cop, what's one phone call?" He tapped a couple of numbers on the phone, told the person who answered who was there to see them and his jaw dropped at the reply. He almost missed the cradle hanging up the phone.

"I don't believe this but they are going to see you." He told Jerry as he typed a temporary name badge for him, "You, young man, have just gotten the golden ticket."

The elevator shot up at super high speed and this made Jerry nervous. He braced himself for a sudden stop that would put pressure on his spine but it came to a smooth stop and opened up to the luxurious offices of FINANCIAL EDGE INVESTMENTS. It was a long day for Jerry and he was getting too cranky and tired to appreciate the beautiful setting or the even more beautiful RECEPTIONIST that brought him lime-infused water and sat him down on a plush sofa in front of a big-screen TV that played a commercial.

A group of small children, perfectly racially mixed, with an equal amount of exceptionally good-looking girls and boys, all with smiles on their faces, playing kickball.

VOICEOVER: Did you ever have one kid take the ball and go home because he wasn't happy because he wasn't winning? It's usually the rich kid. But what can you do? It's his ball.

The children stop smiling as the one boy scoops up the ball and angrily runs away.

VOICEOVER: Now there's Financial Edge Services- we give you the ball.

A limousine pulls up to the sad-faced children sitting on the curb and ED, looking handsome in a nice suit, comes out of the back holding a new kickball and tosses it to one of the girls.

VOICEOVER: Don't like the way currencies are being manipulated? We have our own cryptocurrency backed by real-world commodities and precious metals.

The kids resume playing and now a Kid With Crutches joins the game taking over for the rich kid.

VOICEOVER: Don't like the hedge funds shorting stocks? We have a member/investor-only trading desk where you buy, sell and trade stocks with other business owners and entrepreneurs. If they win, you win.

The Kid With Crutches kicks the ball and hobbles around the bases.

VOICEOVER: Don't like the big boys insider trading? All our information is shared across all of our platforms with all our members.

The Kid With Crutches falls down running to first. All the other kids freeze, not sure what to do until the Pitcher from the other team helps him up and dusts him off.

Ed now speaks directly into the camera. It's the same voice we've been hearing.

ED: The Big Guys have all the money and all the power. But at Financial Edge, we believe money is freedom and knowledge is power. Ask your local Financial Edge Consultant how your business can be a member/investor and have yourself a ball!

The Rich Kid clutches his ball and is crying as he looks out the window and sees an ice cream truck parked behind the limo and Ed and the kids are all eating ice cream.

And after watching this for the twentieth or thirtieth time Jerry had had it. He threw his empty cup at the screen and launch himself, surprisingly quickly, off the sofa.

"How many times do I have to watch this God Damn thing! I bet you play this Damn thing to give your boss time to high tail it out of here," he yelled out at no one in particular, "because he's afraid!"

"What am I afraid of?" a voice asks innocently.

Standing before Jerry was Ed, the same smiling suit and tie that sold you that hogwash while giving little kids ice cream and a kickball. But he's different up close in real life. He can be quite intimidating or charming depending on what the situation called for. In this instance, he was a little of both. At that moment, as he stands in front of him with a warm smile with his hand out Jerry realized the notion of him being afraid of anything is utterly ludicrous.

"Mr. Keene, I'm sorry to keep you waiting."

"Hello, Mr...uh-"

"Just call me Ed. Come on in."

The office is large and sparse but still impressive. He leads Jerry to a clear glass desk with nothing more than a phone, a laptop, and a file folder on it. He motions Jerry to sit in an ergonomic chair while he walks around the clear glass desk. Jerry notices another big screen on the wall behind the desk that shows a moving painting. It almost hypnotizes him but since his default setting is grumpy and angry he gets right into it.

"You people cut off my social security, cut off my pension, denied my medical claims and put a lien on my home and I want to know why!"

"You want a beer? I'm going to have one. I like Stella but you look like a Bud in a can kind of guy."

"Don't act like you know me-"

Ed raises his pointing finger to tell him to hold on one second and then uses that same finger to dive-bomb down onto the intercom button of his phone, "One Stella in a glass and a Budweiser in a can please."

"You think you're smooth like a thief in the night," Jerry spits out through his teeth.

Ed uses that same finger again to press a button on his laptop and simultaneously a photo appears on the large screen behind him of Jerry at a family function at his beach house holding a can of Bud. The photo is from his wife's social media. More family pictures flash on the big screen in a slide show.

Though he stays calm and monotone in his delivery rage fills his eyes as he speaks," I know everything about you. You were a cop for over forty years, your wife, Eve, was a nurse and you had one daughter named Mary Margaret."

The Receptionist brings the beers in on a silver platter and leaves the platter on the desk and walks out without saying a word. Ed presses a button and the slide show switches to Maggie Keene's Facebook page showing pictures of her from college parties.

"Your daughter grew up, got good grades, and got into a good school. But while in school, she got caught up with some rich party boy who got her pregnant and got her hooked on opioids that he sold to other college kids."

Jerry, coming to tears, "My sweet little Maggie."

Then the screen shows images from other people's Facebook pages that mention Eve Keene with posts that say PLEASE PRAY FOR EVE.

"Your wife, the nurse, gets a call to come into work to cover someone who called out sick on the night shift. It turned out the woman she worked with went out the night before and got drastically sick when someone slipped her a roofie. It was a rainy night and she got side-swiped by a hit-and-run driver. She is now a quadriplegic and your daughter currently lives in a crack house in Long Beach. All you need are a few blisters and you'd be Job. So what does that make me? God or the Devil?"

Jerry, head bowed down, doesn't look up until the silence gets a little too long as if Ed expects him to answer the question. But Ed doesn't wait for a reply.

"Let me show you the Devil."

Ed presses another button on his laptop and the large screen fills with an extreme close-up of a red face that is so distorted, that at first glance, does look like the Devil himself. At first, Jerry is terrified as the picture blown up on the screen looks like a hideous demon. But, as he looks longer, he sees that the face is covered red in blood and that the distortions come from a brutal beating that's been given to the person. And as he looks deeper he recognizes who the person is but before he can say anything Ed presses the volume button to play audio and confirm his suspicions.

The video camera pulls back and frames out the picture of a man bound by duct tape to a leather chair. He's an older man, dressed in a sharkskin three-piece suit with the jacket off and the shirt, tie, and vest covered in his blood. Both his eyes are swollen shut from constant beating and his moans are so loud and so guttural they could be mistaken for a demon beast's growl.

The picture shakes a little bit and zooms in and out as the person taping, not seen on camera, sets the camera up on a tripod.

ED (on video): What is your name?

IACOPO: Iacopo G-G-Gunnulli.

ED: Did you order the killing of Eddie Gennaro and his wife Lucia?

IACOPO: Yes.

ED: To whom did you pay to kill them?

IACOPO: I don't remember- some crooked cop.

ED: Do you want me to shut the camera off?

IACOPO: Keene- the cop's name was Keene.

ED: Jerry Keene?

Iacopo nods yes.

Ed shuts off the tape. "Twenty years ago, you were hired by that scumbag to kill my father and mother."

"This can't be..."

"You knocked on my door, in your police uniform, acting as an officer of the law, and told my parents you had an arrest warrant and my father let you in and you gunned them down. But that wasn't all."

Jerry in shock mumbles, "I heard a bump."

"What?"

"You weren't supposed to be home. Your mother was supposed to take you to Easter mass, your sister was in the passion play, and then she was supposed to go straight to your aunt's house for an Easter egg hunt. I was just a beat cop and that was my neighborhood. I used a silencer and was heading out the back door when I heard a bump."

"My sister had just locked me in the closet and I was banging to get out. She heard you coming up the stairs and dragged me out to the window. She told me to jump but I was too scared. I turned back for her and she pushed me out the window just as you fired."

"She saved your life. Your screaming and crying alerted the neighbors and they all came running over. I slipped out the back and I took the call. I was the first on the scene. I was the hero who chased the bad guys away," Jerry interlocks his fingers to plead, "I have a granddaughter. Who's gonna take care of my granddaughter?"

"I am a benevolent God."

Ed sits back, takes a sip of his beer, and lets Jerry sob for a moment before going into his sales pitch. " I'm a God with trust issues, thanks to you. I don't trust any institutions including the institution of marriage. I have a thing against pushy women because my sister pushed me out of a window and I have a thing against family because, well, you know my family. But I don't want to die alone. So here's what I'm gonna do."

Ed pulls the manilla file folder close to him, opens it, and pulls out some of the contents.

He lays the papers out on the desk facing Jerry.

"The Senior Assisted Suicide Act allows for any person or persons over the age of sixty-five to end their life peaceably and all of their assets, including your pension, will go into a tax-free account and held for the descendent or descendants of their choosing and be held until that person's twenty-first birthday. I will personally invest that money so that when your granddaughter Robin turns twenty-one she will be wealthy beyond your dreams."

'Rainbow," Jerry added, "My daughter calls her Rainbow."

"I will see to it that your wife is sent to a retirement home with round-the-clock care so that she may live out the rest of her days in comfort and that your daughter gets the help she needs. Do this, and this video will never leave this laptop."

"And what do you want in return?"

"I want to adopt your granddaughter."

"Are you insane?!"

"I give you my word that I will never harm her physically, mentally, or emotionally. I will love her as if she was my own. She'll live a rich kid's life in a penthouse and not the daughter of a junkie bouncing from foster home to foster home. If you award custody to another family member, I will go after them the way I went after you."

"What are you? Some kind of faggot or you can't get it up?"

"No, but you will become one in prison if I release this tape. If your police brethren let you live long enough to make it to a trial."

Jerry, tried to hold back his tears, "Why are you doing this?"

"Poetic Justice, really. You took my family so I'm going to take yours."

Ed lays out the paperwork in front of Jerry and places a pen beside it. Jerry scratches his name without even looking at the documents. When finished, he threw the pen down.

"There's a special place in hell for people like you."

ANOTHER GOD DAMN
REDEMPTION

There was a long, slow-moving line of parishioners that snaked in the cathedral and out. The people coming out had black smudges on their foreheads. There was no mass, the people funneled in, saw the priest, the priest stuck his thumb in ashes, made the sign of the cross on their forehead, and said," Remember you are dust and into dust, you shall return."

As Edward dissected the long line of elderly people and immigrants the young priest and the elder Bishop Tammany asked themselves the same question everyone else did, "Who is this guy?" Both the Bishop and the young Father David were busy giving out ashes when they noticed this rather large but dashing young man in a nice suit standing by the confessional. As Father David will tell the story years from now, he would swear the clothes were billowing as if they were flowing in the wind.

ANOTHER GOD DAMN REDEMPTION

Father David sidled over to Bishop Tammany, who had taken time from his important duties to give ashes to the congregants, to address him, "Bishop Tammany, who is that man over there by the confessional? Shall I tell him this is not the time for confession?"

"There is always time to save a soul."

Edward smiled at the Bishop as he approached and both men entered the confessional at their respective ends. As the Bishop sat down the screen was slid open and he could tell the man was standing in the confessional. To see a man, over six feet tall, standing in a small space like that was outputting, to say the least.

"Why don't you kneel down?" the Bishop asked.

"I will not do that."

Seeing that he was a big man and athletically built, the Bishop thought he suffered from some sort of knee injury and moved on, "What are you here to confess?"

"I destroyed a man today. I ruined his life ."

"Did you do it on purpose?" the Bishop asked incredulously, "Did you think about your actions?"

"I've thought of nothing else for over twenty years and today was the culmination of my life's work."

"Bow your head in contrition," the Bishop ordered.

"I will not do that."

"The Lord gives forgiveness to all who seek it but remorse is needed to be forgiven. The Lord never lacks mercy it's only those who lack remorse.

"I don't have remorse for what I've done."

"Then why did you come here if you don't seek forgiveness?"

"Today was the greatest achievement of my life and I had no one to share it with. I just wanted to tell someone." Edward leaves the confessional.

"WAIT!," the Bishop jumps out of his seat and goes out into the church. Edward is gone completely. The people and the other priests are too busy with Ash Wednesday to notice his leaving. It was as if he was never there.

The Bishop pushes people out of his way, albeit politely to get outside the church just to catch a glimpse of this man. He looks up and down the street and flaps his arms in frustration, never seeing the black limo turning the corner.

Once inside the limo, Ed's phone rings. It's The Receptionist from the office.

RECEPTIONIST: Bernie Drier called, he wants a redemption on his investment and said he needs it in two days.

ED: How much is it?

RECEPTIONIST: A hundred and thirty-four thousand.

ED: OK, thanks.

He ends the call. He had thought about putting a suspension on redemptions but was afraid it would send up red flags, he wanted people to think he had cash on hand.

ED: Another God Damn Redemption!

POETIC JUSTICE

There was an angry mob of well-to-do young couples outside the Gastropub when Ed got there to meet his childhood friend from boarding school, Jay Bruce, for dinner. At first he thought it was some social justice group protesting fancy food or eating meet but as he got closer he thought they were too well dressed. They were pacing around and stomping there feet. It was the hottest, most expensive restaurant in town but it was too cold to have to wait for a table just to eat dinner. Ed was concerned that Jay didn't make a reservation, Jay didn't seem like the type. But when Ed pushed his way to the entrance he learned that Jay definitely made a reservation.

A makeshift sign written in magic marker read CLOSED FOR A PRIVATE PARTY and scrawled just underneath were the words GO HOME :) which at first glance looked like they were written in blood but Ed later learned that Jay gave the hostess twenty bucks to use her red nail polish.

Ed could see the manager and The Hostess sheepishly staring at each other while beat red upwardly mobile faces were screaming at them on the other side of the door. When Ed went to the window he could see Jay, sitting at the middle table of an empty restaurant dining room just laughing his ass off at the wannabe diners cursing him out. Looking through the glass made Ed think he was looking at a colorful fish at the aquarium but the fish were watching you. When Jay sees Ed he waves him in, his arms flailing in just a grand gesture as if he was taxiing an airplane down the street. He motions to The Hostess to let Ed in.

The Hostess unlocked the door as the others tried to push their way through but with one look from Ed, they stopped and realized their fate. The Hostess took his overcoat and led him into the dining room. It had been a while since they saw each other and aside from the fact that his hair was thinning a little Jay looked the same. When Jay stands up to greet him is when Ed first gets a real up-close look at his funky red suit and dark paisley vest, that if forced to, could only be described as brightly colored western Gothic.

"Sit down, buddy! Glad you can make it!"

"Jay, what the hell is this?"

"I rented the place for the evening. Just me and you and I might have some friends stopping by."

"How much did this cost?"

"What difference does that make? It's only money," spoken by a man who doesn't need over a hundred thousand dollars in two days.

"It's worth every penny watching these idiots stomping around and screaming just trying to stay warm. It's dinner AND a show! GO TO ANOTHER RESTAURANT," he screams back at them before falling into maniacal laughter. He regains his breath and composure and turns on a dime to a sadistic-looking madman, "God forbid these HARPIES stay home and cook a meal."

Jay's mind was like a slot machine, you'd pull the lever and one second it would land on MANIACAL LUNATIC and the next spin would be SADISTIC MADMAN but now suddenly it landed on NORMAL, "We're here to celebrate, buddy. I just got a teaching gig with tenure!"

"Congratulations," Ed cheers raising a glass of water.

"My trust fund was contingent on me graduating, finding a job, and to quote/unquote making something of myself or some such thing my father wrote in his will. Jeez, Dad, I was an only child, I was going to get the money anyway, did you have to screw with me one last time from beyond the grave?"

The Hostess bends down, clutching her hands, trying not to reveal she is terrified, "Shall I get your waiter?"

"NONSENSE! I don't want some boorish unemployed actor trying to impress me because he memorized the specials. I believe in the presentation being just as important as the food and you (he takes a dramatic pause to leer) are a feast for the eyes! Now, would you be so kind as to bring over some champagne and whatever this fine young man will be having?"

"Champagne is fine."

"Aha! A little bubbly for my buddy! And you are, you know, you're my oldest and closest friend."

Ed really couldn't stand Jay. He is, as everyone in the restaurant had witnessed, a weirdo. The only reason Ed is here is that he needs that money. The fact that he laughs at his own jokes was cause enough for Ed to punch his lights out. "I mean really, who does that? How the hell can you crack yourself up?"

Though in a way, Ed was envious. If Ed could make himself laugh like a hyena all the time, between that and masturbating, there would be no need for Ed to ever leave his home.

"Did you ever think that I would graduate school much less become a professor?'

"You were definitely a madman."

"I wouldn't have survived it if it weren't for you."

"I hate bullies."

The champagne finally pops as The Hostess struggles to open a champagne bottle for the first time. "Perfect timing," Ed thought to himself. The last thing he wanted to do is go down memory lane, but it was inevitable. Hopefully, they can talk business.

"You and I were an odd pair, the greaseball and the theater geek, two kids, both of our parents gunned down and we were the only orphans. You were the only one who was cool to me. And so, my good fortune is your good fortune. I want to invest my inheritance with you."

"Thank God," Ed thought to himself, relieved more that Jay wasn't going to bring up any more of their childhood than about the money. He pretends to be surprised, "Oh yeah? How much?"

"The whole enchilada, minus this little get-together. You'll get the check next week. Now, enough business, let's eat! Hostess, bring us two of the chef's finest!"

Ed puts on a happy face but deep down is thinking to himself, "NEXT WEEK? What the hell good does it do me next week?"

"In case the chef asks," The Hostess nervously asks, "Is there anything you're in the mood for?" Jay's impish grin turns into an evil sneer, "Tell the chef to cook a meal that he would serve if his life depended on it being good."

"Oh and some breadsticks," Ed interjects.

"You always know the right thing to say at just the right time."

"Jay, ask me what's the most important thing in comedy."

Always up for a gag, Jay gets into character and plays along, "Ed, what's the most-

"Timing."

Jay almost falls out of his chair from laughing so hard. The laughing fit gives Ed time to contemplate what he really wants to do this evening. Does he flat out ask for money from Jay tonight, does he spend the evening getting him drunk enough to make it seem like it will be his idea to write Ed a check tonight, or should he bail on this whack job and go hunting? The drug dealers were out in force tonight.

The Hostess brings over some breadsticks. Jay grabs her arm.

"I'm having some lady friends stop by this evening and they'll be scantily clad and it's very cold out so as soon as you see them please let them in. They'll be about your age, maybe you know them. Do you go to state?"

"No."

"Shame."

"You hired some dancers?" Ed asks.

"Even better, a sorority of theater majors looking for an easy A. I told you they made me a professor of theater, right? They even gave me tenure at twenty-four. I can work there for the rest of my life and never get fired. They're paying me to mold young minds of mush and to plow through freshmen pussy."

"You are definitely going to make your parents proud,"
"Ed raises his champagne glass, hoping to get him to
drink so that he'll just shut up.

"Ahhh, to James and Bonnie Bruce, their love of theater
was their demise and became my devotion. It was my
eighth birthday when they took me to the theater and
were gunned down by a homeless man after seeing
Les Miserable. It's poetic justice, really."

Poetic Justice–the same term Ed used on Keene–
stops Ed in his tracks. Just the thought that these two
were alike made him suddenly ill...and angry.

"You know, Jay, I have a lot of friends in the police department, I handle their retirement fund. I looked into the
case, you know, to see if I could do something, you know,
with my family connections.

"Eddie! I didn't know you cared!"

"They told me there was no way that homeless guy
could've gotten his hands on a gun."

Jay shoots up out of his chair and throws his
napkin down on the table, "THE DANCING GIRLS
ARE HERE!" As he runs over to greet the girls, Ed lets
out a sigh.

"I can't believe he said poetic justice."

YOU STILL HAVE A SOUL

———————◆———————

Once the girls got there there was no use trying to talk to Jay so Ed left. Jay probably doesn't realize he left. Which was probably for the best. Ed doesn't like revisiting the past and hanging out with Jay it was inevitable, besides if something went down tonight Jay would testify that he was with him all night.

Jay usually asks if Ed had spoken to either Ben Oliver or Alexander Morgan. It's easy to keep track of them, they're both scions of wealthy families but to actually speak with them would be difficult. They probably don't want to speak to Ed anyway and they sure as hell don't want anything to do with Jay. They're partly the reason Ed keeps up the high finance charade to stay competitive with them. He can't have them do better in life than he does and he sure as hell won't give them the satisfaction of them finding out Ed was a fraud. Regardless of how well they do in life, the four of them will never be as good as Kyle Webb, the one boy who didn't make it back from that camping trip.

But Ed couldn't think about that now. He had hunting to do. Ed had become a creature of the night watching as he spent his evenings studying the workings of local drug dealers. He had gone as far to map out the territories of different drug dealers and he knew what soldiers were "clocking hours" and on what corners they did it on. He followed where they went after their "shifts" and all the money led to an apartment on the third floor of a six-floor walk up.

The apartment was leased to the welfare department but the guy who lived there was a Jamaican called SKA and a black man known throughout the neighborhood as SKEETER. On this night, they were watching a horror movie when they heard a noise coming from the hallway outside their door.

SKA motions with a head nod, "Yo, go check that shit out."

Skeeter pulls back the hammer on his gun and sticks his head out the door. He turns back to Ska and shakes his head "no." Ska points motioning him to go further down the hall. Skeeter goes out into the hallway letting the apartment door close behind him. Ska puts the movie back on and doesn't notice the large figure, dressed head to toe in black including a black ski mask come out of the bathroom and lock the deadbolt on the apartment door.

Ed moved so swiftly, so silently that Ska didn't know Ed was even there until he was on top of him.

"OH SHIT, OH SHIT, OH SHIT!" Ska then realizes, "Oh shit it's you, man. The Bump!"

"What?" Ed asks from behind the mask.

"You the Bump! Everyone in the hood has heard bout choo. All the players talk about you. You a legend, man. Niggas be gettin' out of the game cause you!"

Skeeter bangs on the door, "Yo, there's nothin' out here."

"Tell him to hold on."

"YO, chill man!"

Ska whispers, "Boys be chillin' in the crib and they hear a noise, they get up to go check it out, you got them lookin' the wrong way and then you roll up on them fools and you like BAM! I'm telling you, baby mammas be telling their kids to be scared of anything that goes "bump" in the night.

Skeeter is getting pissed, "YO MAN, let me in!"

"CHILL FOOL! It's late! Your gonna wake up the neighborhood!"

Ed demands, "Give me your money."

"I outta me thanking you. You put about half my competition out of biz."

Ed gets impatient, "You've got three seconds.

"It's in the bag!"

Ed grabs the gym bag and looks inside, "Where's the rest of it?"

"That's it!"

"Yo Ska, I'm out in my socks and you watching a horror movie?"

Ska sees that Ed takes out the gun that was in the bag.

"I ain't bullshitting! I gave some of the money to Black Amazon!"

"WHAT?"

"You ain't heard of Black Amazon? I thought you were down! You ain't from the hood, are you? This woman runs an underground store in the basement of the Southern Baptist church three blocks down from here. People in this hood can't go to stores using credit cards or swiping microchips implanted in they hands, EBT ain't shit any more People go to Black Amazon to get food, clothing, medicine, anything they can get and they pay what they can. We help out."

"Yeah, right!"

"I'm a drug dealer but I still got a soul. Ain't you?"

Ed is so angry and frustrated he punches Ska in the face knocking him out cold. He leaves going out the window and climbs the fire escape to the roof. Skeeter was still knocking when he left.

Ska was telling the truth. It wasn't hard to find the church, from the rooftops he could see the neon cross from three blocks away and traveled from rooftop to rooftop till he found a building tall enough that he can leap across the street and land on the other roof. There was a line that went down the ally between the church and the next building. He stayed on the roof and waited until 2 am for the last customer to leave pushing an old shopping cart filled with food, clothing, and children's books.

He came down and looked through the cellar window. He saw the tall black woman, she was light-skinned and noticed some kind of accent but he couldn't tell through the window if it was Brazilian or African. She had a nice ass so Ed was guessing Brazilian. She looked younger than Ed. There were three men total and all three of them were armed. Ed didn't like guns, they were too loud and messy and with the micro-stamping on bullets, they don't even need the gun to know who bought the bullet and where they bought it from. Ed mastered blades of all kinds. He made his own. He prided himself on being able to kill a man from twenty feet away by throwing one of his disks and slicing the jugular and you wouldn't hear anything until the victim hit the floor- you might hear a gurgle or two but it was silent and effective. He told himself that he was going to plant a story in the news saying his name was The Edge. He didn't like this Bump thing.

None of these people deserved to have their throats cut. They were helping people. He'd have to live up to his nickname to create diversions, separate them and then choke each one out. He'll make a noise, two of them will move toward it and one will go back toward the safe, that's the one he'll follow. Ed BANGS on the front door.

One of the guards yells, "We're closed! We close at two! Come back tomorrow night at ten!" The DOOR POUNDING continues totally ignoring him. Now he's pissed. "ARE YOU DEAF?"

He unlocks the door and throws it open and he is instantly met with a left hook aimed directly at the mid-point between his chin and his right mandible. That's where Ed's trainers told him was the human off button. Before he can hit the ground, Ed catches his slumping body and pulls the pistol from his waistband.

Ed drags his body inside with his right hand while pointing the gun at the other two with his left. Their hands shot up where Ed could see them without him asking to ask. They both then hold their guns up where he can see them. Ed tosses them a bag of large zip ties and a roll of duct tape. He points to the unconscious one, "Do him first and then do each other. Where's the safe?" They nod down the hall. "If you make a noise she dies."

She was still doing the books when she looked up from her ledger and saw a man dressed in black with a ski mask standing over her. She reaches for a baseball bat. He points the gun in her face.

"Don't."

She puts the bat down.

"Open the safe." As she does it Ed has to say, "For a woman your age, you have the heart of a lion. But I doubt you pay taxes so why bother keeping the books?"

The door to the safe is now open no more need for small talk.

"How much is in there?

"Over two hundred thousand." Ed still couldn't guess her accent.

"Take out a hundred and thirty-seven thousand and put it in this bag," he tosses her the bag he took from Ska.

"We started with nothing two years ago and now you're stealing everything from us?"

"You can start back up tomorrow with something."

"Am I supposed to be happy you're leaving us with some?," as she tosses him the bag.

He turns to walk out but then turns back around. Her eyes widen as she instantly regrets mouthing off when he was almost out of her life forever.

"YOU...still have your soul."

L'EFFET PAPILLON

———————❖———————

When Jerry Keene applied for Suicide Assistance, the Police Union hosted a memorial service in his honor that was sponsored by Financial Edge Investments. During the proceedings, Ed, who showed up just to pay his respects, was asked by the crowd to say a few words. He resisted at first, not being one to ham for the camera but relented nonetheless. He just wanted to "thank Officer Keene for his service" but then got so caught up in the emotion of it all announced to Jerry and everyone that he would like to adopt Jerry's granddaughter.

There wasn't a dry eye in the place and, with the help of the Financial Edge Public Relations Department, the media ran with it. GURU WITH A HEART OF GOLD was the headline in papers across the country and was the bottom third scrawl on cable news channels for months. A ploy to kiss up to the Policeman's Union ended up endearing Ed to the

world and making Robin a celebrity while still in dia-
pers. And Jerry, the honoree of the event, surrounded
by his brothers-in-blue that would've shot him like a
dog if the truth came out, never said a word.

True to his word, Ed officially adopted Robin and
raised her as his very own and she never knew any
family other than him and his. He stayed in touch
with his family and, in the beginning, took her to
family functions but for the most part, it was just the
two of them.

Discipline became her second parent as Ed trained
her more than he raised her. In her early years, Ed
surrounded her with aunts and nannies and the occa-
sional girlfriend to teach her all the things little girls
needed to know and he taught her everything else. He
taught her geometry, gymnastics, and jiu-jitsu while
the other girls her age went to Gymboree.

He was hard on her but never cold. In the brief
time he had with his mother, the thing he took away
from it was the feeling of being loved uncondition-
ally. So, if other girls were mean to her she told him
about it. If she was jealous of someone they talked
about it. If he felt something was bothering her he
would ask her about it. It was his answers that set him
apart from other parents. He always put things into
context, seeing things in the big picture, "playing the

long game" as he called it. That's how he survived his childhood.

For instance, one day they were in the car driving somewhere when Robin was little and a monarch butterfly landed on the windshield while they were at a red light. Robin turned to him and told her she loved butterflies and that her Aunt Marie (Ed's cousin) told her whenever she sees a Monarch butterfly it's really her mother's spirit watching over her and she even bought her a butterfly pendant.

Ed took this opportunity to teach her about life. "Butterflies are pretty but they don't live very long, maybe about a month. So, a month to a butterfly is a lifetime. (Monarch butterflies can live up to a year but Ed doesn't know everything) Half of that life is spent as a caterpillar and then in a cocoon. So, it's only beautiful for half its life. Beauty is fleeting and life isn't that long so make the most of every day. Do you know what a butterfly's defense is?"

"It's what?" she asked already regretting starting this conversation.

"You know, nature gives all creatures a predator and a way to defend themselves. Sharks have teeth, tigers have claws, bats have sonar. Do you know what butterflies have?"

"I know! Their beauty! They are so pretty other animals don't want to hurt it."

"No, it's beauty that other animals want to destroy because they don't have it. The thing that keeps a butterfly alive is that it tastes awful and other animals don't want to eat it."

"Really?"

"Yep. Now, do you know what the butterfly effect is?"

"No. What's that?"

"Well, a scientist once said that a butterfly flapping his wings in Brazil can cause a hurricane in Texas."

"Is that really true?"

Ed liked it when she pushed back and questioned things- to a point. It told him that she wouldn't grow up to be a sucker.

"Well, it's impossible to prove. But I think nature is a little too resilient. But I can give you an example in business. One time I was on my way to work, this is back when I first started, and I was going to go to the store to buy ink for my printer to print out an agreement before a big meeting. A bicycle messenger was zooming along and a butterfly flew into his eye and he crashed into me. He said he was OK but we exchanged business cards and left but it made me late for my meeting. The person I was dealing with demanded a signed agreement right there and then. When I printed it up on my printer-the ink was low- so the 8 looked like a 3. We signed it and they left. A paralegal working for their lawyer noticed the mistake and they demanded a new agreement revised and signed and submitted to the commission before five o'clock that day. So, I printed up a new one and signed it and I called the bike messenger that hit me. I figured I'd do him a favor. He sends it over there, they sign it and they have him send it down to the commissioner's office before five o'clock. It turns out the guy was really hurt from our accident, he had internal bleeding and he pulled over his bike and died before ever getting the paperwork in. The deal went in and I made an extra five million dollars.

"Is that really true?"

"It's impossible to prove."

"But what do you think about butterflies!"

"Well," he thought for a moment while driving, "my favorite movie is Papillion which is french for butterfly."

"What's it about?"

"It's about a guy who escapes Devil's Island."

Ed didn't mind his cousins and relatives filling her mind with silliness. He loved his cousins and they meant well but he knew that his parents were murdered for "business reasons" and those in his family that weren't complicit in the act were definitely complacent with it. They knew it too and that's why they sent him away to school far, far away.

That's why it was sometimes hard coming home for breaks and holidays. He'd come back just in time to have the seven fishes with the family on Christmas Eve and then open presents with his cousins and on summer breaks, he'd go stay with his rich friends at their summer homes but he always came back in late August because that was when the tomatoes were ripe enough to make sauce. He wanted Robin to have these experiences too and he wanted sure as hell wasn't going to send her away to school after what happened to him.

He wasn't just raising a girl he was creating a living weapon. The first thing he taught her was what he called "The Rule of 90." That was that ninety percent of fighting is first showing up and being ready to accept a challenge or meet aggression head-on because ninety percent of the people you have run-ins with don't want to fight. If you have a run-in or a disagreement with them give them an out so they can save face or stand up to them and they'll back down. Of the remaining ten percent, ninety percent of them don't know how to fight. As soon as you show good form and that you really know how to throw a punch, they'll know they're in trouble and the fight will end soon. Most fights don't last more than ninety seconds anyway either a teacher or principal or school guard will come to break it up. But the ten percent left out of that group simply couldn't handle an onslaught of ninety seconds of well-timed punches and kicks with speed, power, and good form. They can't handle it physically, they can't handle it mentally, they don't have the cardio and they would collapse after the adrenaline dump.

Robin, being the smart girl she was, asked the question that begged to be asked," What if I find that ten percent person?"

"Then you'll have a worthy opponent. You should feel lucky. Try to make them your friend."

Robin was the only real thing in his life, everything else was bullshit. He created the financial business just to gain the power to vanquish his enemies and to impress the people he went to school with and his late-night excursions, dressing up in head-to-toe black and beating up drug dealers wasn't about fighting crime or seeking justice it was about revenge on the Canto crime family and as an outlet for his rage.

He started beating on what they would call "soldiers" and taking their money just to make it look like robberies or rival gangs ad he would hit other gangs so no one would know he was singling the Canto family out. He knew how they operated because they used to brag about their crimes at family functions. He stopped going to them because everyone would be wearing black and crying about their loved ones and Ed couldn't keep a straight face anymore.

There was one instance where he went to the funeral of a "capo" in a "rival family" and got drunk on Sambucca. When someone asked him how he thought this "serial killer" could be so "familiar" with mob activities.

Ed replied. "Hey, you can't spell familiar without familia."

Pretty soon, he was hitting everybody Mexicans, Russians, Blacks. Then, an unexpected consequence happened. The streets got safer. Crime was all but eliminated. He would later learn that all the precautions he took not to get caught really didn't matter.

There was never a 911 call saying they were being attacked by "The Bump." No D.A. ever called for an arrest to "The Bump." The cops were not going to go out of their way to find someone no one was looking for and crooks felt is was easier just to be a regular, honest, working schmo than to take all the danger and risk of being a criminal just to have some guy swoop in the middle of the night to kick your ass and to take all the money you risked your ass to get.

When Ed ran out of criminals to beat up at home he had to take the show on the road. Things got a little complicated. Ed would go on these business trips and have to take Robin with him. He simply didn't trust anyone else with his kid and with what happened to him and his sister; could you blame him? He thought that someone somehow would figure out who's doing all this and they'd go after her but no one ever did. And she became his alibi. What does a man going snorkeling with his daughter have to do with drug dealers going missing on the beaches of Mexico? It would be like telling a farmer in Texas to blame that tornado that destroyed his barn on the butterfly flapping his wings in Brazil.

The Legend of "The Bump" grew. It spread throughout the ghetto, the barrio, and all the way to the halls of congress. Someone in the federal government made money off of drug trafficking and the sex trade because satellites and drones were picking all this up but somebody was paying them to look the other way. But then, it turned out the "Bump" was good for business. The number one problem for Democrats was they were soft on crime. The people will put up with a lot from incompetent politicians higher taxes, stifling regulation, silly agendas but when they no longer feeling safe walking in their own neighborhood, people have to go. But, no matter how soft they were on crime, no matter how many criminals they let go, no matter who or what they let come over the border crime went down. And it was all due to "The Bump."

He started taking her on what he called "hunting expeditions" for the most dangerous game. And when they traveled he didn't leave her asleep in the hotel room. At first, he kept her safe mainly as a lookout. But then she learned how to crack safes, disarm security systems, and plant bombs. It was her inclusion that got Ed to step up operations and invest in Kevlar suits and safer, hi-tech equipment. As she got older she became more integral in the operations. She then graduated to being the "bump."She was the one that would make the noise that had the victim looking in the wrong direction and in some instances she became the bait.

When a warehouse fire in Jakarta destroyed an entire year's supply of product the company had to double their order from their supplier who was a member/investor of Financial Edge Markets, Robin went ice skating at the Taman Anggrek Mall.

When Ed was seen at the Cannes Film Festival with a supermodel an Arab sheik was found dead on his yacht. A Lebanese businessman testified that he had just sold him an underage white girl for sex minutes before. He later died in prison.

A member of the Chinese communist party had stolen software and intellectual property from a small design firm in America. The man was seen playing baccarat with Ed at a hotel-casino in Hong Kong at the same time a virus was uploaded to the Chinese government mainframe from the laptop in his hotel room. Security cameras show that the only person who enters the room was the cleaning woman. The General's Ferrari crashed a week later when its brake line was cut. The design firm's patent made a fortune for Financial Edge Investments.

They stopped when she became more recognizable than him and she started missing too much school. By then, he didn't mind leaving her alone. He knew she wouldn't have parties because the doorman would tell him if people came over. If she went out partying or clubbing he would find out about it on the news.

One weekend he told her that he was leaving to go on a "safari" in Africa and she wanted to go.

"Don't you have a French exam next week and a science project due?

"Oui."

"What are you going to do the science project on?"

"L'effet papillon."

CHILDREN CAN BE
EXCEPTIONALLY CRUEL

———————◦———————

"IT'S BEEN TWENTY YEARS?" Ed blurts out.

"Yep," The Receptionist confirms, "This was my first and only job out of high school and my high school reunion was this weekend."

"How was it?"

"I made a point not to stay in touch with any of them after high school so when I told them I work for you they couldn't believe it. Then they all couldn't believe I never got married while they all got fat and all their husbands were hitting on me but I think they were doing it to try to get to you. Everybody has an idea they want to talk to you about."

"Sounds like you had a good time."

"I'm feeling it now. Now I feel twenty years older."

"You look the same as you did the day I hired you. Do I look the same?"

"Better." She lets that linger in the air for a moment and holds eye contact.

After her comment about not being married, it comes clear to him what's been going through her head all these years. He hired her for her looks just to be eye candy but she turned into an incredible asset. She could run half the companies on Wall Street if she wanted to but she stayed for him, just in case he ever saw the light. But Ed was self-aware to know that being with him would be a nightmare.

She goes back to business, "This came for you and there's someone at the lobby here to see you."

She hands him a thin shipping box with no markings on it. He shakes it (he could never be too careful) and something in it rattles about. He waits until she's out of the room before opening it. It's a folded letter with a wax seal. The emblem on the brand is a triangle inside a circle with three little L's. "Circle L Investments.

What the hell do they want?"

He checks the security cameras images from his laptop. A camera in the lobby points down on the people waiting by the bank of elevators. One man sticks out in the crowd. "He's huge!" Ed thinks to himself. "He's minimum four hundred and fifty pounds."

Ed watches in stunned silence as the other people shy away from him as if he was going to bite one of them. The man keeps to himself and Ed can't see his face because his hat dips down low. He's wearing a very large overcoat and is carrying a large briefcase, Ed reasons he must be some kind of salesman with samples and since it's not that warm for a large coat like that the obese man probably reeks of body odor and people are backing off. Only Willie, the elderly black janitor says something to him. Ed can't hear what they're saying but he knows the man shook his head no.

When an elevator arrives, the man waits for others to get on. He even motions to a young lady to go ahead but she ignores the offer. He proceeds and has the elevator to himself.

Ed presses a button and switches to the elevator camera. He sees the man press the button to the top business floor. The Financial Edge offices. Over the past twenty years Ed bought the building and made his office on the top floor and had a penthouse built where he and Robin, strike that, she goes by Rainbow now, where he and Rainbow live.

Ed gets on the intercom, "A very large man is coming in. Please send him through to my office."

Ed takes the moment to read the letter.

He can hear The Receptionist greeting someone just outside the door so he folds the letter back up, sticks it in the box, and leaves his chair to greet the man.

When The Receptionist leads him in Ed is standing there waiting for him.

"Hello, Mr...?"

"Po. Maximillion Po."

"Poe like Edgar Allan or Po like the river in Italy?"

He hands him a business card, "My father called me Massimo."

"Oh, so you're a Paisan! What did your mother call you?"

"Bambino. But please, call me Max."

"They believed the Po was bottomless so you are aptly named."

"My family shortened it at Ellis Island from Ponzi so that we weren't associated with scam artists so if you see my family don't tell them we met."

"Touché! That's probably why you didn't set an appointment."

"I've tried for weeks to set up an appointment with you and my employers were getting impatient. So, I won't take up too much of your time. I represent a group, a consortium if you will, that deals in commodities, precious stones, and metals.

Ed reads the card aloud, "Visionary Ventures? I like the alliteration."

We want to diversify their portfolio and invest with Financial Edge. We have vast mineral holdings But our cash reserves are currently tied up investing in deep-sea mining, we have the equipment such as custom-built submarines but there's a lot of pressure in deep-sea mining."

"Are you referring to political pressure?"

"Especially navigating the tricky waters of international rights which is something they are hoping you can help them with."

"Well, as you know, when you become a member/investor you get full access to our trading desk, our currency market, the entire platform, the whole nine yards. We have a very thorough vetting process."

"You have a fiduciary responsibility to your constituents we understand but please time is of the essence."

Max opens up his case and pulls out a stack of papers five inches thick, "Here are copies of our financials if you need any more please email me, it's on my card, and I can send you whatever you need."

He slaps the papers onto Ed's waiting arms, "We'll get right on it."

"Before I go, my employers want me to give you a present," Max reaches into his left side pocket and pulls out something wrapped in a handkerchief. He unwraps a one-inch round bright red diamond, "This is a sample of our holdings. They call it The Red-Breasted Robin in honor of your daughter and they read somewhere that your daughter's twenty-first birthday is soon approaching and they wanted her to have it.

He holds it up so Ed can bask in its brilliance.

"Is it real?" Ed asks in awe.

"Very, but I told them a gift of this value might be mis-construed as a bribe so I advised them against giving it to you."

Max wraps it back up, sticks it back in his left pocket, and pulls something else out of his right pocket. He then unwraps another handkerchief revealing an even bigger sparkling crystal diamond and he holds it up into the light.

"Is that real too?"

"No. It's actually Moissanite. They call it a Rainbow diamond and as you can see when the light goes through it creates a rainbow effect. And so I told them that since your daughter likes to go by Rainbow and since this is a lower-priced item it might be a more appropriate gift."

He hands it to Ed.

"Why thank you."

Max puts a smile on his face. "I know I shouldn't, this usually never leaves my office safe but I wanted to show you our crown jewel. He reaches into a case and pulls out a black box and holds it against his wide stomach as he raises the lid to reveal a blue diamond the size of a softball.

"As you can see, if we were to simply liquidate our assets to raise the cash it would cry havoc in the marketplace. After all, we are all slaves to supply and demand. But I just wanted to show you that we can back any stake we claim."

Max snaps the box shut and that snaps Ed out of his hypnotic stare. He sticks out his hand for Ed to shake, "I want to thank you for your time."

Ed comes to, shifts the folders onto his left arm, and shakes his hand with his right. Years ago, a businessman told Ed that when you shake someone's hand always twist your wrist so that your hand is over his. It subconsciously implies dominance. Now, the guy told him that while they were at a Walmart so Ed never took much heed in it but he still did it anyway. And, for the first time ever, Ed can't turn the man's wrist. In a brief moment, a millisecond, Ed tries again but the wrist wasn't moving and it gets to the point where the handshake was going on a tad longer than usual but Max was too strong and his grip nearly broke Ed's hand. It was as if he was making these diamonds by crushing coal in his hand. For the first time in his adult life, Ed gives up.

"No problem."

Max closes up his case and turns to leave, tipping his hat as he goes. Ed plops the papers on his desk but seeing his laptop reminds him of something. He turns back to Max.

"I noticed on your way up, our janitor Willie said something to you. What did he say?"

"He asked if I'd feel more comfortable taking the service elevator. I told him it wouldn't be necessary."

"I'm sorry. I'm going to have a talk with him."

"Please, it was nothing."

"It must be hard–for you -sometimes.

Max ponders his answer for a moment, "Yes, children can be exceptionally cruel."

TIME TO EAT EVERYBODY

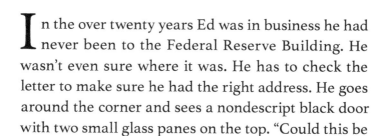

In the over twenty years Ed was in business he had never been to the Federal Reserve Building. He wasn't even sure where it was. He has to check the letter to make sure he had the right address. He goes around the corner and sees a nondescript black door with two small glass panes on the top. "Could this be the place?" He wondered to himself.

Though he was over six feet tall, Ed needs to get on his tippy toes just to look inside through the glass. It was dark inside. He put his hand above his eyes like a little kid looking through the candy shop window to see if they were open. He gives the door handle a little tug but it's locked.

Two soldiers burst out the door with rifles drawn. One white guy and one black both in full commando uniform and both were pointing their M-16s at him, "Can we help you?"

Ed appreciates the politeness but was still taken aback, "Is this the Federal Reserve? My name is Edward Gennaro, I have an appointment with the chairman Peter Simon."

He reaches into the breast pocket of his suit jacket and they both raise the barrels of their rifles. With just his thumb and index finger he pulls out the letter with the broken wax seal still on it and with his pinky and ringer sticking as far as they could he hands it to the white guy in front of the black guy. The white guy snatches it and holds it up over his head and back to the black guy.

They both shuffle their feet backward retreating back until the door closes behind them.

In all the times' Ed had a gun pointed at him this time was by far the most disturbing. He wasn't breaking into a bad guy's lair as The Edge, he was knocking at the door of the Federal Reserve, the people's bank, the place designed to protect the American citizens against the evils of capitalism and free markets since 1913, as a billionaire who was invited.

A young man wearing a suit and a bow tie opens up the door with a big smile on his face, "Hi Mr. Gennaro, I'm Josh Taggert with the Federal Reserve, come on in.

They walk through the door toward a security desk with a metal detector entrance. A tall, balding elderly man hurried over to meet him. Ed knows right away that it's Peter Simon, chairman of the Fed and brother to the President of the United States.

"Mr. Chairman, thank you for inviting me," Ed sticks out his hand and Peter offers him the equivalent of a bored wet fish for a handshake. For the second time today and the first time in his adult life he doesn't bother with the twisting wrist handshake. What would be the point?

"Just see your way up, I'll be along in a moment," Peter mumbles as he turns away.

"UH, Mr. Chairman! Mr. Gennaro is not in the system."

Peter turns to Taggert, "He's not?"

"No."

Peter turns to Ed, "You've never been here before?

"No," Ed answers.

"I thought you had." Peter turns to Taggert, "Give him full access security clearance." He turns away and scurries back to where he came from with his feet scuffling along the floor.

Taggert turns to Ed, "Are you chipped?"

"Yes." Ed ticks his hand under a red light until the light turns green.

"There you go. Welcome to the Federal Reserve. They are waiting for you in the conference room. Please excuse us, we have a tour of fifth-graders going on," Taggert walks away.

"Great, I have as much access as fifth graders."

Only one of the double doors to the conference room is open but he can see LEO EPSTEIN smiling at him and waving him to come in. He greets Ed with a hug like they're long-lost friends.

"Edward! How are you? Come on in! Have a seat! You know my associates LEON GOLDBERG and LUPE CRUZ."

"Ed smiles and waves hello as he takes his seat at the conference table, "The whole Circle L brain trust is here!"

All three were older than Ed but not by a whole lot. Leo was probably the oldest. He has grey hair but he has a youthful bounce about him and Leon has silver hair but he keeps it long and combs it straight back like a rock star. Lupe was a little older than Ed and there was something sexy about her. She had that thing where one eye was a different color than the other which usually freaks people out but on her, it was a turn-on.

Leo plops down in his chair, "I'm the brains, he's the balls and she's the heart. The gangs all here!"

A voice comes from the back of the room behind Ed, "I wonder what body part that makes me."

Ed spins around. There's a CUTE WOMAN dressed in black smiling from the back of the room setting up aluminum trays of food to be heated up for lunch. She's holding a Sterno can in her hand.

Ed smiles but thinks to himself, "WHERE THE HELL DID SHE COME FROM? Ed prided himself at scoping out a room before he entered it. He did it as if his life depended on it because oftentimes it does. "She could've slit my throat and I never would've seen it coming!"

"Hi, I'm Lucy!"

She was adorable almost pixieish but Ed couldn't tell what she was. She seemed Asian but had an Audrey Hepburn vibe going on, maybe with a little Linda Rondstadt thrown in. Maybe Ed was still spinning from the surprise or maybe he finally needed glasses because she wasn't THAT far away. But he wasn't looking at her face. He was staring at the Sterno can in her hand. He didn't see her light it but he could've sworn it was aflame and she was just holding it like nothing. Maybe it was time for him to get glasses.

Ed turns back around to Leo," A fourth L?"

"No, no, no, Lucy is just here to serve," Leo said while staring down Lucy, and judging by the emphasis he put on the word "serve" he seemed a little perturbed.

Lucy responds bubbly, " I usually don't serve at Circle L, as a rule, but this is a special occasion."

Leo gets right back on track, "Yeah, we have a lot of exciting things going on and we wanted to tell you about them so we thought, 'Let's invite him for lunch.' Even though I've invited you to come on my jet to go to the Hamptons, West Palm, Davos and you always say no. So I said, 'Let's meet him at a restaurant, you know, neutral territory' and then Leon said, ' Great, I'll call Squawk Box and see if they can do a live remote,' and then Lupe recommended we do a Food

Network tie in, you know, maybe find a sponsor to offset the cost and so I said OK, OK, OK, I get the picture! So then Lucy recommended this. If the Chairman of the Fed invites the largest investment firm in America (referring to Ed) to lunch it's no big deal, if he invites the second biggest investment firm in America, that's no big deal. If those two firms were to meet, the market would go into a frenzy! So, we thought we'd keep this under the radar."

Ed gives a wide smile, "Ahhh, the proverbial free lunch. I mean, I am the one being fed, right?"

As if on cue, a very tall, very intimidating black man enters the room wearing a full-length leather coat over a hoodie that covers his face and leather gloves on his hands. And the oddest thing about him is that he's wearing work boots covered in wet mud and they're in the middle of the city.

"C'mon buddy, why would you say something like that?" Leo asks not even acknowledging the man who enters the room.

"Because there's a rather tall man wearing a hoodie so I can't see his face and he has gloves on. It's not that cold in here. So maybe he doesn't want his face on security cameras and he doesn't want to leave any fingerprints..."

"Now you're being paranoid," Leo says.

"He's with me!" Lucy pipes up.

"Yeah man," Leo says trying to sound hip, "We didn't introduce you to Thade? That's Thaddeus Isidor but he likes to go by Thade. But he's cool! He in our tribe!"

Ed gives Leo a look like 'what the hell are you talking about?'

"He's an Ethiopian Jew," Leo explains.

Lucy turns to Thade, "You can wait outside. It's OK."

Leon getting angry, "Tell him why we're here!"

Now Lupe is mad at Leon, "Dios Mio! Can't we at least eat first and get to know each other!?"

"Leon's right Edward," Leo tries keeping it light and positive, "At Circle L we believe if you can't beat him, buy him and we want to buy your company. The country is moving forward with nationalizing the economy and they want one investment company to deal with. I mean, they still want to keep outside investments and keep certain private companies but the economy is going totally digital and they don't want any competing currencies.

"And what if I say no?" Ed asks.

Leon getting impatient gets to the point, "The government is broke. They finally ran out of other people's money and now they're taking ours. They want us all to keep working but they want all the money going to them."

Leo tries to soften the blow, "Edward, you've built something great! You've helped the little guy get ahead and you leveled the playing field. Now the playing field is going away and we want you to hit the showers."

"Or take a bath," Ed fears.

"Edward," Leo answers, "We are about to make you the wealthiest man who ever lived. You will be the world's first trillionaire. But we want it all the crypto, the investments, everything."

"What about my customers?"

"Ed," Leon steps in, "The country is going broke. China is ready to eat our lunch. We can't have your people playing in your sandbox and sticking money under the mattress where the government can get at it. There's only going to be one global currency and it's going to be ours."

"Well then," Ed claps his hands with a big smile on his face, "I guess there's nothing left to discuss. Where do I sign?"

Leo pumps the brakes a little, "Let's do a handshake deal for now. We still gotta do our due diligence, you know, take a look at your books, kick the tires, make sure everything is kosher, make sure you have everything you say you have."

"You'd better hurry up. I have a retired couple from Palm Springs just offered me two trillion last week," Ed jokes making everyone laugh and relax.

Leo still smiling, "Let's make it official next month. We'll do a big reveal. We'll have trumpets, the works. Just don't say anything until then."

Lupe has an idea, "Invite him to the island."

Leo acts like he was hit by lightning, "Yeah! We're having a big blowout on the island on the 28th of next month. Have you ever been out to my island? Oh, you'll love it! You'll get lost in paradise! Peter is going to be there (he points outward referring to the Chairman) his brother Joe is going, too. Peter will be flying on my jet and Joe will be on Air Force One, of course.

The conversation gets a little rapid-fire as everyone steps over each other's words.

Ed: I can't. It's my daughter's birthday that weekend.

Lupe: Bring her along! They'll be plenty of girls her age.

Ed: I'll bet.

Leon: The leaders of the G7 are going to be there?

Ed: Only seven?

Leo: How come you never bought an island?

Ed: Are you kidding? I didn't like cutting the lawn back in New Jersey. To take care of an island?

Lupe: There's so much to do there.

Leon: The BRICS are giving us pushback but they'll come around.

Leo: It gets kind of expensive but we set up a pharma lab out there.

Lupe: What does she want to do? She should model. She's so pretty. There's going to be a lot of fashion designers coming.

Leo: We even set up a hospital for the natives. It's our way of giving back. We're doing some groundbreaking work there. It's going to be a future growth market.

Ed: Growth market?

Leo: Yeah, we're not going totally socialist. We got a lot going on in bio-med.

Leon: Ed doesn't want to hear about this.

Lupe: Does she want to get into medicine?

Leo: We originally got the idea from the Chinese.

Ed: What idea?

Lupe: Charity work! I bet she wants to get into charity work. Leaders from Planned Parenthood will be there. So will a lot of celebrities! She'll love it!

Ed: Charity?

Lupe: Oh yeah, to help with the stigma of abortion we're having young girls, who want to take control of their health, they can come out to the island, they're allowed to bring up to three guests if they want to bring the parents we offer free colonoscopies for the fathers or maybe they just want to make it a girls trip we cover all expenses. We call it procedure leisure.

Ed: Catchy.

Leo: The Chinese track everyone through social media, they've got everyone's health records, they know who eats what, who's not taking care of themselves, do they drink or take drugs.

Leon: Ed doesn't need to know all the details.

Lupe: People are living longer, happier lives and we're reducing overpopulation.

Ed: Are you talking about organ harvesting?

Leo: We're making real breakthroughs in cloning.

Ed: If you can't pay an arm or a leg how about a kidney or liver?

Lupe: We're lessening our environmental impact.

Leo: We can't create life but we can save it!

Ed: By copying it?

Leo: HEY! Our hospital saved 144, 000 lives last year, buddy!

Leon: ENOUGH!

Lucy rings a cheerful little bell, "Time to eat, everyone!"

It's a trap

────────────•:•────────────

There's a throng of anxious reporters at the entrance of Ed's building when he gets back.

"How the hell did they find out so soon?" he thinks to himself as they pulled up. "Was it that Thade guy?"

Once Lucy served them the lunch was actually enjoyable after that and Ed had a good time. Everyone seemed happy when they left and Ed promised to revisit the trip to Leo's island. They promised to stay quiet, cover their tracks and Ed had the limo come pick him up about a block away from the Fed and take him straight home. Ed was soon to be the richest man ever and all was right with the world and now this. "Play it cool like you always do," he thought to himself.

He doesn't wait for the driver to come around and they pounce on him as soon as he opened the door. A Boom mike descended on him as cameras rolled and flashes were popping.

"Mr. Gennaro," the REPORTER asks, "What's your comment on Rainbow's credit card?"

"What?"

The Reporter elaborates, " Your daughter's credit card was denied at Chez Josephine today while she was having lunch. Her bodyguard had to pay. Are you punishing her or do you really have financial problems?"

A million things ran through his head at that moment. "If these people knew where I had just come from and what we discussed, 'What the hell is she doing with her money?' 'Will this ruin my deal?'" Anger rises up in him like never before and he grabs the reporter by the head with his face firmly in Ed's palm and throws him down to the curb. He then storms off into the building as the other reporters hover around the Reporter to interview him. He's now victim du jour.

For about forty minutes Ed felt sorry for himself. Why does this always happen to him? He's so close to making a big deal and something bad happens. Now he's got to do something drastic just to make it right. He went to work on a new plan. He didn't want to, but since when did he ever have a choice?"

Speaking of victims, Ed had the big screen on in the background and the 24 HRS News Channel was interviewing the Reporter. "He was sure making the most of his fifteen minutes of fame," Ed thought, "I'm sure he'll get a book deal out of this."

His self-pity was replaced by disappointment in himself. He had never let "The Edge's" anger develop in him. He had never lost control, especially with a reporter- on camera! He wasn't sure what triggered him exactly. Was it talking about his daughter or that he may lose this deal? It didn't matter now. He had work to do.

He had to find out all he can on Visionary Ventures. All he had was a business card. He had a contact at city hall messenger over everything they had on the business and the building. He had blueprints and building permits but not much else. They were a new company and had recently bought the building and he found a permit for a new elevator but nothing on any vaults being installed.

Anyone who tells you a rainbow comes after a storm never met Robin "Rainbow" Gennaro. She bursts through the door, slams her expensive handbag to the floor, and dives onto the sofa.

"My credit card was denied today!"

"I heard."

"It was awful! The manager came over and my friends were so embarrassed for me! Larry had to come over and pay!"

"I heard."

"This is the worst thing that has ever happened!" as she kicks the arm of the sofa.

"I heard the Holocaust was pretty bad."

"Wait until Perfecta hears about this! That cow! I wish I could just go to the desert in Sonoma and just stay at the spa for like forty days and come back when this is over and my trust fund kicks in!"

"Sedona is in Arizona. Sonoma is in wine country," Ed says while still working.

"Shut up! This is all your fault! What's going on? Are we broke?"

Ed doesn't respond so she gets up in his face, "Oh my God! You are the world's worst businessman!" She gets practically nose to nose while he's still reading documents, "YOU WOULDNT KNOW WHAT A PROFIT WAS IF IT WERE SCREAMING IN YOUR FACE!"

He remains unphased. She decides to change tact, "Admit it, this isn't for you. Let's go out to Hollywood. You can be my manager and work for me. I've got agents calling me every day."

"Let them take you out to lunch."

This enrages her as she knocks papers off his desk. He doesn't even lookup.

She looks down at the papers, "What are you doing? Are you casing a joint? Do you have a job? I thought you were done. When do we start?"

He finally puts down what he was reading, "I don't think it's going to work." But then he tries to change the mood. He gets up and pulls out the Rainbow diamond Max gave him and holds it up to her face.

"That's some rock," she says, "Let's fence it and turn it into some bread."

"It's a Rainbow diamond. I got it for you."

"We're broke," she starts, "and YOU bought me a diamond and give it to me a MONTH before my birthday."

"OK, sit down." He waits for her to plop on the sofa, "I got an offer today to buy everything, my whole operation."

With her arms crossed, "How much?"

"A trillion dollars."

She leaps up, "HOLY-"

"I need to cook the books a little, settle some accounts that are arrears and to do that we need some quick cash. I'm looking at the office of the gentleman that came to see me today. He gave that to me to give to you and he's got more in a safe in his office. I don't see any work permits on a vault, I found one for the elevator but that's it."

"Rainbow and The Edge are back, baby!" She runs out of the room.

He reaches down and picks up all the papers she threw on the floor. She comes back in holding up two Kevlar jumpsuits. One is brightly multicolored and the other is bright red.

"Which one do you like?"

"Does this one have a sign that says, 'Hi, my name is Rainbow'?"

"Don't hate."

"You know the idea is not to be seen."

"These are state-of-the-art! They're like twelve grand each."

"No wonder your credit card got canceled."

"I think they put a little tickle in tactical."

"They certainly don't have the tact."

She throws them down on the sofa, "OK, what's the plan?"

"OK," he leads her to the plans on his desk," The building is not that far away. We can reach it with the zip line gun."

She points to her suits, "This building is way taller. Let's just jump off this building and fly over to that building. These come with skydiving wings."

"No, it's too windy. With the zip line, we stay off the street cameras but below the radar. When we're done, we can skydive to the park a few blocks away. No chance of us getting blown into a building. I can have a drone drop off some clothes in a tree so that they're waiting for us. We get dressed in the park and hit Chez Josephine for a late dinner. We'll make the news and that'll be our alibi.

"I like my idea better."

Later that night, the two of them go out to their penthouse patio in their tactical suits. His all-black and her bright red. He's covered head-to-toe with protective headgear and she has red goggles so her hair can flow. They set up a large air-powered gun with computer-controlled trajectory, he bolts the legs down while she aims it through the viewfinder. He then attaches about a mile of zip line to it.

He taps her shoulder letting her know it's ready before standing back. She fires it.

It makes almost no noise but it shoots the line over ten blocks and hits the metal access door on the roof of Max's building. The magnet attaches to the door and the camera mounted on it shows that it's secure.

"Bullseye!" She high-fives him.

He hands her the zip line handle, "Remember, jump off before you reach the door."

"OK, old man."

She attaches the handle to the line, gives it a tug to make sure it's secure, and then gets a running start, jumping off the building and riding the line the entire 10 blocks with him not too far behind. They travel the ten blocks in under a minute with her screaming all the way like she's on a rollercoaster. He's shaking his head the entire time.

She applies the hand brake so as soon as she's over the roof it slows down so that she can simply let go and step off onto the roof. His descent isn't as smooth since he's twice as big he comes in twice as hard and has to do an uncomfortable tumble onto the roof. He pops up in a ninja fighting stance and she cracks up laughing.

They pop off the doorknob and take the fire stairs down to the top floor offices of Visionary Ventures.

"I'm going to night-vision," Ed says as he presses a button on the side of his goggles.

"Congratulations," she says snarkily.

The offices are not impressive at all. What furniture they have is cheap rental stuff.

"Look at this cheap crap," she says.

"Let's find his office," he says.

They do find a door with a plaque that reads: MAXIMILLIAN PO ESQ.

He goes inside and it's a simple eight-foot by ten-foot room with a desk, chair, and phone.

Rainbow comes in behind him, "Is this it?" She kicks a hole in the wall but it's just sheetrock, "There's nothing here!"

"What the hell!" he says angrily, "Let's look around a little."

She pushes past him and leads the way back out to the lobby. THE ALARM IS TRIPPED.

SIRENS GO OFF. LIGHTS FLASH.

"Let's get out of here!"

He heads for the stairwell they came down. A FLASH BANG goes off! Seeing the bright flash through night-vision goggles disorients him.

He hears a HISSING SOUND as smoke fills the room. He sees little sparkles in the smoke.

"TEAR GAS! PUT ON YOUR GAS MASK!" He pulls a breathing apparatus out of a compartment in his belt and attaches it to the front of his mask.

"I DON'T HAVE ONE!" she fires back in anger and fear.

He goes over to the elevator and hits the button. The doors open with a DING. He turns to her "Let's go!" He turns back and there's no elevator just an empty shaft.

"I've tripped a wire! You gotta jump!" she yells.

"Not without you," he garbles behind the gas mask.

"IT'S A TRAP!"

He turns back to her and a large explosion knocks him down the shaft as he falls twenty stories and lands on the concrete with a thud.

The suit absorbs a lot of the impact but he's still immobilized. His last vision of consciousness are the bits of flame flittering down from the top floor. He sees the entrance to the basement floor elevator door twenty feet above him. He couldn't get up there if he was healthy.

Paralyzed, all he can do is look up toward the fire coming out of the top floor creating light at the end of the tunnel that he'll never reach.

His body is in shock, feeling no pain, he drifts off.

NO REST FOR THE WICKED

His body feels lighter but he's sinking, no wait, the concrete floor is rising, engulfing him. He's not sure what's happening. He only knows it's dark he can't see. Panic kicks in. He feels a weight on his chest, more like pressure. He can't move and the weight on his chest makes it harder to breathe. His gas mask will give him hours of breathing that will keep him alive. That's bad news. The thought of it shoots through his mind. He thought he was peacefully drifting off but now he's fully aware and it's torture. In his panicked state, he snorts a little dirt that sifted through the mask. He starts shaking. "Wait!," he thinks, "I can feel my arms and legs."

"I'M ALIVE!" he thinks to himself. "This is dirt. I'm covered in dirt. Whoever did this took me out to the woods and buried me alive! But they messed up. I'm alive and I'm gonna make them pay."

It's the thought of revenge that gives him new life and new focus as he tries to dig himself out.

Totally disoriented at first he realizes that they must've thrown him feet first in a shallow grave.

"Mistake number two," he thinks as he's already plotting his revenge.

It's the realization that he has to punch up and not out that allows for his hand to break the surface. He can feel it...air...freedom. This empowers him even more. He still claws frantically but now it's in a certain direction. Controlled chaos puts his mind at ease. Now, he has both hands over the surface. From here he needs to dig. He used to spend hours on the mountain climbing machine in his home gym. He did it because it was good cardio. He never thought it would be the perfect training to dig himself out of his grave. His pumping legs loosen the soil around him as his wiggling arms get more room. His arms are free to his elbows. "PULL GOD DAMN IT! PULL," his mind screams. He feels freedom but he can't see it.

He pulls himself up to his waist, his feet kicking all the while. He finally pushes his way out to freedom. He lays on his back exhausted. The incredible energy it took, to pull himself out of hundreds of pounds of dirt and rocks with absolutely no room to move had taken its toll. And now, after the adrenaline dump, with nothing left in the tank, he lies victorious.

The first thing he does is pull out his cell phone and tries to call Rainbow but he can't get a signal. He shuts it off to conserve power.

As he takes off the mouthpiece and knocks all the dirt off of it he feels a slithering sensation throughout his body. He takes out his flashlight and it still works. He has to slap it once or twice buy it still shines. It's always been his most reliable tool and weapon. He's won more fights by blinding his opponent in the dark and then whacking them with the heavy end of the flashlight than with knives or guns. And it came through for him again.

Before he can even get his bearing straight to see where he is the light on his body shows he's totally covered by worms and maggots. The once exhausted Ed is now on his feet brushing away all the creepy crawlers covering him. If not for the tac suit they'd be all over him.

It's totally dark. He can only see the ten or fifteen feet the flashlight gives him. "Where the hell am I?" He thinks to himself, "How far out did they take me?" He realizes he is out in a forest or a jungle but he can't be sure. He would've had to have been out for days for someone to take him out to a jungle. And who would waste the time or travel to do that?

The lack of sight must've heightened his senses because the smell of rotting flesh is unbearable. It brings him to his knees. He puts the air filter back in his mouth. He can't see, he can't smell, so he listens. All he hears is a buzzing sound so loud and so encompassing he thinks it's ringing in his ears like some form of tinnitus. He soon wishes it was that. "WASPS," he realizes.

The swarm is upon him and they're angry but once again the suit is his savior. H reaches in his belt for his butane torch pen. He originally bought it thinking he could cut locks with it but it doesn't get that hot. Then he figured he'd keep it for soldering circuitry in alarm systems but he's never done it. He has pulled it out when he wants someone to talk. He's never had to use it. As soon as he fires it up they tell him what he wants to know. He's never used it exterminating. He picks up a dead branch and is able to light it enough to keep the swarm off him as he waves it around.

He needs to find out where he is and how to get out. He comes to a tree and tries to climb it but the first branch he grabs snaps off with a sound that he swears is a scream. The branch is brittle. But even though it's bone dry there's some kind of sap that comes out of it that looks like blood.

One of the amazing things about Ed's tac suit is the gloves. The exoskeleton built into each hand has servo motors that can give him the strength to twist and tear a padlock but they also have sensors that are so sensitive they can detect the tumblers on a bank safe. They also can analyze certain substances and send the images to his headset via graphite wires. The motor is mainly made with polymers, but there is some metal in them, but not enough to set off a metal detector. He tries to run an analysis but there's no internet connection.

For now, he pulls out two of his knives and drives them into the trunk of the tree, and uses them to climb up the tree like the pegboards in his high school gym.

Each time he drives a knife into the dry dead wood more of the red fluid sap comes out. The servo motor on the exoskeleton of his tac suit makes it easier for him to drive the knives in and be able to pull them out. He sees that all the trees around him are dead. It's warm out and there are no leaves. It makes it easier for him to see far. As he makes his way to the top he can see that there's a clearing not far off, a meadow. And beyond that, he sees a light that must be from some kind of a building. "Run toward the light," he tells himself.

Just then, the tree gives way and he plummets to the ground with a thud. It's not the worst fall he's had and compared to the last one but it's bad nonetheless. "Was there a nuclear war?" He thinks as he lay there in pain. To him, it makes sense. Maybe the bombs hit just as they were in the building or maybe they hit when he was deep underground. If there was a nuclear winter it would kill all the trees and all the mammals leaving only hungry bugs, wasps, and worms. He doesn't know if it's true but it sure as hell feels that way.

Until he hears a growl coming from a distance. He hopes the wasps come back. Maybe they'll ward off whatever's coming. "Screw it," he thinks, "run toward the light."

He runs as fast as he can through the darkness with the flashlight leading the way by only about ten feet. The pivoting to avoid tree trunks, the ducking to miss low branches, then sprinting at full speed not knowing what's in front or behind you, no Olympic athlete could do it better than him.

He makes it to the meadow. Now it's a foot race between him and whatever it is chasing him. He has a light to guide him. He shuts off the flashlight and holds it ready to whack whatever comes near him. At this speed, uneven ground is just as treacherous as a tree or a branch but he doesn't stop. He falls but does a duck and roll and gets up at full speed without breaking stride.

Something is gaining on him. He can feel the slight vibrations in the ground. It might be more than one thing but he doesn't turn around to look. He can see the light from the entrance of the building. It's big. It looks like a hotel. And there are people out front. A line of them. He's safe! He's made it! Should he yell for help or warn them that something is coming? They don't seem to care. They're trying to get in. "Oh, God! The place ain't open!"

Out of breath, he comes to a stop on the driveway before the building. There is silence as the people in line and the ones crowding around the door look at him as they ask each other with their eyes, "Where the hell did this guy come from?"

Ed pulls himself together and walks with a confident stride toward the door. He turns back to see if any animals are coming toward them but nothing is there as far back as the tree line.

"Nobody seems to care so why should I?" He asks himself self-consciously. He feels out of place wearing an all-black tactical suit with mask and goggles but he notices some of the people are fully naked and shivering while others wear tattered rags. "They must be refugees from the nuclear attack," he reasons as he makes his way to the door.

"Hey, mister," one of the people asks, "Can you get us in?"

"Yeah, do you know somebody?" Another one chimes in.

"Hey, buddy! Let us come in with you?" Another one asks.

As Ed ignores them, their requests become demands and they start clawing at him. At first, he politely pushes them aside but then they become savage in nature and swarm him. "These people are incredibly strong, even the women," he thinks but writes it off to desperation, adrenalin, and his own fatigue. Now he must unleash powerful punches to the face as well as elbows and knees. They go down but another one follows.

Attached to the inside of each forearm are telescoping taser batons that can go from a billy club to debilitating cattle prod with the touch of a button. He only uses these to inflict severe damage and never on civilians but this is a different story. He jabs a naked woman in the rib cage and she goes down to her hands and knees. She looks up at him and hisses like a wild animal and he delivers a devastating downward backhand to her nose. Blood pours out like a faucet but she

NO REST FOR THE WICKED

doesn't go down or even scream. "What the hell?" He asks himself as he slips through the door.

When one man tries to force the door open Ed applies the taser dead center of the man's forehead sending him back and allowing Ed to slam the door shut. Then...silence.

Ed is in the lobby of a quaint hotel lobby, smaller than you would think when looking at the building from outside. For all the commotion outside the inside is eerily quiet. He takes off his mask. The air is fresh without the horrible smell outside. The sights, sounds, and smells from the outside are totally abandoned once inside. On the front desk, there's a little bell. He taps it. Ding!

When no one comes he bangs it two times DING! DING! Usually, at this point, a man of Ed's means and lack of patience would be screaming for the manager but he's different now. The situation is different now. He walks to the other side of the lobby and sticks his head inside the hotel dining room. There are about ten tables, all empty, and the kitchen is closed.

As he walks down the hall he comes to a set of double doors which open to a large banquet hall. Inside are about twenty ten top tables. Sitting by himself at the center table is a man, VIRGIL STANHOPE, drinking champagne out of a bottle. Ed enters the room stepping on confetti littered all across the floor and kicks several balloons strewn throughout. Across the back wall over the stage hangs a banner: HAPPY NEW YEAR.

The man, wearing an old-style tuxedo with wingtip shoes looks up to see Ed and a smile pops upon his face. "SAY HEY! OLD MAN! You missed one helluva fine party tonight! But don't worry every night is New Year's Eve around here. And an hour feels like a day and vice versa, depending on what you're doing that is. Ed, still bewildered, walks toward him without saying anything. "Put it in the ol' vice, fella!" He sticks out his hand and Ed shakes it. "That's some grip on you. Virgil Stanhope's the name from Buffalo, New York, well Rome actually...

"I'm Edward Gennaro."

"Oh, I know all about you. The boss wanted me to stay here to meet you." Virgil says in a fast-paced Transatlantic accent that Ed struggles to keep up with.

"The boss?"

"Yeah, he'd be here himself but he's tied up on the ninth floor."

"I'd like to speak with him."

"You just can't see the boss. You have to be summoned. But don't worry, he'll pop up when he wants to be seen."

"Where are we? Was there a war?"

"There's always a war, pal. Always was and always will be."

"Where are we?

"You, my friend, are in the grand banquet room of the Way Station Hotel just outside Lake Gehenna."

"Where is everyone?"

"There half-seas over." He can tell Ed can't keep up with his slang. "Half in the bag, sozzled. Like I said, you missed a real humdinger tonight."

"What about the people outside?"

"Those ragamuffins? Forget them! What goes on outside is none of our beeswax. Say, let's take a load off and get bent."

"What?"

"You know, have a bit of the bubbly." He grabs another bottle of champagne that was sitting on ice. He pops open the cork and it flows all over. He then hands it to Ed who gulps it down like a man in the desert. As Ed drinks, Virgil keeps talking, "The boss doesn't like to deal with the other guests because all they do is cry and moan about the accommodations but not you. He wants your stay to be very extra special. That's why he wants me to be your guide because I know my onions. My job is to get you stuff before you think you even need it."

Ed puts down the empty bottle. Virgil shakes it to make sure it's empty, "Another dead soldier."

Ed cuts right to it, "Is this hell?"

"Now you're on the trolley," Virgil jokes. He sees the serious look on Ed's face, "It's no secret that you've done some bad things in your life but the boss has big plans for you. I'm telling you this place ain't so bad. I like it here. Hey, life might've been a breeze for you but it was no Queen Mary for me let me tell you. I never stood a chance.

"Is there any chance of getting out of here? Have you ever seen anyone leave?" Ed asks desperately.

"Here? Yeah maybe. But the other place? No way."

"There's got to be a way out." Ed tries to convince himself.

"One time, I saw the big guy himself reach down and pull a guy out. It was like a beam of light coming down and he just grabbed the guy and whoosh. They were gone."

"I'm not a jailhouse lawyer but I spent a little time in the joint here and up top and everyone thinks they're innocent or don't belong here or the boss made some kind of mistake. The boss doesn't make mistakes. And when I was down there I never saw someone who didn't belong there. And I've seen them all. Come on, let's get you a room."

Virgil walks toward the door. Ed doesn't repeat the question because he really doesn't want to know. He sits there for a moment to let it all sink in.

Ed has to hurry to catch up to Virgil who is tapping away on the bell at the front desk.

A woman comes out of the back wearing a red skirt with a matching red vest over a white collared shirt. She looks like she just came off the runway in Milan with blown brown hair, tan skin, and full lips. She has the "look" of a European socialite or what Rainbow would call "resting bitch face." The name tag pinned to her vest says CHARON.

Ed smiles but she doesn't smile back. He notices something that wasn't there before. "I've never seen a hotel front desk with a tip jar before." He points to it but she doesn't react. Ed's not used to women resisting his charm especially servants.

"A room please for this fine gentleman."

She looks at her book, "Huc non pertinent. Et mortuus est."

Virgil replies," The boss said everything is Jake."

"Vuolsi cosi cola dove si puote. CIO Che is vuole." She turns around and reaches into one of the many cubby holes on the wall behind her and pulls out a key and slams it on the counter.

Virgil takes the key and with his other hand reaches into his pocket and pulls out a silver dollar and flicks it with his thumb into the tip jar. "Don't take any wooden nickels."

As Virgil walks away Ed leans in toward her, "Grazie." She doesn't react still looking at her book. He tries one more time, "Is it pronounced Sharon or Char on?"

Virgil turns back, "Come on! Shake a leg!"

When they get to the elevator the door immediately opens and Virgil walks in. Ed sticks his head in first. "What's the matter? Never been on an elevator before?" The two of them stand in an old-style elevator where a hand above the door tells you what floor you are on.

"Don't tell me," Ed jokes, "Thirteenth floor."

Virgil shakes his head," Don't be silly. The joint's not that big. We're going to the sixth."

"That was my next guess."

They walk along the brightly lit corridor that seems to go forever until they get to his room.

The first thing Ed says when he sees the room is, "I thought it would be bigger."

"Oh, so you've thought about your stay here before?"

"No windows?" Ed asks already knowing the answer.

"I'll have the house tailor send up some clothes so you can get out of that ridiculous get-up," Virgil offers.

"Don't you want my measurements?" Ed asks.

"The devil is in the details," Virgil cracks, "Sorry! The devil made me do it!"

Ed is not amused, "Have some food sent up, I'm sure you know what I like, and find a duffle bag for my get up.

"There's the big shot that nobody loves," are Virgil's parting words as he walks out of the room.

Ed peels off the Kevlar suit and piles all of his equipment on top of it. He enters the bathroom and turns on the shower. The water is piping hot so he lets it run for a moment as he looks around and finds a robe in the closet. Now the room is filled with steam so thick he can barely see and the temperature of the water hasn't gone down a degree. He doesn't notice that as the mirror has fogged up that someone had written with their finger DEPART FROM ME, YOU CURSED, INTO THE ETERNAL FIRE.

He sticks his hand under the shower and it's still scalding hot, "Youch!" All he can do at this point is stick his towel under the water and wipe himself down with the wet towel. He doesn't even see the message left on the mirror when he wipes it clear with another towel.

He dives onto the bed and he's so tired he doesn't care how hard the mattress is because he knows it could be much worse.

As soon as he gets comfortable there's a knock at the door. "Go away!" He yells but Virgil still walks in. He has a suit on a hangar draped over his shoulder.

"Knock, knock," he chuckles as he lays out the suit on the bed.

"What the hell!?" Ed is furious, "Doesn't this place have locks on the doors?"

"The boss has put together a little surprise for you downstairs," Virgil announces.

"I'm sleeping. Come back tomorrow," Ed replies.

"You'll have time to sleep when you're dead. Just kidding! A little gallows humor. Come on! Up and at 'em! You said you were hungry so I pulled some strings and got them to open the kitchen for you."

"Oh, I can't wait...for breakfast...in the morning!"

"Look, I even got you a new suit. I picked the tie myself. And I think you'll like these shoes. They say shoes are the first thing people notice subconsciously."

"You did all that in the short time you were gone?" Ed asks dubiously.

"I told you that a day feels like an hour but also an hour can feel like a day," Virgil responds.

"Why did you get the honor of pissing me off?"

"I got the winning ticket because I had hospitality experience. It's no secret my parents owned the Grand Niagara Hotel and Resort. You ever been?"

Ed with his face buried in a pillow gives a muffled yell, "No!"

Virgil tries to shove him awake before clapping loudly by his ear, "Now come on, there's no rest for the wicked."

DO WE HAVE A
SURPRISE FOR YOU

———————◆———————

"You look like a real Dapper Dan with those new glad rags," Virgil tells Ed as he comes out of his room with his new suit on. "A real cake-eater."

"I wish I knew what the hell you were talking about."

"Your wish is my command," Virgil jokes as the elevator door opens to the lobby. He gets out first when a hulking man with silver hair and dressed in an ill-fitted suit pushes him out of the way.

"Hey, watch it, Palooka!" Is all Virgil can get out.

The large man stands before Ed confronting him with his hands out to the sides as if ready to attack but doesn't. He stands there staring at Ed until he cracks a smile and then grabs him in a bear hug and lifts him off the floor.

"Ciacco!" are the only words Ed can get out of his mouth while his breath is being squeezed out of his lungs, "How the hell are you?"

"I can't believe you're here!" The big man squeals like a kid at Christmas.

"Well, there goes the surprise," Virgil says as he lights a cigarette.

"You'll never guess who's here!" Ciacco Argenti blurts out as he puts his arm around Ed and walks him over into the dining room where they are met by two men who look about the same age but the smaller man seems much older and they wear clothes from totally different eras. The first one is Iacopo Gunnulli, the man Ed had beaten to a pulp and videotaped, and Giovanni Canto, the man who started the Canto crime family. Gunnulli is dressed in a flashy sharkskin suit while Canto is dressed in a plain black suit with a thin tie similar to what they wore in the 1950s.

Iacopo greets Ed, who is leery, with a big smile, "Ciao, Bella!" He too gives Ed a hug and a kiss on the cheek.

"Don Gunnulli, it's good to see you," Ed says cautiously.

"Edouardo, allow me to do the honors," Gunnulli says as he guides Ed over to meet the small, balding man in the plain suit you wouldn't look twice at if you saw him on the street. "This is Giovanni Canto, our patron. The man who started it all."

Ed shakes his hand and bends down to give the small man a kiss on the cheek.

Virgil rolls his eyes at the reverence but plays along anyway, "The boss wanted to put together a little welcoming committee so you would feel more at home."

A group of waiters already come out with trays of food scurrying around the table pouring water glasses, wine glasses, and bringing over baskets of fresh bread. The men take their seats.

Virgil calls out, "I'll be sitting right over there having a drink and a smoke if you need anything. I'm just a fly on the wall."

"Preform, is accomodi, Canto says with a smile.

"What's the food like here?" Ed asks.

"Well, I don't think it'll be as good as some of the places in Little Italy or Arthur Avenue."

"How about Hell's Kitchen?" Ed quips. Ciacco roars like a lion who's had his belly tickled.

They immediately stick the cloth napkins into their collars and begin to eat.

"Mangia," the old man says as he lifts his wine glass, "Salud." The other three return the gesture and take big gulps of wine.

"Don Giovanni, I never thought I'd ever be sitting with you breaking bread, it's an honor," Ed starts with, "I can still remember the dry cleaners you owned on the corner of our street.

"That was my first business," Canto looks back wistfully, "My only legitimate business. I had wish I'd stayed.

"My father used to walk me down to the corner and we'd go pick up the suits, but this was long after you stopped working there."

"Did I know your father?" Canto asks.

"Gunnulli jumps in, "Yeah, his father used to cut lawns in the neighborhood and then started a landscaping company and then bought a backhoe and then started an excavation company and then started renting out the equipment and made a small fortune. He did some work for us after I took over the family after you passed. Some of the toxic dry cleaning chemicals were sweeping into the groundwater out on Long Island so we had his dad go dig some of it up."

"And then you had him killed," Ed adds without skipping a beat.

"What are you complaining about? You killed me. I killed him. Ciacco, who killed you?" Ciacco nods toward Ed while he sucks a long string of linguini into his mouth. "Get out of here!" He chuckles, "But in all seriousness, your old man was a worker, a real earner, a climber."

"Is that why you had him killed?"

Gunnulli turns to the other two," He's not gonna let this go is he?" He then looks directly at Ed, "I had your father killed because he was Sardinian."

"WHAT?" Ed is dumbfounded.

"You gotta be Siciliano to be a boss. Or at least Italian." Gunnulli explains.

"It's the next island over!" Ed uses his hands to show they're close.

"What are you gonna do?" Gunnulli shrugs as he goes back to his meal. He takes a few bites and motions to Canto,

Argenti decides to jump in, "Don Giovanni, you should've seen the building Ed owned. He was a billionaire! Easy! No problem. And he was legit. Well, not too legit. He is sitting here with us!"

All four of them laugh and it eases the tension. Until Gunnulli asks," How come you never let any of us get our beaks wet? My son went to you for a job. Why did you turn him away?"

In between chews Ed answers, "He was a dummy. Besides, I never hired anyone whose name ended in a vowel. That was my rule. You see, when I started, I knew you needed others to make money for you. And, quite frankly, I didn't have the balls to go into someone else's home and give them the line of bullshit I was selling and take their hard-earned paychecks. So, I got other guys to do it, gave them commissions, and called them brokers. So, one day, I guess I was feeling gutsy, I decide to hit the Indian market."

Argenti interrupts, "Whadda ya mean? Like Casinos?"

"No," Ed laughs so much he needs to stop.

"You mean Indian like Tonto?" Argenti tries to clarify.

"No, like Ghandi. Now shut up and let me finish my story. So, I hire this Indian kid, nice kid, went to Penn, everyone I hired went to Ivy League. Anyway, I start sending him to Indian people's houses."

"Oh God," Gunnulli starts up, "That smell! What the hell is that?"

"Curry," Ed continues, "So, he comes up to me one day and he says, "Why do you always send me to Indian people's houses? I was like, 'cause you're Indian. He says to me 'Indian people hate other Indian people. They didn't come all the way to America to buy something from another Indian. They want to buy something from John Wayne, not a Slumdog Millionaire.' And then he says to me,' The Chinese stick together because they're like midgets in a land of giants but not Indians.' So, I said to myself, 'Wow, this kid makes a lot of sense,' and then I fired him. But the point of the story is everyone wants to buy the American dream and they want to buy it from a WASP because people, all people, are nostalgic for WASPS. They're like an endangered species. And people yearn for the old days when WASPS ran everything. People love it when they kick their ass but they won't admit it. Like a broad or Ciacco over here." That last joke sets off an eruption of laughter.

For the first time in a long time, Argenti looks up as he sticks a piece of bread soaked in clam sauce into his mouth and confirms, "It's true."

"And that's why, if you had a T-O-N at the end of your name I hired you. If you hand an Ington at the end of your name like Worthington or Remington I made you a manager."

Canto puts down his knife and fork because he's still laughing, "The two of you are better than Martin and Lewis. How'd you get to be so funny."

Ed says to him, "Ask me what the key is to being funny?"

Canto asks, "What's the-"

"Timing."

Ciacco Argenti almost chokes from laughing. Ed points to the other two, "It's gonna take both of you to give him the Heimlich. Let him (pointing to Virgil) give him mouth-to-mouth."

"And how did you instill loyalty if you hire strangers?" Canto asks.

"I paid them insane commissions. And that was the key. These rich kids came from rich families and went to expensive schools. Anyone in their right mind would've known that there was no way to give that much commission off of such tight margins and still make a profit but these kids thought they actually deserved it. That it was their right to go to Aspen in the winter and Nantucket in the summer. And the best part was they were all liberals. When I started this carbon credit scam they sold the shit out of it because they believed in it."

"You built an empire at such a young age," Canto marvels.

"I'm not that young," Ed starts off, "I recently went to the doctor to get my prostate checked because you should get it checked when you start feeling old. So, the nurse tells me to take off all of my clothes, put on this hospital robe and bend over the table and wait for the doctor to examine me. So, I'm waiting there with my ass hanging out and the doctor comes in, puts on this rubber glove, and says, 'OK, Mike, try not to get an erection.' I said, 'Doc, my name is Edward and he says, 'I know, my name is Mike." Ed makes himself and the others laugh.

Canto stops laughing long enough to say, "You know who he reminds me of? A young Jack Pontiac."

"Hey," Gunnulli says to Canto, "Don't let this slick son of a bitch fool you with his nice suits and funny jokes he's the most vicious person I've ever met. He's the one that put most of the people in here."

"He killed me and my brother," Ciacco adds.

Canto is amazed, "You killed him and his brother?"

"They were bullies. They used to steal my stuff when I went off to boarding school. " Ed says.

"We were busting balls!" Ciacco explains.

"Ciacco used to be my enforcer. We used to call him Iron Fist, his brother too, but what Ed did to them was brutal. I mean, you should've seen the beating he gave me. I died from it. But, you know what, they asked me who did it to me and I said 'no one, I fell down the stairs' and the cop said, 'Of what? The Empire State Building?' But I didn't rat. I rolled over on that lousy Irish cop but not you. Did you kill that prick?"

Ed gets somber for a moment, "No. Listen, is my ...have you seen ...my parents?"

All three look down at their plates but Ciacco says, "No kid, I haven't seen them."

"Thank God!" Ed says with a sigh of relief.

"WHOA, WHOA," Gunnulli warns, "Don't say that word! Are you trying to get us killed?" The men laugh some more. "I mean Jesus Christ!" He puts his hand over his mouth like he let slip a dirty word.

Canto asks. "We're you married? Did you have kids?"

Ed answers, "I had a daughter."

Ciacco says, "Ed was a real lady killer. What was the name of that girl you used to date when we were kids? You know, the one with the hot sisters?"

"Erin Fury," is Ed's response.

"All four of them, this girl and her sisters, they were the hottest girls in the entire town and I think they all wanted Ed, even the oldest one. Did you ever do a threesome with the sisters?"

"No way! I wouldn't have even tried. Besides, we were young and Erin was the oldest so her sisters were really young." Ed explains.

Argenti concurs, "Oh yeah, real jail bait."

Virgil gets up and walks out of the room. They notice but they don't act like it.

"Oh yeah, I knew the mother, Gail. Back in the sixties she became a flower child and got into all that hippy-dippy free love crap," Gunnulli remembers. "Ain't that right, Ciacco."

"Yeah, I think all four of them had different fathers. It messed with their heads, they got into drugs and became whores."

"That's why you need a strong man to lead a family, "Canto says as he looks out to make sure Virgil is gone. Canto moves in closer to talk business, "There's a prophecy. A man that comes and he brings white, brown, black and yellow together and they overthrow the one who runs this place.

"He's right," Gunnulli adds, "With our help, you can run this place."

Argenti chips in, "Yeah, and the way this pansy kisses your ass the powers that be must really have a hard-on for you."

"Do you think we can get out of here?" Ed asks encouraged.

"Get outta here?" Gunnulli scoffs, "who wants to get the hell out of here? Get the hell out of here with getting out of here."

Canto offers his advice, "He's right. We're not in the dark place. This place is manageable."

"He's right," Gunnulli adds," down there we're just wise guys but up here we're made men. When we're with you we're good as long as we all stick together."

Argenti joins in, "That's right, familia!"

"Besides, Gunnulli reasons, "you ain't never been down there. If you had been you wouldn't even be thinking about getting out of here. This place is paradise compared to there. There ain't no hope down there. This is better than that Club Fed joint in Connecticut compared to going to the state pen. Hell, you spend a day down there you'd be begging to go to Supermax with all the Muslims and all the sickos.

"He's right," the other two both agree.

Virgil comes in and stands over the table. Before he can speak Gunnulli says to him, "Why don't you make yourself useful and get us four shots of Sambucca."

"None for me," Canto pipes up, "Maybe a little decaf."

"Sorry boys, the kitchen's closed," Virgil announces before slapping Ed on the shoulder, "But boy, do we have a surprise for you!"

HELL HATH NO FURY

After they say their goodnights, Virgil walks Ed back up to his room. "Hey, I hope I didn't come off like a Killjoy but those Capones were feeding you a lot of applesauce and I don't want you to be the one holding the bag. Besides, you're going to love what's waiting for you on the other side of the door. TRY to get some rest and I'll see you tomorrow."

He pats Ed on the back and walks back toward the elevator. Ed opens the door slowly, rather cautiously. He turns on the light and there are three very beautiful and extremely naked women lying in his bed under the sheets. ALEXIS is a fiery redhead, TRISH is a beautiful blonde and MEG is a lovely raven-haired vixen. They were seductively playing with each other until Ed walked in and now there are six eyes on him as they speak in unison, "Hi, Eddie!"

"Hello, ladies," he sings as he takes off his jacket and lays it over a chair before getting undressed. "You seem to know me but I'm at a loss."

"You don't remember us, Eddie? I'm Alexis, " she teases.

"I'm Trish."

"And I'm Meg. We're Erin's sisters.

"It can't be," Ed is amazed, "we were just talking about you tonight."

"He's so hot but so dumb," Trish reports.

"Where's Erin?" Ed asks.

"Alas," Alexis begins, "she won't be joining us this evening."

"You see she's no longer with us," Trish states.

And then Meg says, "That's OK, she never did like to share her toys."

Ed, to all three, but especially Meg, "How old are you?"

"Old enough," Meg shoots back.

"Oh, that's right," Trish says, "this will be our little sister's first time. Bye-bye virginity."

"Let's send her off with a bang!" Alexis jokes.

Tired of the small talk, Ed dives on the bed and pleasure ensues. And the first few hours are the most pleasurable he's ever experienced but not even his cardio is infinite and it becomes too much of a good thing. The sexual play goes from kinky to painful. At this point, he's exhausted and in a lot of pain.

"Hey girls, let's take a little nap. What do you say?"

"WHAT? Alexis almost explodes," I've been sucking you off getting you hard for these two and now I want to finish!"

"Calm down, " Trish says as she's used to this reaction. "No, you calm down! I've been generous all night and now it's my turn!"

"You've been generous!?"Meg reacts, "You two have been hogging him all night. This is MY first time! I want it to be special! You two always get the boys!

The three girls get into a knockdown drag-out fight with plenty of scratching and hair-pulling. Ed tries to break it up and at first, he's collateral damage getting a stray kick or punch but then it seems they turn on him a little. The fighting becomes vicious and these women get increasingly strong. Ed reaches for the duffle bag with his suit and weapons he left under the bed. He reaches into the bag and pulls out some zip ties he uses to subdue his victims.

The door opens and all three go from a frenzy to complete silence as their oldest sister, Ed's old girlfriend ERIN enters the room.

"WHAT THE HELL?" Erin screams. "MY SISTERS?"

"ERIN!" He scrambles off the floor as he goes right into guilty, apologetic boyfriend mode, "They told me you were dead!"

"No, I said she's no longer with us." Trish corrects him with sass, "We got into a fight."

"I AM DEAD!" Erin screams. "I killed myself over you!"

"WHAT?" Alexis goes to lunge at him but Trish and Meg hold her back.

"What do you mean? I thought you OD'd." Ed asks.

"I did! I killed myself over you! I couldn't take the pain anymore!" Erin cries out.

Trish turns angry, "You killed my sister you son of a bitch! Now I'm going to kill you." As she says it she crawls over the bed to get inside the bag and pulls out a knife from Ed's weapons. Ed tries to hold her back but at this point, all four of them are savagely beating on him. He fights them off long enough to run into the bathroom and lock himself in.

He sees his robe hanging up so he puts it on before sitting on the toilet with his head in his hands," This is unbelievable!"

He can hear the women scheming over the constant pounding of their fists and feet on the bathroom door.

"I got his bag!" Meg yells.

"GIRLS!" He yells through the door. Don't touch anything in there. It's dangerous! Someone can get hurt.

Trish sings loudly, "That's the ideeeeaaa!"

As he listens to all the scurrying around and going in and out of the room at least one of them, if not more, continues the steady and violent banging on the door. Then the FIRE ALARM GOES OFF! "Thank God," he thinks in relief.

He can hear Meg yell out, "I got this out of the hallway but I set off the alarm. It said shatter glass in case of emergency!"

Eddie heard this and says aloud, "Uh oh!"

That's when the chopping begins. Two of the sisters work together to swing the ax at the bathroom door. Pieces of wood fly in his direction. Another whack and a hole opens in the door.

Erin looks through the hole and with a devilish grin, "WHEEERE'S EDDIE!"

Ed knows he has to do something. No matter how loud the fire alarm is no one coming to his rescue. He looks up at the shower and comes up with an idea.

He turns the water on in the large jacuzzi bathtub and checks to make sure it's still scalding hot. He then turns on the shower and lets it run. By this time the women have shattered the door enough that they kick it in and come running through.

Erin is the first one through the door and she comes at him full speed wielding the ax with a crazed look in her eyes. She swings the ax at him but rather than back away he steps into it and using an aikido move flips her over into the tub of hot water. She wails in pain like a banshee.

As the other three fight over each other to get to him he takes the movable shower head off its cradle and sprays them with scalding water. They curl up and scream in agony as the fire rains on them. They finally are able to backtrack and run out of the hotel room completely naked.

Virgil shows up as the women run past him. He walks into the bathroom and holds his hands up speechless. He sees Ed sitting on the toilet with his head down.

Virgil sits down on the edge of the bathtub next to him. He surveys the damage.

"They're really going to regret doing this later. They're the housekeepers." Virgil sticks his hand in the water and pulls it out in pain. "Hell hath no fury."

Virgil convinces Ed he should go down to see the hotel doctor to do something about all the cuts and bruises he received. He actually insists on it. "Besides," Virgil adds, "There's something I'd like you to see.

They go down a flight below the lobby and they find a small office with an old-style look from a black and white detective movie with the name DR. WILLIAM BENNET painted on the door.

Ed, dressed only in his bathrobe and slippers, greets the physician with, "Wow Doc, I didn't expect you to be so young."

William Bennet was young-looking. With his shirt, tie, a white lab coat, and a stethoscope around his neck he looked more like a young man playing a doctor on a soap opera than a learned man of medicine.

"What seems to be the problem?" The young doctor asks but it doesn't seem like he's even interested in the answer.

"I had a little dust-up. I don't know if you heard the alarm or not."

"Was that you?" The doctor asks with less curiosity than the last question. He reaches into the pocket and pulls out an amber pill vial that rattles when he hands it to Ed. "Take as prescribed."

"Don't you want to find out what's wrong with me?"

"Nope," the doctor turns away and walks behind his desk where he sits down and pretends to read something. "It doesn't really matter."

"Then what are these?" Ed asks as he holds up the vial and shakes it.

Without looking up the doctor replies, "They're sugar pills. Around here hope is the only narcotic."

All the while Virgil, who's been standing in the corner steps up to the center of the room. "Hey, doc, why don't you show him the infirmary."

The doctor doesn't even look up from his reading, "He doesn't want to see it."

"Sure he does," Virgil cajoles.

Annoyed, the doctor gets up and walks over to the door on the other side of his room. They go into the next room, the small examination room, and walk right past it into another adjoining room.

This second room is much, much bigger. It's dark but lit up by the lights and flashes of life support machines. We can hear the beeps of the machines and the constant WHOOSHING sounds from the ventilators.

The doctor holds his hand out as if to say "here you go" and the look on his face reads "Happy?"

Virgil taps Ed on the shoulder and motions "Let's go."

They walk out into the hallway heading back upstairs. Ed looks at him and asks, "What was that all about?"

"All those people in those beds were doctors. Doctors who had lied or fudged numbers or did something they knew were wrong all for, what they thought, or were told, was the greater good. The young doctor there was a research lab assistant at the University of Pittsburgh while they conducted experiments using baby fetuses. They would grow human body parts on the backs of mice in hopes of one day being able to regenerate human tissue and save people's lives. Now, his job is to monitor all those people on respirators fighting for every breath knowing he can't do anything about it. He stopped caring a long time ago."

"But they were trying to do good or at least they thought they were," Ed reasons to him.

"Oh, I get it. The whole can't make an omelet without breaking a few eggs thing, right? A for effort."

"Right!"

"That's why they're here and not the other place." Virgil goes up the stairs leaving Ed to ponder.

Ed goes back up to his room by himself. He opens the door and the room is immaculate. It's just as it was when he first came. He walks over and the bathroom door is good as new.

There's a KNOCK on the door. Virgil walks in and this time he has a tuxedo, "I got your prom suit right here! New shoes, bow tie, the works!"

"Oh no," I'm not going out tonight! I need some sleep!"

Virgil hangs the suit up, "Come on, tonight's New Year's Eve!"

The evening arrives like a freight train and Ed greets it with a new tuxedo courtesy of Virgil. He enters the banquet hall and the place is full of people, all sorts of people, in all sorts of dress. It's a who's who of no good-doers. The first group that catches his eye is three men wearing Nazi-era uniforms and commiserating in German. They stick out in the crowd but there are all sorts of regular people who you'd think were decent people but something brought them here.

"Do these people really think it's New Year's Eve?" He wonders to himself until he sees the servants. Men and women all dressed in black pants and black shoes with white jackets, white shirts, and black bow ties. They also wear the same fake smile. Ed knows when someone is miserable and painting on a smile, he's done it himself for years.

Virgil, already visibly drunk, struggles to get out of the old-style phone booth in the lobby. The door is like an accordion and he's not sure if he should push it out or pull it in and the bottle of champagne in his hand makes it more difficult. He finally manages to stumble his way out onto the lobby floor where Ed witnesses the buffoonery.

"HI HO, my good man," Virgil belts out, "I'm glad you could make it for the fest- fest-festivities." He struggles to keep his balance while slurring his words. He puts his hand on Ed's chest to hold himself up. "I'll be master of ceremonies for the evening so I won't be able to spend much time with you. But, that doesn't mean I didn't think about you. I pulled some strings and I got the singer from that rock band you like to play for us tonight. My pleasure!"

"He's dead?" Ed asks honestly struck by the news.

"It's a shame really. He thought smoking was what gave him his raspy voice and he never ate so as to stay thin for the ladies but he couldn't stay away from the candy," Virgil says as he points to the inside of his elbow."

Some young girls dressed like flappers brush between them and Virgil turns and follows them leaving Ed alone at the doorway.

He's met at the door by Argenti, "Happy New Year, Edge!" He says as he gives him a bear hug.

"You too, Iron Fist," Ed replies using his school-yard nickname.

"Hey, we got a table over here. There's somebody Don Giovanni wants you to meet before we all get too crazy to talk."

As they walk over to the table Ed looks over toward the stage at the big band playing big band era music and he notices a small man holding up a stand-up bass and plucking away.

Ed points over toward him, "Isn't that the lead singer from that band?"

"I was always into disco," Argenti says as he leads Ed to the table.

They arrive at the table and Gunnulli and Canto are the only ones at a ten-chair table whispering to themselves. They light up when they see Ed. They go to get up but Ed motions for them not to bother.

"Happy New Year!" Gunnulli says with a smile.

"You too," Ed returns much less enthusiastically.

Canto gets right into it, "Eddie, I told you that you reminded me of someone, a great man and a great leader. You see, in my day, before you were born, we were really making strides in politics and we were getting our seat at the table. There weren't a lot of Italians in national politics but we still had some good friends in our corner and none better than Jack Pontiac. He's here tonight and I'd like you to meet him.

"Jack Pontiac?" Ed is borderline stunned. "I did my thesis on him in high school. He was a hero of mine."

"He was a hero to everybody," Gunnulli adds.

From across the room he strides over. Tall, thin, and at least six foot four with slicked-back grey hair and pearly white teeth that shine from a distance. He sticks out his hand and Ed, too surprised to stand, shakes it and his grip is as strong and as smooth as a velvet vice.

"Ed," Jack says with a smile, "it's good to meet you. I've heard a lot about you."

"Senator, it's a true pleasure," stumbles out of Ed's mouth.

"Sit, sit," Canto begs.

Jack sits down and offers an audience with him. "This is great!" Argenti squeals.

"Listen, Ed," Canto starts, "there's a prophecy of a great man that comes and unites everyone to overthrow our oppressors and you're that guy. I have an eye for talent. That's how I became the head of the largest family in the country. In the fifties and sixties, we were nation-wide and we did it with the help of Jack and now we got the team back together! You two together, forget about it, you'll be bigger than Mantle and Maris."

"Don't forget Joltin' Joe," Gunnulli jokes.

"Hey," Jack kids, "I was a Washington Senators fan!" That gets a big laugh, "Just kidding, I'm Detroit Tigers all the way! If any of my constituents heard me say that they'd have thrown me out of office."

"When I saw what Sam did in Chicago for Joe Kennedy and the ruin it brought upon us I said 'Never again' and I vowed to get Jack into the White House," Canto concedes, "but it didn't work out that way."

"You see, Ed" Jack explains, "I was a true Democrat. I was for the working man. I was union all the way, baby!" He does a little fist pump at the end of that sentence.

"And we owned the unions," Canto adds.

"Ed, I was always a man of the people. The working-class men and women that built America. When Kennedy came in it became the party of rich college kids and you saw what happened. When Johnson had him killed I kept my mouth shut. And how do they repay me? I would've brought the party together. Humphrey and Muskie were weak and Wallace was a loudmouth redneck. LeMay loved me but I wouldn't have made in VP, I would've made him secretary of defense but not VP."

"Who would've been your veep?" Ed asks.

"You see?" Canto jumps in, "He's smart enough and bold enough to ask the right questions."

"You're not going to believe this but I had talks with George Romney and Spiro Agnew!"

"Ain't that something!" Gunnulli jumps in, "And that's straight from the horse's mouth. You ain't gonna find that in any history book!"

"You see, Ed, " Jack continues, "I really am an uniter. I can help you bring all the people together."

"Listen, Ed" Canto gets in, "I backed Jack but I never bribed him. He was an honest guy. He wasn't in it for the money. I wanted to help him to help the country.

And a strong country with strong unions is good for the country. It was all legit."

"Then the Six Days War," Ed concludes.

Jack turns to Canto and smiles, "This kid IS as sharp as a tack. Yes, you're right. I was against Israel in the Six Days War and it made me look bad. And since the Jews own the media I was done. But I knew the truth. Come on, man! You're going to tell me if all your neighbors decide to attack you one day that not only are you going to beat them but you're going to end up with more land? Come on, man! That's a fairy tale!

If you were so great then why are you here?" Ed asks with a prosecutorial tone.

There's silence at the table, they can't believe he has the balls to ask that of the great Jack Pontiac. For the first time, Jack shows his teeth but not with a smile. He turns away, looking back on his life when he says with a slight growl. "I blame my savage wife for my torments."

Ciacco Argenti uses this moment to break in and change the subject. "Listen, I've been talking to one of the waiters, his name is Ruggieri, he's a paisan, he said if something goes down he'll help us out and give us a heads up if the bosses are onto anything."

Ed looks past them as he notices someone, "Is that Enzo?" He stands up and walks toward the man he recognizes trying to make his way across the dance floor.

Jack is insulted, "Where the hell is he going? We're right in the middle of serious negotiations here."

Canto puts his hand on his shoulder, "He sees his uncle. His father's brother. It's a Sardinian thing."

Ed comes over with a smile on his face happy to see him, "Uncle Enzo! It's me, Little Eddie!" Ed gives the man a hug and he cries on Ed's shoulder. "Why are YOU here?"

Unable to look him in the eye and with his lip quivering Enzo replies, "Sodomy."

Ed gives him a look of understanding, "Did Larry and Aunt Fran know?"

He shakes his head no, "I was good about hiding my true self."

Ed puts his hands on both shoulders holding the crumbling man up so that he can look him in the eye, "Listen to me, when my parents and sister were killed you took me in and Larry became my little brother. More than anyone else you taught me how to be a man and I will be eternally grateful and we can be stuck here forever and I could still never put into words how I feel."

Virgil appears to Ed for the first time tonight on stage with the microphone in his hand and shouts out "LIMBOOOO TIME!"

The crowd cheers and the dance floor divides. People clearing the center happily push Enzo and Ed apart. Enzo, with his head down in shame, is relieved to be sent away and Ed doesn't fight the smiling faces pushing him away.

Ed turns away from the dance floor and puts his head down and tussles his hair trying to make sense of this world and the one he left. He walks against the current of happy people who can't wait to crawl backward under a broom.

When Ed does look up he sees one young woman who doesn't rush to the dance floor. Ed recognizes the strawberry blonde hair from a distance. "It can't be," he says to himself.

As he walks toward her a man dressed in black stands before him blocking his path. He looks up to see the white collar of a priest. It's Bishop Tammany dressed as a regular parish priest.

"Hello, Edward." He greets him with a polite smile.

"Bishop Tammany! What are you doing here?"

Regretfully, "I guess I really didn't believe."

Ed slaps him on the shoulder, "I bet you do now," and pushes him out of his way and keeps walking toward the woman.

When he gets there he sees Mary Margaret Keen, Robin's mother, as the younger version of her when they first met and he swears she's glowing.

"Hi Eddie," she greets him with a smile.

"Maggie, I never realized how beautiful you were."

"That's because you were always looking for revenge and never looking at me."

"I'm so sorry. I always-"

She cuts him off, "How is she? We can't see what goes on up there."

"She's beautiful, she's rich and she's popular. I mean like internationally famous. She's a role model for young girls everywhere. She's like a Regal. She likes to go by Rainbow."

"That's cute," she says with a smile holding back tears.

"ITS GETTING CLOSE TO MIDNIGHT SO EVERYONE BETTER GRAB A GLASS" Virgil booms on the microphone.

It's so loud it jolts Ed and he turns around to say, "Already?"

When he turns back around she is instantly transformed into the way she looked when she died, twenty years older, twenty pounds thinner with pale blemished skin and ratty hair wearing jeans and a tee-shirt. He takes a step back and she hides her face and runs away.

"WAIT!" He tries to run after her but Virgil gets in his way.

"Why are you chasing that wallflower? I hear there are some real hotsy-totsies here tonight!"

"You're like some psycho-pimp!" As he pushes Virgil out of his way to go after her, but everyone in the hall, led by Canto, Iacopo, and Ciacco is holding up their champagne glasses to him and chanting, "PAPE SATAN! PAPE SATEN ALEPPE!"

He runs out of there and out to the lobby. He looks around but she's gone. He decides to call it a night and go to bed.

When he gets to the door of his room he takes off his bow tie and opens up his collar.

When he opens the door he sees a woman sitting in his bed waiting for him. The room is dimly lit, the only light coming from behind the closed bathroom door. He can't see the woman but he can make out her silhouette and it's voluptuous. The woman gets up on her knees at the edge of the bed, "Come here, baby."

He can't help but go to her and they embrace with the most sensuous kiss he's ever experienced. He can't help his arousal and as their bodies merge he can tell that she's not shaved. He eventually pulls off her full lips to grab a breath of air and to take a look at her.

It's at this moment he hears the shower running and muffled screams coming from the bathroom. "Is there someone in the bathroom?"

"It's just my husband." She says.

He squeezes his brows together trying to make sense of it before running into the bathroom.

There's a man in the glass-enclosed shower and he's screaming in pain. Ed tries to open the door but the metal handle is much too hot so he has to palm the outer sliding door and turns off the scalding water.

The man collapses into the tub with his upper body hanging out of the open shower door. The man's face is so blistered and swollen Ed can't even make it out. Ed looks around the room for a towel-or something-when he notices the amber vial with the white cap that the doctor had given him.

He grabs it and holds up the man's head, "Here, take these!"

The man is barely conscious when he asks, "What, what is it?"

"They're pain killers! They're REALLY strong! They work instantly! Let me get you some water!"

Just the word 'water' snaps the man awake," NO!"

Ed funnels the pills into the man's mouth using his hand as the man gobbles them up, "They're really strong so be careful," Ed lies to him again hoping it will help him believe they work.

"Thank you, Ju-Ju," as the man collapses again.

Ed jumps up practically falling into the sink out of fear as if he's seen a ghost. He scrambles out of the room barely able to grab the doorknob he's so scared.

When he comes out, he turns on the lights to find the woman is waiting for him with open amorous arms.

"M-mommy?" That is all he can get out.

"Yes, baby," she comes clean, "come to bed and mommy will make it all better.

He crumbles to his hands and knees from the weight of it all. The twenty-eight-year-old Lucia Gennaro is waiting for him in bed as her thirty-year-old husband lies in his bathtub.

"NO! NO! NO!" He yells as he punches the floor.

"Eddie come to bed now!" She tries to use a forceful motherly tone to coax him.

Ed reverts to a little baby crying, "WHYYY? WHYY?" He needs to suck up oxygen after each cry just to be able to breathe.

"Your father was in too deep," she explains.

"BUT WHY YOU?" He cries back.

"Because I knew and I still loved him. And I didn't protect you and your sister."

Ed, still sobbing on the ground, "What about-"

"My sweet angel is in heaven."

That little bit of news saves him. The thought of his sister being here would be too much for even him to bear. Still, on all fours, he pulls himself together and wiping the tears from his eyes looks under the bed where he can see his duffle bag.

He scurries across the floor to get to the bag. For a moment, Lucia sees him as he was when he was trying to walk for the first time. But she knows what he's doing. A mother always knows.

"No, baby, no baby don't! Please Eddie come to bed! If you leave they are going to send us back! Please, Eddie, I can't go back!"

Ed pulls the bag out from under the bed and opens it to take a quick inventory when he HEARS the SHOWER turn back on. "NO!" He yells toward the bathroom.

"He has to suffer, Eddie. Even now, this is the first time he's been out of the lake of fire but they won't let him stop burning, not even for a minute."

Ed looks up at her, "Do you suffer?"

"They m-make me..." she can't even say what they make her do in front of her son.

Ed zips up the bag, gets up, and heads for the door.

She grabs him pleading," PLEASE! I CAN'T GO BACK!"

He turns to look at her. His heart breaks with each tear that rolls down her cheek. He stares at her beautiful round face one last time before walking away.

She pulls him back, "Please! Let me suck your dick!"

He pushes her off of him as she falls back on the bed. He runs out slamming the door behind him. He can hear her cries all the way down the hall.

"NO, PLEASE COME BACK! PLEEASE!"

He makes his way down the hotel corridor to the elevators but something weird happens. The red-carpeted floor feels soft and unsteady. He loses his balance and falls to the floor. His hands break his fall and the bag falls down beside him. The floor feels wet and porous. He lifts his hand and feels the moisture. The hallway gets dark. He notices the floor is moving. He tries to get to his feet but he can't stay up because the floor is too shaky. When he falls down again the floor is much softer. This time he recognizes the moist feeling of a tongue. The floor has become a tongue and the hallway looks like the throat of a demon.

He buries his face into his arm and screams out, "NOOOO!"

He's losing his mind and recognizes that in his descent into madness is him being swallowed up whole. This is where his true nature is revealed. What makes him such a fierce competitor in business and an unbeatable foe in fighting isn't his unwillingness to lose but his undying need, his insatiable want to inflict so much pain on the other that they regret even challenging him. If he is going to be swallowed up whole he will leave such a bad taste on the monster's tongue that it'll lose its appetite and die of starvation. It will slowly waste away to nothing spending every last second of its miserable existing regretting it ever laid eyes on Edward D. Gennaro.

He reaches into his bag and pulls out a boot and slides one of his daggers out of the side compartment. He then raises the dagger and drives it so far into the tongue of the beast that the whole building shakes from it and blood gushes up into the air. He drives it in again and again and again quicker and harder each time not stopping until he hits carpeting on a wooden floor and the lights come back on and the hallway is back to normal.

Now that his world is somewhat normal, he regains his composure, gets to his feet and walks over to the elevator, and punches the down button so hard he almost punches a hole in the wall. As he waits for the doors to open he takes off his blood-covered tuxedo shirt and pants. And by the time the elevator lets him off into the lobby he is fully dressed in his tactical gear and ready to go hunting. But he's too late.

When he gets to the doorway of the banquet room he sees that someone has written over the door in blood: ABANDON ALL HOPE. He walks in to find a blood-bath as the wait staff turned demonic and killed all the guests save for one, Jack Pontiac.

He walks by a group of waiters literally ripping Argenti apart and eating him with bones and body parts strewn on the floor.

Standing behind them, jumping up and down and banging two drum cymbals together like a monkey, is the Rock Star cheering them on. Ed steps over Argenti's remains and pushes the demonic waiter out of the way to get to him.

The Rock Star sees him and cries out," I'm not doing anything! I'm just standing here!"

"This is for your last album," Ed says as he reaches back and punches him harder than the Rock Star's five foot seven, one hundred and thirty-pound frame can take. His nose is driven into his skull. The beating is so horrific that the demons are aghast.

He keeps on walking to find a group of demons beating on Gunnulli who is sitting in a chair the same way he was when Ed beat him to death. He raises a shaky hand as Ed passes by begging for help but he can't say the words. Then Ed comes to find Jack strangling Canto with his bare hands. When Jack sees Ed standing beside him he drops Canto and the little man's head hits the dance floor with a thud. Jack pulls out the handkerchief neatly showing from his breast pocket and wipes the sweat off his face and then he pulls out a comb and combs his hair back giving him time to calm down, regain his composure, and try to reason with him like the true politician he is.

Jack holds his hands up and says, "Satàn just wants peace."

"Don't assume I came here to bring peace. I brought a knife," Ed holds the knife up menacingly as he walks toward him.

Before Jack can say another word, Ed reaches into his mouth and grabs the politician's tongue, and cuts it out of his mouth as his garbled scream gets the attention of the demonic waiters. Even they back away in fear as Ed passes by them.

Ed walks out of the banquet hall and heads straight for the front desk where Charon cowers along the back wall as he approaches.

"Quid vultis mecum?" she asks quivering. "Ne me torqueas!

She tries to avoid him but he reaches over the counter and grabs her by the hair and drags her over the front desk and throws her to the floor.

"Daemonium loqui anglicus!" He demands as he bangs her head on the floor after each word.

"You don't belong here! Go back from the pit from whence you came!" She growls.

"Maybe I like it here. I think I'll stay. Now, what shall I do with you?"

"Allow me to go out to the pigs!" She pleads.

He stuffs Jack's tongue into her mouth and he lets her get up. She runs to the front door and bursts through it where she is immediately swarmed by the starving people outside who immediately claw and grab her ripping her clothes off her body and eventually tearing into her. Ed uses this opportunity to walk right past the melee. It's when of the angry mob sees that the entrance to the hotel is open at they leave her on the ground and pour inside.

Ed is running to the clearing when Charon calls out to him," PLEASE! WAIT!"

Against his better judgment, he turns back toward her. She makes it to her feet and offers as an olive branch, "My name is Ka-Ron."

He looks at her and wonders what to do with that knowledge when just outside his periphery he sees a large lion casually strolling around the grounds. He sticks his hands out as if to say," Stay put, don't move," but the words don't come out.

"Please take me with you," the battered, bruised, and bloody woman pleads.

Ed's eyes dart to the right as he watches the nostrils of the lion flare as he smells the blood and launches himself a distance of over thirty feet with his front paws landing on her shoulders. He can HEAR the CRACK of her neck as the lion lands on top of her and he can only watch helplessly as the lion tears into her flesh.

She reaches out with one hand and both eyes toward Ed as she asks him to," Help me," as the lion eats her alive.

It was already too late. She'd be dead before he could take two steps forward so he turns back and runs across the meadow to the tree line. It's dark and all he can hear is the sound of his breath and the pounding of his boots but he senses something gaining on him like he's standing still. He realizes whatever it is coming at him it's no use trying to run from it. He must stop and confront it. He has one grenade in his belt that he made with his 3D printer and he never thought he'd need it to fight off a wild animal but he's happy he has it nonetheless.

How will he throw a grenade at something he can't see? By the time he throws it this thing will be on him and moving so fast that the blast will kill them both.

He's going to have to stop and turn on his flashlight. At this point, whatever is tracking him can probably smell him so it's not like he's giving up his position. So he stops and pulls out his flashlight.

It's a spotted leopard that runs past him and turns back around. "What's he doing?" Ed thinks to himself. Ed turns to face him realizing too late that the leopard was setting him up for something else coming from behind. He hears the barking and growling of the grey wolf coming before its paws make an impact on his back.

He's able to spin himself around so that he's on his back facing the wolf and was able to jam his left forearm into the wolf's mouth. It's the Kevlar and the baton mounted on his forearm that keeps the wolf from biting his arm off completely. He flashes the flashlight into the wolf's eyes and briefly notices that the wolf has two different colored eyes before he flips the flashlight in his hand and smacks the wolf right on the nose, stunning it and making the two colored eyes tear as the wolf steps back and sneezes.

Now he's on his feet and both his batons are out, extended, and fully charged. Now it's a little closer to fair.

"Come on!" He yells, "I got something for both of you!" But they don't charge. He's smart enough to know that they're not afraid, they're waiting for their friend.

On cue, a bolt of lightning flashes the sky followed almost instantly by a thunder BOOM.

He moves cautiously, slowly knowing he has no time before the lion arrives but doesn't want to make any sudden moves. He lowers to one knee, pulls out a grenade and his butane pen torch, and places the two next to each other gently on the ground. The two animals are transfixed by the bright light and something they think might be food. He takes this time to tiptoe out of the light and then sprint to the tree line as the rain comes down hard. By now the lion is on the scene and the wolf, the leopard, and the lion quizzically stare at the flame before it explodes.

The force from the blast actually pushes him forward a little faster as his legs have to keep up. He runs to the first tree he sees and climbs up it. It was extremely difficult climbing the dead trees when it wasn't raining but now it's almost impossible. Almost. As hard as it would be to climb a greased pole there is something about being chased by beasts from hell that allows you to open up your ability to adapt to the situation.

"I'm in the clear," he says aloud but as massive as the blast was he knows they'll eventually come back so he decides to stay up in the treetops. He kept his flashlight because he knew he'd need it to find his bearings. He climbs up a small tree until he can perch himself comfortably atop. As the rain comes down in sheets, he pulls out what he calls his "wrist rocket" and attaches it to his right forearm, and pushes up the retractable sight on it. He then takes out a collapsible grappling hook and extends it before tying it to something very similar to a fishing line and loads the rocket with it.

He awaits the next lightning strike to aim for the next tallest tree in his sights. BOOM the rocket is fired just as the thunder comes and the hook is buried into the taller tree off in the distance. The electric motor kicks in and the rope pulls him up to the next tree. Like rooftops, you cover more ground quicker in the treetops but it's a lot harder. But even in the dark, from the top of the canopy of dead trees he knows he'll need to do this several more times to get to the pit, he came from. Like most of his life luck has always come into play but this time it's bad.

He hears a blood curdling SCREECHING like a banshee or, what he thinks might be a pterodactyl, swoop in, dig its claws into his shoulders and lift him out of the tree like he was a chickadee. Usually, the rule of thumb when dangling high in the air is to never look down but in this case, he keeps looking down trying to figure out what's going on and where he is. He fights to get one hand free as the talons of this flying monster dig into his clavicle. He looks up to see it's a human-looking bird with a wingspan of at least eighteen feet. He pulls out his long knife and digs it deep into the beast's breast and through his glove, he can feel human flesh.

The flying beast lets out an even louder, higher pitch scream of pain as it lets him go, an intended consequence that he wasn't ecstatic about. The dead branches break off easily but hurt just the same as he hits every one of them, slowing his fall, but brings him a meeting with the muddy ground below.

He sinks into the mire like quicksand as he can only look up as the rain hits his eyes and the lightning flashes long enough to see the flying beast circle around him. He closes his eyes to cover his eyes from the pouring rain until he stops feeling the rain hit his face and he feels the rushing air of giant flapping wings upon him. It lands on top of him and sinks its talons into his chest. He opens his eyes just as the lightning flashes to put him eye to eye with the winged vengeance with the body and face of ...Maggie! She screams at him just as he cries out in pain.

But all he hears is the voice of Max Po shouting, "CLEAR!"

LOOK WHO'S COME BACK
FROM THE DEAD

E d opens his eyes to a blinding light that makes his eyes tear. And for one brief moment, he thinks that he's survived Hell and is now on his way to Heaven.

"Ed, Edward, Mr. Gennaro, can you hear me?" A voice calls out to him.

"Wait, God wouldn't call me Mr. Gennaro," he thinks. It's that realization that brings him out.

Behind the glare of a penlight pointing directly in his eyes is the face of Max Po," It's Max Po. Can you hear me?"

"Yeah, did you lose weight?" Ed asks groggily but still perceptive.

Max turns back to two other men in the room, "He's alive."

"That was intense," an unseen voice says.

Ed was right, Max Po does look much thinner than when they first met. Still somewhat overweight but closer to three hundred pounds than before when he was closer to five hundred. Ed notices that he's wearing a white doctor's coat as he goes over to confer with two other men that he can't see. The room is not a hospital room, at least not from what he can tell, but he can only see the ceiling and there are no windows. He is on a hospital bed and there is an IV drip next to him but the defibrillator they used was the kind you can find at any restaurant.

It's at this moment that he learns he can move, he's no longer paralyzed like he was back at the elevator shaft but he's strapped into the bed. He jerks around trying to get free. When he can't free his escape mentality kicks in and he tries harder to get free shaking the bed and almost knocking over the IV.

THEODORE WAY, a little older than Max, with long, curly, salt and pepper hair and wearing wraparound shades comes over to calm him down by putting his hand gently on his shoulders.

"Hello, Mr. Gennaro," the man says as welcoming as possible, "welcome back to the land of the living."

"WHO ARE YOU? WHERE AM I?" Ed barks not as loud as he would like but still forcibly.

"You are in a townhouse a few blocks away from our building you broke into," the man reassures.

"So, I'm your prisoner?"

"No, not at all. When Max found you he brought you back here. He thought you might've broken your back and he brought you here and stabilized you."

"Wheres my daughter? Is she still alive?"

"She's still alive but she isn't here. Mr. Gennaro, you've been out for over twenty-three days." "WHAT?" Ed can't believe it. He felt like he was only at the hotel only one full night.

"We received an alarm that someone broke into the building. When Mr. Po went to investigate he found a small fire but nothing else," the man explains.

"I thought it was a false alarm," Max jumps in defensively, "I mean who breaks into an empty building? Maybe kids or squatters."

"FALSE ALARM? You booby-trapped the place waiting for me to break in."

"It wasn't until we reviewed the security camera footage that we saw you and who we presume to be your daughter in the lobby and the explosives went off."

JOHN BRADY IV, in the corner of the room and out of Ed's line of vision chimes in, "You did say that a rat always takes the cheese."

Theo turns back toward Ed and says apologetically, "I meant that as a metaphor not as a pejorative. I didn't think you'd actually come and steal the cheese!"

"And they call you The Visionary," John chuckles. Max has to turn away and put his head down to hide his laughter.

"Who the hell are you?" Ed asks pushing back on his restraints.

"Well, you already know Max's name. And, I don't know if we're quite ready for real names. It's not that we don't trust you but, well, we don't trust you. After all, you did try to break in and steal from us and it's been revealed that you are an international criminal wanted in six continents, we're not sure about Antarctica, and that you were the mastermind behind the largest Ponzi scheme ever, next to Social Security,

I don't think we're on a real name basis yet. So, I guess you can call me The Visionary. And you can call my other associate the Alchemist."

John (AKA The Alchemist) sticks his head into Ed's vision and sings, "But you can call me Alllll, call me Al."

"Really?" Theo says in distaste.

"You know, from the song. What? Too soon?" John wonders aloud.

"Come on, man! Read the room!" Max chastises.

"I think we've embarrassed ourselves enough for one day. Let's let Mr. Gennaro rest for a little while. I'll come back in and check on you." Theo escorts his two friends out with him.

Ed tries to call after them but he falls back exhausted and finally falls off into a deep sleep.

Ed wakes up when Theo re-enters the room. What feels like a moment to Ed is another whole day. "You're wearing different clothes," he points out.

"Yes," Theo answers," You were still pretty tired. You slept all night. Max put in a feeding tube when you first got here and he's not sure if you're ready for solid food so I brought some of those meal replacement shakes in different flavors."

"I thought he was a lawyer," Ed asks by stating.

"He got his law degree after he went to medical school. He never had a practice in either but he is licensed in both," Theo explains.

"So what happens now? You turn me in or hold me for ransom?"

"Neither. As soon as you're healed we send you on your way. But I need to repeat, you've been out for quite a while. Your situation has changed drastically."

"Where's my daughter?"

"We don't know. She left the building and a few days later reported you missing and then reported you dead. They had a memorial TV special in prime time on all the channels. Your daughter sang, it was quite emotional. I taped it for you."

"Why didn't you tell them that I'm still alive?"

"We thought that might not be a good idea for your sake. We didn't set those traps for you. Your daughter said she set off the traps but the video is inconclusive.

It looks like she might've been the one that set you up, we can't be sure. But what I can tell you was that somebody wants you dead so I thought it best to let them think that way"

"So you didn't set those traps?"

"Who would put explosives in their own building? The Fire Marshall would have a field day with that. The video shows you getting blown into the elevator shaft. When Max looked down he shined the light to the bottom and didn't see anything. He assumed you climbed up and out. After all, you do have all that equipment on that suit of yours. By the way, we tried to keep as much of it intact as we could but we had to cut it open to get to you. Oh, and Max got shocked when he tried to get your mask off. He wasn't happy about that. It seems you're the one who booby traps things. It wasn't until your daughter went on TV and announced that you were missing and presumed dead that we went looking for you. If your suit had a little more color you would've been easier to see."

"You're not the first person to tell me that. So, how did you get me out of the shaft?"

"Max got you out."

"How the hell did HE get me out."

"Let's just say that he's got a big heart and leave it at that."

"What's with the sunglasses... are you...blind?"

"Me? No" he chuckles," If I were it'd be kind of cruel calling me 'The Visionary" he does finger air quotes as he says it.

"It would be like calling Max 'slim.' If I'm not a prisoner then why am I still strapped in?"

"Max felt it best to immobilize you due to your back. He induced the coma to help with the healing process and to save you from the pain. While you were sleeping you must've had some intense dreams because you were thrashing around quite a bit. That's why we restrained you."

Theo adjusts the restraints so that Ed can move his hands.

"Thanks," Ed offers as he rubs his wrists.

"I brought you some books to read if you get restless. I'm embarrassed by how so few I have. There's Dante's 'Inferno', Milton's 'Paradise Lost' and of course, the Bible. This one is not as heavy but it's pretty good, it's called New Jerusalem, New Jersey. It's a murder mystery set in a small town where all the characters are people out of the Bible."

"I think I sense a theme," Ed kids.

"You're right. Maybe I'm not the only one who sees things around here. But the New Jersey one is really good and it's an easy read," The Visionary recommends as he places the books on a nightstand. "Max closed the hole for your feeding tube. How are the sutures holding up? Have you had any more bad dreams?"

"Don't tell me you're a psychiatrist."

"I don't believe in psychiatry. It excuses bad behavior by making exceptions into rules. I just thought if you wanted to talk, " Theo turns to walk out.

As he opens the door to leave, Ed starts talking, "It felt so real. I don't think it was a dream. It was more like..."

"A vision," The Visionary finishes for him.

"Everything looked OK, but it was all...dead. The trees were all there but if you touched them they crumbled in your hand. The people were alive but they acted like animals. And the animals, they were...evil... like... people. It felt like the end of the world."

"'Do not fear what you are about to suffer. Behold, the devil is about to throw some of you into prison, that you may be tested, and for ten days you will have tribulation. Be faithful unto death, and I will give you the crown of life.' Do you know what that's from?"

"The Bible?" Ed guesses.

"Revelation."

"So, tell me," Ed starts to change the subject, "If you weren't trying to set me up, then why did you create the whole story about you wanting to be an investor and showing me that phony diamond?"

"What I wanted no longer matters. What I was trying to avoid has come to pass." "What do you mean?"

"Are you familiar with 'Democracy in America'? I mean the work of Alexis de Tocqueville. He wrote about America, as an outsider, almost two hundred years ago. 'If despotism were to be established in present-day democracies, it would probably assume a different character. It would be more widespread and kinder. It would debase men without tormenting them.' That's the path Bush the first set us on when he alluded to a kindler, gentler new world order."

"What does that have to do with me?"

"He also wrote, 'The vices of those who govern, and the ineptitude of those governed, would soon bring it to ruin, and the people, tired of its representatives and of itself, would create free institutions or would soon revert to its abasement to one single master.' When you "died" your scheme collapsed, it caused a run on the market and that led to a crash. A crash greater than ever and President Simon used it to "temporarily" seize control of all financial markets including those of Financial Edge Investments and your Carbon Offset Markets. You were too big to die."

"So, you're afraid America is going to run by socialists," Ed concludes.

"No, he said 'one single master.'"

"So you were going to use my company to destroy the economy?" Ed asks indignantly.

"I didn't have to be a visionary to see that your scheme was a house of cards and all it needed was one little bump at the right moment."

"You sound like a cheap comic book villain," Ed scoffs.

"Coming from a jewel thief who dresses up in a costume... It turns out you were the one who destroyed the economy."

"YOU'RE LYING!" Ed yells as the straps and the pain stop him from lunging at him.

"I'd give you my laptop," Theo offers, " to search the internet but I'm afraid that if there are people trying to kill you, they'll be monitoring your accounts and if you were to try to contact somebody and since we use our neighbor's WiFi they might go after him and kill him. Poor guy doesn't deserve that. It's bad enough we steal his internet. He's a quiet guy, doesn't bother anybody, keeps to himself."

"He sounds like a serial killer. Wait a minute! You have million-dollar diamonds and you can't pay for internet?"

"You said it yourself; I'm trying to destroy the economy not contribute to it. Between that, the cable and the landline, it's crazy! I'm going to go out and buy you a TV with a digital antenna. I was going to order it online but-"

"Don't tell me, Amazon is evil."

"Now, you're getting it!"

"What's stopping me from breaking out of these straps, breaking your neck, and leaving here with the diamond?" Ed asks menacingly.

"Please don't do that. I was the one who convinced the other two to let you stay here. If you were to break out and kill me I'd die of embarrassment before you even got your hands on me. I doubt The Alchemist cares if you live or die, so if you kill me, there's no one to stop Max from killing you."

"What's he gonna do? Sit on me?" Ed mocks.

"I'm sure you're a very formidable man, but when Max gets going I don't think there's a human being that can stop him."

"HIM?"

"You see, that's why he doesn't like you! You judge people based solely on looks. He finds you intellectually debased and superficial. He sees a mirror-loving, pleasure-seeking mediocrity."

"ME? A MEDIOCRITY?"

Ed has been called many things but no one has ever called him a mediocrity. And in all the years of hardening, it was thought that no person's words could touch him much less hurt him. But those stung. Because, after all, he's been through, his death, the betrayals, and the failure of his company, for the first time he thinks they might be right.

"I came here to make sure you were doing better not to make you feel worse. But I also wanted to prepare you for the things you are about to learn about yourself, your family, and the world."

"I guess I should be thanking you for saving my life," Ed concedes.

"I didn't tell you those things because I wanted to reveal my plan. I'm not a comic book villain. I told you those things to tell you that my friends and I were planning to destroy the economy to keep it out of the hands of the one single master. They were willing to join me knowing that it would end our lives as we knew them and make us into villains. Those two have more abilities and more opportunities than any other humans on the planet and they were willing to throw it all away to help their fellow man and for the greater good. Those men should have statues made of them and cities named after them. But no one will ever know who they are or what they did for them. I'm telling you this because I want at least one other person to know."

Ed leans forward, "If they're so great then why do they follow you?"

"My companions saw the light but did not understand the voice of the one speaking to me."

"What did you mean prepare me for things I would learn about me? How bad is it?"

"There is no fall so deep that grace cannot descend it and no height so lofty that grace cannot lift a sinner to it."

Ed stares out into space when he asks," What if you're wrong?"

"What if," Theo repeats giving him time to think, "If you can talk with crowds and keep your virtue, Or walk with kings nor lose your common touch if neither foes nor loving friends can hurt you if all men count with you, but none too much, if you can fill the unforgiving minute with sixty seconds worth of distance run, Yours is the Earth and everything that's in it, and, which is more, you'll be a man, my son."

On that note, he walks out and closes the door behind him.

The next time Ed wakes up he opens his eyes to find a television with an old VHS player underneath it and a digital antenna above it. There's a cassette tape sticking out of the VCR along with a remote and a note that reads: JUST PRESS PLAY.

The recording is that of the network broadcast of the live funeral service for Edward D. Gennaro. He fast forwards through the beginning just stopping to see who the hosts are. "He says to himself, " They got the nightly news anchor to do this? Wow, they must be taking it seriously!" Until they cut to the cohosts of the morning news shows, "And now they bring in the vidiots!" So he fast forwards through a lot of their talking. He does play it back when they discuss all of the charitable works he's done, "Even I know a lot of that is bullshit!"

They do a video biography only saying that his parents and sister "died tragically when he was just four years old," mentioning nothing about them being murdered or his father's criminal history, or his mafia connections.

They do bring up his childhood at boarding schools. They show yearbook pictures from when he was young and they show a picture of a young Ed alongside Ben Oliver, Alex Morgan, and Kyle Webb. Ed freezes the frame and mumbles, "I think Jay was in that picture. I don't believe it!

They digitally erased Jay. I guess it's for the best. I wonder if they even tried to reach out to him for an interview? They probably did and realized he's a lunatic."

Ed fast forwards some more and they're still on Ben Oliver. They show him at his office, then they show him walking through one of his manufacturing plants, and then they show him throwing a ball to his dog in the countryside, "What are they doing? This is an infomercial for Oliver Industries. The son of a bitch looks like he's a model for L.L. Bean. Who gets dressed up to play catch with their dog in front of a camera crew? I can't believe he uses my death as a way to promote his company. This is more like an online dating profile than an interview about a lost friend."

The program then moves on to Alexander Morgan who as the commentators point out, "Hasn't done in an interview in years but has decided to break his silence to discuss his dear friend Edward Gennaro." Ed rolls his eyes and thinks, "Dear friend? I haven't talked to him in fifteen years and that was only at a ski resort in the Alps."

The interview takes place in one location in front of a dark backdrop. "At least he's didn't do it from his corner office or his penthouse apartment," Ed credits. But as he fast forwards through the piece they show the old photograph of them at school and the picture zooms in on the young Kyle Webb. "No, no, he's not going to talk about Kyle." Ed turns OFF the MUTE button.

ALEX: It was around this time that we had an English teacher named Mr. Hart and he had the class read "The Three Musketeers" and during recess, Ben Oliver, Edward, and myself told ourselves that we were the musketeers. Now, another student who was new and was on scholarship wanted to join our ranks, and Ben and I said 'no' but it was Edward who stepped in and said, 'You know, there were really FOUR Musketeers. So, we said, 'he's right' and we let him join and we were all dear friends until the fourth boy was killed in a tragic accident. And now that Edward is no longer with us our ranks are shrinking evermore.

A rush of emotions hit him all at once. First, he couldn't believe that Alex had the audacity to mention Kyle and then not to at least say his name. Either mention him or don't bring him up at all. Secondly, Ed doesn't even remember reading the book much less wanting to be one of the characters. He wonders, "When did Alex come up with that one? Probably while the sound guy was pinning the mic to his shirt. And then to call what happened to Kyle a tragic accident. "What the hell was that?" Was he afraid to tell the truth? Was he worried about retribution after all these years or was his thinking more in the line of Ed's in that it wasn't worth digging it back up. And Mr. Hart? Why did Alex have to mention his name? It's true, they all liked Mr. Hart. He was everyone's favorite teacher. But he was killed along with Kyle and it was never certain if he played in it. Rich kids are the least inquisitive because they know it's not worth ruining a good thing. But their lives are haunted just as much, if not more, than anyone else's.

He fast forwards through the painful bull and stops when he sees the President of the United States JOSEPH R. SIMON step onto the dais. He has to turn the volume down due to the roar of the crowd who loves this president.

SIMON: My fellow Americans (he has to raise his hands to lower the cheers) Let me have your attention.

A female voice cries out, "WE LOVE YOU, JOE!"

SIMON: I came here to bury Edward, not to praise him. The evil that men do is remembered after their deaths, but the good is often buried with them. It ought to be the same with Edward. His beautiful daughter is here with us today.

The camera cuts to Rainbow wearing a very bright multicolored pantsuit with dark sunglasses. "There's my baby." He thinks to himself as a single tear escapes one eye. "She still won't wear black," he says aloud as he wonders if she's really crying behind the shades.

THE CROWD GIVES HER A HUGE APPLAUSE as she sits stoically. The president lets the cheering go on for almost an entire minute and Ed is grateful for every second. He thinks to himself how everything he's been through is worth it just to see that his baby girl is not only alive and fine but also loved and admired.

SIMON: Rainbow told me that he was ambitious. If that's true, he was ambitious to a fault and he's paid dearly for it. With her permission, and everyone on stage with me.

The camera cuts back to show Rainbow sitting with Leon, Leo, and Lupe along with a lot of famous people, most of them Ed knows and some of them he likes, and a few that actually liked him. But, he spots Thade, the shadowy figure from the Fed, sitting behind Rainbow, dressed in all black and he's crying. "What in the name of-" Ed can't even finish his thought so stunned by what he's watching. Thade, a man he's only met once, and Ed thought he was there to kill him, is crying non-stop at his funeral. Everyone is sobbing, and Ed's ego is bathing in those tears but, "Why is this man crying?"

SIMON: I have come here to speak at Edwards's funeral. He was my friend. He was good to me.

He never lied to me. At least not that I know of.

THAT GETS A BIG LAUGH FROM THE CROWD.

Even Ed concedes as he laughs, "That was pretty good."

SIMON: But Rainbow told me earlier that Ed liked me and Rainbow is an honest person so that's good enough for me. Ed helped a lot of people out of poverty and brought wealth to millions of Americans while he was alive. Was that his ambition? You all loved him once and not without reason. Ambition can turn men into brutal beasts. Trust me. I'm in politics. I know these things.

HE GETS ANOTHER BIG LAUGH OUT OF THE AUDIENCE.

SIMON: So, don't think about what he took from us. Think about what he left behind. His gift to us! The beautiful Rainbow.

Rainbow gets up out of her seat and walks toward the President who gives her a big hug and kiss that Ed finds very inappropriate and many who were watching cringed at.

THE CROWD ERUPTS as she walks over to the podium and takes a handheld mic waiting for her and goes right into a song.

RAINBOW: It must've been cold there in my shadow, to never have sunlight on your face.

She sings to a large portrait that Ed had commissioned by the famous artist Robert Crosby. When Ed met him he was Bob Crosby and Ed hired him to paint a boat he had docked in the Outer Banks. They were the same age and they hit it off. Over many, many drinks he told Ed that he did want to be an artist and that his parents had supported him for years but it just wasn't happening.

So the first thing Ed did was to buy an old warehouse and made into a studio for Bob (and later remodeled it–with Bob doing the work) into a museum that was free to the public and then hired Bob to paint as many paintings as he could and then he had his PR team go to work in making Robert the most amazing new talent of the twenty-first century.

Ed used to tell Robert about Joseph Duveen, Ed described him as "an art dealer who used to cal himself Baron" as having said when asked how he made his fortune said, "Europe has a great deal of art and America has a great deal of money." He just went along with the times and sold Robert's art to Russian oligarchs and Chinese Communist Party members. He would then take that cash and buy other works of art from real artists, or what his accountant called "like-kind exchanges" and as long as he did it within one hundred and eighty days after the sale he wouldn't have to pay the tax on it.

Robert used to call Ed "Patron" and joke how he had to be careful around him because he was worth more to Ed dead than he was alive. To which, Ed would respond, "Yeah, but who's gonna scrape the barnacles off my boat." It's not that Ed didn't think about it but he knew with the way Bob drank his liver wouldn't hold out and there'd be no need.

It turns out, Robert shared one trait with all great artists, he was crazy and got drunk one night on Bacardi 151 (Ed later changed it to Patron tequila—he felt that gave Robert a motive and that would make the story resonate more) and splashed it all over the paintings and burned it all to the ground costing Ed millions. The only painting of Robert's to survive was the one Rainbow was singing to.

"Thank God for NFT's," Ed thinks to himself as he briefly remembers Bob. He liked Bob and he liked his work. It was very realistic. So much so, on some of them, you'd swear it was a photo. His style led to Ed selling digital reprints of his work as Non-Fungible Token Art when the blockchain technology became available making back most of his money. Unfortunately, a lot of non- Robert Crosby art was in the museum as well.

RAINBOW: You were content to let me shine, that's your way. You always walked a step behind.

Ed always knew she had a beautiful voice. Of course, he paid for singing lessons as well as dance lessons but he refused to let her take acting lessons. "She doesn't need someone teaching her how to lie," he reasoned. Ed thought it was ironic that she sings this song. She always complained how Ed held her back and kept her from acting and singing and modeling. He always felt it was beneath her and he didn't even want her in that world.

That makes him think about the future. With him "out of the picture" who knows who would try to sink their claws into her. Especially with the Circle L people sitting right next to her.

He can't watch anymore. He reaches over, wincing a little from the multiple injuries, presses stop, and ejects the tape. The television switches over to broadcast TV. He doesn't have many stations but he's able to find the news. A beautiful female anchor opens the report.

FEMALE ANCHOR: New details have come out about the President's plan to save the economy in the wake of the Gennaro collapse. The graphic on the screen shows the logo to Ed's company: FINANCIAL EDGE with the words OF COLLAPSE added in fiery red. Here to tell us more about it is Jennifer Stevens.

An even younger and more beautiful woman comes on to explain it.

JENNIFER STEVENS: President Simon announced today the U.S. Federal Reserve will commission what he's calling the Krugman Coins after the late economist Paul Krugman. They will create 30 specially made coins that will be valued at one trillion dollars each. They will eventually be sent down to Fort Knox, Kentucky where the United State government will borrow money and use these coins as collateral. This will allow the government to buy back huge amounts of debt and stabilize the markets.

FEMALE ANCHOR: A trillion-dollar coin? Is this legal?

JENNIFER STEVENS: It's still legal tender backed by the full faith of the American government.

FEMALE ANCHOR: What do the experts say?

JENNIFER STEVENS: The politicians are divided by party lines and economists are divided by ideology but the American people en masse love it.

They cut to a clip of people cheering as the President gets off Air Force One. One group holds up a large banner that reads: WE ARE SIMANIACS.

JENNIFER STEVENS: Since his speech at the Edward Gennaro funeral and how he's handling the crisis his approval rating has hit ninety percent!

FEMALE ANCHOR: That's Jennifer Stevens reporting. When we come back we'll show you more families devastated by the collapse of Financial Edge.

Ed gets out of bed for the first time in a while. He sees a bedpan they left for him and tosses it aside. "Screw that!" He thinks to himself.

It's the first time he's been out of bed and the straps are strewn in the corner of the room. At first, he has trouble walking due to stiffness, soreness, and having a catheter put in him. He makes it to the door and tests the knob. He can't believe the door is unlocked. He cracks it open just a little to peer out into the hallway. It looks like a regular hall in a regular house without guards, cameras, or any security device.

He comes out cautiously, looking around to get his bearings. He knows he's in the basement level. He looks for a bathroom but comes across an indoor gym. He peeks inside. What he sees compels him to go in and see more. Ed knew the smell in an instant, the mix of sweat and burnt rubber from what they call "bumper plates" or dumbbells made from recycled rubber. There were probably a hundred of the forty-five-pound plates laying around. There were specially reinforced bars safety equipment. There was a "squat rack" constructed so that a person could do pull-ups and dips but also rack weights to do bench, squats, and other exercises similar to Smith machine. But everything was mounted to the floor and secured into the foundation of the house. Ed counted the weights left on the curl bar. Whoever was working out down here was doing curls with four hundred and fifty pounds. And over by the dip rack was a belt, using an anchor chain, with over seven hundred and fifty pounds. Ed liked to do dips with a leather belt he had seventy-five pounds attached to it. This was ten times more. Based on the weights left near the bars, there were no racks as you would find at a local gym, there were just too many plates for that, whoever was down here was benching over a thousand pounds and only God knows how many weights they were putting on the bars. There was a pile in the corner of forty-five pound bars, two inches wide on either side and they were warped from having too much weight on them- and these were the kind used in the Olympics.

Ed had to get out of there. The smell was getting to him and he still had to go to the bathroom. "Not even

Goldilocks would stick around here no matter how good the porridge might be," he said to himself.

The next room over was just as impressive but for a different reason. They called the one guy "The Alchemist" but Ed wasn't sure exactly what they meant by that. It would only stand to reason that he would have some kind of lab and he did. But there weren't many beakers or Bunsen burners. But there were equations all over the whiteboards on all four walls. There was also an old high school-style Periodic Table of the Elements taped to the wall.

Just as Ed knows his way around a weight room he's no dummy either. He remembers the basic elements though he probably hadn't looked at one since high school. He did recognize some things scribbled on the whiteboard: OS was for Osmium, RH was for Rhodium, Pt was Platinum, Ir was Iridium and Re was Rhenium. He thinks he knows that from watching "Jeopardy."

Scattered on the desk in the middle of the room was a newspaper with the headline: "Krugman Koins to Kill Kollapse" and images of the Fed building that Ed had visited weeks ago. A giant lump of coal rests on it as a paperweight alongside random pieces of copper, diamonds, and cubes of gold. Over on a bookshelf he sees tubes that look like they may hold blueprints. "What the hell are they planning?"

Now his bladder is demanding he leaves the room and finds a bathroom. As he makes his way to the end of the hall he comes to a set of stairs and judging by the noises coming down in sounds like it leads to the kitchen but before he can get upstairs he finds a half bath and uses it. He is charmed by the decor and alarmed to see the full beard on his face.

Now, about a liter lighter he ascends up the stairs until he comes to the kitchen where sits The Visionary, The Alchemist, and Max Po. The first two look like they're done eating while Max is still eating away. The table is covered with food as if they are the last three remaining from a holiday banquet. To Ed's amazement, they seem actually pleased to see him.

The Alchemist raises a glass, "Look who's come back from the dead!"

THE CHRISTIAN THING TO DO

"Please, have a seat!" Theo welcomes, "He and I are having coffee but Max is still eating.

Ed acts a little shy but pulls up a chair in front of mounds of food. Steak, shrimp, sausages, mashed potatoes, gravy, mixed vegetables, and French bread among other things. He looks at Max as he shovels food into his mouth. He notices that, though the jacket is off, Max is wearing a shirt and tie button up and the sleeves still buttoned as well, with a bib that looks more like a poncho. What Robin's grade school art teacher would call a "smock."

"Dig in," The Alchemists offers, "You probably haven't eaten in a while and you must be starved."

Ed looks to Max awaiting medical advice. Max sees this and puts down his knife and fork. "Just take it slowly. Your eyes are bigger than your stomach right now."

"Don't be bashful," The Alchemist says invitingly.

Ed digs in. Piling food on his plate that you normally wouldn't mix together while The Visionary and The Alchemist sip on their coffee. Ed becomes self-conscious when he sees John, The Alchemist out of the corner of his eye, staring at him.

"What?" Ed asks with a mouthful of food.

"You can ask us," John teases.

"Ask what?" Ed gets out in between chews.

"I know there's a question your dying to ask us. I'm sure there are many but one in particular," John says at he looks at Theo, The Visionary, who looks down at his coffee cup.

"What are you guys? Are you some kind of cult?"

John gives one loud clap like he just won a bet. Max drops his knife and fork and jerks his head toward Theo, "What did you say to him? Did you start quoting Bible verses or something?"

Theo reacts defensively, "I quote Kipling, de Toqueville, and the dummy still didn't get it!"

"No, no, no," John puts his hands up to make a point, "This is good. This is a teachable moment. It lets us become aware of how we come off to other people. Please, tell us your thoughts and be honest. Don't worry about hurting feelings."

Max shoots him a look and without saying a word conveys to Ed, "Worry about hurting my feelings!"

"Well, since your asking," Ed states upfront, "He seemed like he wanted to change the world for religious reasons. Like a zealot. And it seemed like you guys were a cult."

John lifts a plastic pitcher and raises it to Ed, "Would you like some Kool-Aid?"

Ed looks at John's big grin while Theo almost spits out his coffee and Max laughs so hard he has to stop eating.

Ed, realizing the jokes on him, pulls back from the conversation but John asks for more. "Do you think the world needs changing?"

"I think there are natural laws to the universe and the people who play by them the best win. The people who don't want to change the rules. It's more about fairness."

"Oh, so we're jealous zealots," John adds. The makes Max snort and shake his head.

"Well, what do you call yourselves? Does your team have a name?"

"We're not professional wrestlers," John jokes, "We're more like a coffee klatch."

"We're a circle of friends," Theo decides.

"Yes! We're a circle of friends!" John concurs.

"Ed, even from your vantage point you have to see that something is definitely wrong with this world," Theo relates.

"We are still a democracy. The people chose this," Ed fires back.

"Another thing de Tocqueville said," Theo starts.

Max breaks in," Let me apologize for my clients. They invited you to eat not an episode of The McLaughlin Group."

"Theo continues without missing a beat, "They, meaning Americans, derived consolation from being supervised by thinking that they have chosen their supervisors."

Max apologetically, "They're not usually this much fun. I think John made the Kool-Aid a little too sugary."

"It takes away the cyanide after taste," John piles on. That actually makes Ed laugh.

"Come on," Theo pleads, "You actually thought that was funny?"

"It was the delivery. I'm a big fan of a well-timed joke." Ed says, "I'd lift a glass if I had something to drink."

"John, get the guy something to drink! He's our guest!" Max orders. "He thinks he tonight's entertainment but he's not even a good host."

"Oh, so we're using real names now?" John fights back.

"Ok, ALCHEMIST, please make the man a concoction! No cyanide, please." Max fires back. It even makes Theo chuckle a little.

"Oh, that you find funny?" John pretending to be upset as he gets up from the table. "Would you like beer or wine?"

"No beer," Max commands.

"Is there a difference medically?" Theo asks.

"Nah, I was going to watch the game tonight. He's allowed to have a domestic beer or boxed wine, doctor's orders."

John turns to Ed, "And I'm a bad host, right?"

"You can have anything you like. It's probably not the gourmet food you're looking for me we focus more on quantity than quality around here," Theo says looking at Max.

"I'm only joking," Max says smiling," I repaired your suit as much as possible."

"You're a man of many talents," Ed says in a thankful manner.

"I have a little experience with special suits," Max replies.

"Why don't you reveal your secrets to him like you gave away my real name?!" John says to Max and then turns to Ed, "I'm John Brady the fourth."

"Don't forget the fourth!" Max jokes.

"Ah yes," John says as he picks up the spoon he used to stir his coffee and holds it long ways with his left hand while he slides his right index and thumb over it. As the fingers slide along the handle it's transformed from stainless steel to solid silver right before Ed's eyes. "I too know a little something about eating with a silver spoon."

He hands the spoon to Ed who scans it thoroughly with his mouth wide open but is able to get out two words, "What the-."

"Oh, so we're doing parlor tricks tonight?" Theo asks in a slightly perturbed manner. "You'll have to excuse my friend, he aspires to own a dinner theater and wants to be the only act."

"You know my agent and lawyer, Max Po, and here's my manager Theodore Way," John says going along with the joke.

"It's a pleasure to finally be introduced properly. Though, I must say I was beginning to answer to "The Visionary. I think I'm going to make that the new password for the WiFi."

"You mean the WiFi you steal from your neighbor," Ed kids.

"We've got to stop piggybacking his signal. I don't trust that guy. He seems like a serial killer," John says, "But for now, the password is 'the zero way'- you know- Theo Way but with a zero in the middle. 'The way, get it?"

"Well, they needed at least six letters and one number, so...," Theo tries to explain its not hubris but changes tact, "You're more than welcome to surf the internet but as I said, someone may be looking for you, and we don't need you bringing your enemies to our door."

"Don't worry, I'm leaving tomorrow," Ed assures them.

"What are you going to do?" John asks.

"I'm going to find my daughter. I think I know where she's going to be," Ed replies.

Theo turns to Max, "Do you think he's OK to travel?"

"Airplanes? Yes. Elevators? Well, as a doctor I say 'look both ways' as a lawyer I say 'call me next time you find a faulty elevator." They all laugh but Ed especially appreciates the humor.

"I don't think you realize how bad things have gotten," Theo warns.

"He was right, you know," John says to Ed. "He predicted this crash. THAT'S why we call him The Visionary."

"That's why you tried to sabotage the market? In hopes of preventing a market crash?" Ed asks.

"A whole lot of good it did us," Max chimes in.

"At least we got to make a new friend!" John jokes. "And a celebrity at that."

"That's right," Ed says, "I heard you weren't a big fan of mine."

"I told him to watch the thing Oliver Stone did on you. Then he would love you! But he didn't."

"Yeah, right," Max says with disgust, "Oliver Stone, give me a break! After he made Jim Morrison out to be some weirdo and I don't know what he was trying to do with JFK but the final straw with that guy was when he did that documentary for Showtime about everything that's wrong with the world and what does he blame everything on? The 'evil corporations that run AM talk radio stations! Liberals always find some way to blame conservatives! Rush Limbaugh is the one who destroyed America! His biggest sponsor was pet vitamins and he seduced the country and sent us down a destructive path. And then he makes a fluff piece about you of all people? The world hates you now just wait until they find out that you get dressed up in black ops gear and rob people."

"Then why did you save me?" Ed demands.

"Because it was the Christian thing to do."

WHAT DO THEY NEED ME FOR

The next morning Theo knocks before entering the room where Ed was stretching and doing some exercise for the first time since waking. Theo comes in with a large gym bag and a plastic shopping bag. He drops the large bag on the floor and puts a plastic bag on the already made bed.

"I got you some clothes," Theo says as Ed inspects the bag.

Ed pulls out a tracksuit, a zip-up hoodie, socks, underwear, and the same Velcro strap sneakers that Jerry Keen wore. "Did you put a tracker in the shoes?"

"The fact that you're asking me that is disturbing. There's a receipt in the bag if you want to return them for cash or if you ever feel the need to repay me."

Ed says thank you with a look and hands him back the silver spoon, "Here, before I forget. How did he-"

Theo pushes it back and says, "Hold onto it. The set is already ruined. Hock it for some cash."

"You mind if I use your shower?" Ed asks.

"No, not at all. Do you want a razor?"

"No, I think I'll keep the beard. If things are as bad as you say maybe it's better not to be recognized. You know, being dead and all."

"Good idea," Theo says, "Max said he made some adjustments on your suit. He separated the chest plate and says you should wear it as much as possible to help keep your back aligned."

"Good to know. Tell him I said 'thanks.'

"He'd be here to see you off but he's still sleeping. He needs his rest."

"What are you going to do since I ruined your plans?" Ed asks.

"I'll think of something," Theo answers.

"You're not going to stop, are you?" Ed asks rhetorically.

"The rich have sold their souls and sold us out just so they can compete with the Regals for their spot on the food chain. I cannot abide by that."

Ed picks up the gym bag and puts it on the bed, "You might be right," as he inspects the bulletproof chest plate and the rest of his uniform, "but it's a dangerous game you're playing."

"What about you? Are you going to maintain your extracurricular activities? You're a smart guy. You don't have to steal from people."

"I created a persona, I call it 'The Edge' as a way to exact revenge on people who'd wronged me before I used it to extract money from criminals."

"Most criminals are victims first. Many of us have something traumatic happen to us when we are children. It's usually a betrayal. And it teaches us not to trust," Theo states. "The fact that you call 'it' a 'persona' tells me you know it's wrong and you absolve yourself from it."

"I thought you weren't big on psychology," Ed responds."

"I'm not. I don't know exactly what happened to you, I didn't see the Oliver Stone documentary either, but I can tell you that our parents, especially our fathers let us down in life, I know mine did, and you need to forgive them. They were young boys, like us, at one time. And no matter what happened, or who betrayed you, you have a Heavenly Father and he won't let you down."

"Thanks for the sermon, Father," Ed quips as he takes weapons out of the bag and inspects them.

Theo picks up one of Ed's many knives, "I too, wanted revenge as a child but when I became a man, I put away childish things."

Theo drops the knife on the bed and turns to walk out. Ed calls out to him before he leaves, "'For now we see through a mirror, darkly; but then face to face: now I know in part; but then shall I know even also I am known.' You're not the only one who went to Catholic school. I'm going to need The Edge one last time if I'm to save my daughter."

"Things didn't work out the way I envisioned them," Theo concedes. "That turned out to be a good thing. If they had, you'd be in jail and we'd be hunted."

"Are you telling me to not go looking for my daughter?" Ed questions.

"I'm telling you that things may not work out the way you hope."

"You're right. Things are looking bad right now but I'm still alive. I make my own fate. If your God has given me a second chance it's for a reason but I decide what that reason is and nothing in heaven or hell is going to stop me from finding my daughter."

"You've had a good life, better than most. You've reached the pinnacle of success. The same things that drove you to reach the pinnacle of success also drove you to put on a dark costume and steal from criminals. You've raised your daughter to be a powerful and successful woman but you also drove her to leave you to die."

"You're saying 'forget my daughter?'" Ed inserts.

"I'm saying bury it. Bury it and start anew. Start a new life without the demons that drove you. Bury them along with your old life and watch your daughter from afar. I know it's painful but there's a reason childbirth is painful."

"That was powerful," Ed says in amazement.

"I'm just going to walk out now. Good Luck," Theo says as he walks out and closes the door behind him.

"YOU COULDN'T JUST LET ME HAVE THE LAST WORD, COULD YA?" Ed yells through the door.

Theo's voice is muffled as he is calling back from down the hall, "Nope."

Ed can't help but chuckle as he packs his bag.

When Ed walks out of the townhouse he looks around to see where he is. The street sign says STRAIGHT STREET. "They weren't kidding," Ed thinks to himself, "we are just a few blocks from the office building and even closer to the park."

He throws the gym bag with his suit over his shoulder and pulls the hood from the hoodie Theo bought him over his head and keeps his head down as not to be recognized as he makes his way down the street. He eyes as much as he can without picking his head up or making eye contact with anyone. He does not like what he sees. Once thriving shops now have soaped-up windows and though there are still people hustling and bustling their way to work they must avoid hitting homeless people wandering against the flow as if it were a real-life video game.

The park, where people used to go picnic or play frisbee is now pop-up tents and lean-to shelters as far as the eye can see. It makes it difficult to find the tree hiding his drone. He has to cut through encampments and step on people's things to get where he wants to go. That also means pushing needy and belligerent people out of his way.

He comes to the right tree and once up close can see the drone along with a carrying case attached sitting high up in the green-leaved branches. "If these people weren't so busy looking down and just looked up they'd find something of real value," he thinks to himself as he approaches the tree.

Though still not at a hundred percent, it is still much easier for him to climb this vibrant tree full of life than it was those dead trees that broke off in his hands. He looks around to see if anyone is watching and sees that no one even notices, "In the land of the crazies it's normal to do crazy things," he thinks to himself.

Once he reaches the drone, he grabs it and the cases attached to it and descend down the tree. Once on the ground, he kneels down, enters the security code, and pops open the prize. Inside are a designer suit and shoes including a tie and billfold. There's no cash, only credit cards which he deems are now worthless. He then pulls out the biggest prize of all, his cell phone. He tries to turn it on but the battery is dead. He closes the case and folds the drone collapsing it small enough that it will fit in the bag.

"Now, to get out of these clothes," Ed thinks to himself as he looks for a place to change. Edward Gennaro is one of the few people on earth that are more comfortable in a tight-fitting suit worth thousands of dollars than he is in a casual sweatsuit and sneakers. "SOCKS," he yells in his head. He forgot to pack socks and will have to use the cheap cotton white socks they bought him.

Ed comes from behind the row of tents to the main pathway toward the one public restroom in the park. It's at this time the people notice the big guy wearing clean clothes as one brave soul approaches him.

"Hey, Mister-" is the only thing the Homeless Man can get out as Ed backhands him so hard the poor man does an involuntary backflip and lands face-first on the pavement not to awaken. The message has been sent and quickly spreads throughout the park, 'don't even approach this guy.'

When he comes to the brick building known by the occupants as "the brick shit house" Ed makes a beeline for the door marked "men's" and doesn't have to say a word or waste time threatening people or pushing anyone out of the way. In fact, the man who was up next in the mile-long line to use it not only waits for Ed but holds the door open for him.

Not even Clark Kent in a phone booth with Lois Lane's life in danger can change clothes quicker than Ed does in the disgusting men's room. For years Ed had trained himself to strengthen his lungs to hold his breath for an incredibly long time. He did this for many reasons, be it using tear gas, underwater demolition, or even in battle but he never thought it would be used for public restroom utilization.

He kicks himself for thinking that for a criminal mastermind and taking pride in his planning ahead on everything that he forgot dress socks and whether he packed the case wrongly or there was turbulence on the trip but his suit was wrinkled. He didn't care though. He was back, baby!

He left the park and walked down the street with his head held high. He was happy to be alive. The air smelled fresher, the birds chirped louder and every woman on the sidewalk was prettier than ever. The world had definitely changed since he was away more so than he could've imagined. It used to be when Ed walked down the street, every head turned in his direction, woman, man, gay, straight it didn't matter. Walking down the street wearing a scruffy beard, a wrinkled suit and a cheese-eating grin he didn't have the magnetic effect he used to have. That Ed was dead. This Ed says, "Hi, how ya doin'" to every woman that walks past him and turns away ignoring him. Not even a "Beautiful day, isn't it?" could conjure up a smile from average-looking women. Perhaps this was Ed's biggest fear come to life. He was now a nobody. A shlub just like everyone else. And like the mere mortals he looked down upon, he needed cash. He sees another long line of disgruntled people. The line wasn't as long as the one in the park and the people were nicer dressed and had actually bathed but they were angry. Ed could tell as he passed them by the looks on their faces and the bits and pieces he caught them saying to each other that they felt they were too good to be in this position. Ed surmised that weeks before they had regular, good-paying jobs, probably in mid-level management and now they were in desperate need of money. Unlike the people in the park, they had something that they felt had some kind of monetary value and that they didn't feel they had earned this fate.

Ed, who had developed a pretty good memory for faces, a skill he developed in business and for basic survival could even spot out faces that weeks before were waiting outside the Gastropub for a table. Now, they needed to hock their jewelry to buy cereal for their kids. If only they knew that the man walking past them was the cause of their misery in both instances.

Ed, being Ed, goes straight to the door. After all, he is who he is in any scenario and the people let them know they're not happy about it. Ed wonders to himself if they knew who he really was if they'd be so emboldened or not.

It's not until a POLICEMAN in full uniform comes out of the Pawn Shop's door that Ed puts his head down and keeps walking as if he had no intention of even going in the place.

"Sir, sir," the Policeman calls after him, "it's okay, the broker will see you now."

Ed stops, turns around. "Are you talking to me?" Not even hiding the look of guilt on his face.

"Yes sir, please come in." The Policeman says invitingly.

Ed enters the Pawn Shop to a chorus of boos and the jingle of the bells attached to the quaint shop's door.

"He'll be out in a second," The Policeman assures him as he returns to his post leaning on the front door.

"Thanks," Ed says as he looks around the shop. He can see behind the cage that is the counter that the news is on and the scroll on the bottom of the screen has some stock prices and just so happens to show: GOLD IS AT $3000 AN OUNCE SILVER AT $30 just as Ed looks at it.

THE PAWNBROKER comes out from the back room. "Sorry if I scared you. I was in the back watching the security camera and I saw you wearing a nice suit and I figured you might have something worth of value so I sent Mike outside to get you."

"How did you know I needed money?"

"Everybody needs money," The Pawn Broker answers, "Now, whadda ya got?"

Ed unveils a solid silver tablespoon and hands it to him. "Solid silver," Ed says.

The Pawn Broker pulls the glasses resting on his forehead down onto the bridge of his nose. "I'll be right back," he says as he goes in the back.

Ed looks out the window and doesn't even recognize the city anymore. Ed spots crimes happening all around him and he spots uniformed policemen, like the one standing next to him doing nothing.

Right outside the window, he sees a man, who is definitely a JUNKIE terrorizing the people in line with a knife. Ed turns to the cop who stares inside the store with his back to the outside.

Then The Pawn Broker comes on over an intercom, "Can you take care of that, please? He's bothering the customers.

Without saying a word, The Policeman goes outside, pulls out his billy club and whacks the Junkie in the forearm. The crack of the bone is just as audible as the switchblade hitting the sidewalk and The Junkie falling to his knees sobbing where The Policeman then commences beating on him with his billy club relentlessly.

The Pawnbroker comes out from the back room, "I'll give you eighty bucks."

"Do you have a phone charger, too?" Ed holds up the phone so he can see the model.

"Lemme check," he says as he looks under the counter.

"Do all the stores hire off-duty cops as muscle?" Ed inquires curiously.

"Off duty? There is no more off duty? The city went bankrupt and let all the local cops go. It's all run by the National Police," he curtly explains.

"National Police?" Ed wonders out loud.

"Yeah, where ya been the past month? In a coma?" The Pawn Broker cracks.

"Actually, yeah. Now, what do you mean National Police?"

"Yeah, when the market crashed all the municipalities and the police pensions were with Financial Edge. The cities are all broke. The cops' retirement is gone. The Federal government had to step in and make all the soldiers and border patrol agents into local police. That Gennaro screwed everyone."

Ed instinctively turns away at the mention of his name. He looks out the window and witnesses a man grab a woman, in real-time, drag her between two parked cars and push her to the ground.

"Hey, a man is raping a woman. Can you get your boy to go handle it?"

"Is it on the sidewalk?" The Pawn Broker asks.

"It's right on the curb," Ed responds anxiously.

He dismisses the request. "Not my problem. I pay him for everything in the store and out to the curb. But don't worry, the National Police tanks should be rolling by any minute now with the water cannons. Now, I'll give you eighty dollars. Take it over leave it?"

Ed looks out the window to see The Police Man still beating on The Junkie. He opens the front door, to a chorus of jingles, passes the crowd of people staring at the "junkie beating" and goes over to where the woman is being sexually assaulted by a hulking bald man. Ed takes a step with his left foot and swings his right foot like an NFL placekicker and kicks the attacker, as his hands are down unbuckling his belt, right in the face. Ed can see the attacker's teeth flying up in the air as the man rolls out in the center street. Ed helps the woman up but out of fear and shame, she pushes Ed away, adjusts her skirt, and runs away as fast as she can, in high heels. Ed has never seen a woman flat-out sprint, that hard and that fast before. Except for that one time when a reporter saw him coming out of the courthouse and wanted an exclusive.

He casually walks back into the shop and announces, "I'll take it."

"How about I charge that phone for you as well, huh?" The Pawn Broker asks intimidated.

Ed smiles and says, "Much obliged."

Ed leaves the store just as he hears a loud rumble of heavy machinery. A tracked Armored Personnel Carrier comes rumbling down this small side street tearing up the asphalt below it with its heavy tracks.

Ed goes out to see if the man he kicked is still out cold and lying in the street. He is. The APC has a water cannon mounted on top of it and the soldier operating it blasts it at full strength at the sleeping racist blowing him right off the street like a bug being blown off a windshield.

Ed can only watch horrified and amused at the same time. The machine is so loud that it makes the glass storefronts rattle and all he can do is cover his ears and wait for it to go by so that he can use his phone.

He turns on his phone and checks the messages. The machine announces: YOU HAVE ONE THOUSAND AND THREE HUNDRED NEW MESSAGES. TO ACCESS YOUR MESSAGES PLEASE CONTACT CUSTOMER SUPPORT ABOUT THE REMAINING BALANCE ON YOUR BILL. "The company didn't even pay my phone bill while I was gone!" He thinks to himself.

He then finds ROBIN in his contact list and dials it only to hear: THE NUMBER YOU HAVE REACHED before hanging up. Discouraged, he puts the phone in his pocket, picks up his bag and starts back up on his way to his old building to be on the lookout for her.

He buys a cup of coffee from his pawnshop profits and camps out across the street from his old building, The

Ivory Tower. The first thing he notices is that there are no more news vans, cameramen, or reporters lurking in front of the building. The traffic in front of the building is minimal as most of the company is now defunct. He does see one lone figure, a small man with dark hair and wearing an overcoat. He has a steno pad, a pen and approaches people going in and out of the building. Ed watches him for hours as he walks up to people, exchanges a few words Ed can't hear and the people either brush him off or push him away. "When is this kid going to take a break," Ed wonders to himself.

Finally, the man decides to call it a day, and Ed follows him from across the street taking an intercept angle as he finally confronts him as the man is about to cross the street.

"Excuse me," Ed calls out to him. The man turns, looks at Ed but decides to keep walking.

"It's kind of ironic, isn't it?" Ed asks aloud, "How you spent all afternoon approaching people on the street but when someone approaches you you don't engage. Isn't there some kind of reporter code or something?"

"I'm not a reporter. I'm a writer...not that it's any of your business." He barks back.

"What are you writing about?" Ed asks in a friendly, curious manner.

"None of your business," the man fires back.

Ed stops following him, "I thought maybe I can help you."

The man stops and turns around. "My name is Scott Rosenberg and I'm writing a biography on Rainbow Gennaro."

"Do you know her?" Ed asks.

"UNauthorized biography. Now, who are you?"

Ed ignores the question and asks another, "Do you know where she is?"

"She's not here," the man concludes. "I was just trying to get some background interviews. You know, the doorman or maybe a friend or coworkers of her father."

"There's been no mention of her anywhere? Newspapers? Magazines? I've been away for a while without internet."

"My guess is either she's in a studio cutting her debut album or in Milan for fashion week. But we would've heard something if she was there."

"Why do you want to do a story about her? Are you a fanboy?"

"No! Well, kind of. I just think she's been through a lot and there's a lot of b.s. written about her and I just want, for once, someone to treat her like a real person."

"What kind of b.s.?" Ed asks.

"Well, you know how the internet is, everything from her doing drugs, to getting involved with some kind of cult, to her being the one that killed her father."

"My God," Ed blurts out.

"I know, right! You must be a fan of hers like me!"

"Big fan! Listen, give me a card. When the time is right I'll reach out to you. I'll tell you the real story. I promise it'll be worth your while."

"Here's my card. It's just my name and email address."

"Good enough. Listen, what do they say about her father?"

"Oh man, that guy was no good. They say he molested her, that he killed her mother and her grandparents and some people say she trained her to be an assassin.

He hears his phone ring. "Hey kid, I have to get this. Beat it and I'll call you when I got something good for you.

"Yeah, whatever," Scott says dismissively as he walks off.

Ed drops his bag to answer the phone on the corner of a busy intersection... People have to avert walking into him. Some give a dirty look as they pass by. He doesn't even notice, he's too happy that he's got a call, thinking it's her.

"Hello!" He answers enthusiastically.

"Hi Ho, stranger!" The familiar voice answers back. "Long time no hear!"

"Who- who is this?" Ed's voice quivered as he asks.

"How quickly they forget! It's your old buddy, your pal, your amigo, Virgil Stanhope. You know me, from the hotel!"

Just the sound of that over-enunciated Transatlantic accent sends a shiver down his spine. The phone just falls out of Ed's hands and he drops to the ground, his knees and the phone hitting the sidewalk at about the same time. He's now on his knees unable to get up. Not only do people not check to see if he's alright, but they are also angry they have to walk around him.

He can hear the distant voice of Virgil still on the phone, "Hey! You there? Quit your lollygagging! I need to speak with you. We hear Virgil loudly whistle and then say, "Helloo, little birdie! Pick up."

Ed, his head down on the cement struggles to find the phone, swatting his hand blindly until he hits it and brings it to his ear. "Huh?" That is all he can muster.

"Let me tell you, that was some Sockdollager you threw the other night. They're still cleaning up the joint! You got everyone worked up into a real leather!

"Wha-" Ed mumbles, almost about to faint.

"Now listen here, It's no secret you double-crossed us and played us for a bunch of saps and left me holding the bag! And let me tell you, the Big Cheese was hot under the collar and how! He even canceled the New Year's Eve party this year. But I think there's a way we can take these lemons and make lemonade and turn his frown upside down. There are a few demons that have escaped recently and they plan on starting trouble up there. The boss wants you to bump 'em off for him. You do that and everything will be Jake with him. They might be hard to find. They're going to come off as humans but they've got what you and I call superpowers. Be on the lookout for anyone like that. But be careful, these guys aren't your run-of-the-mill palookas they're real torpedoes! If you come across anyone like that get on the blower and let me know. I'll be your contact down here. They might have some big plans and they might try to get you involved with them so just let them beat their gums but don't do anything until you ok it with me. You see, these demons lust for idolatry so they want to do something big to make a name for themselves. You do this and you'll be sitting pretty again with the big guy. And don't let these guys send you on any trips for biscuits. And look out for anyone who tells you they know the way. Alright, I'll see you in the funny papers.

"IT CAN'T BE," his scream is muffled as he bows face down on the pavement, arms covering his head, "IT WAS ALL REAL?"

Still, on his knees, he lifts his head to the sky and shouts, "HELL IS REAL! HELL IS REAL!"

The people passing by actively avoid him but he reaches out to them trying to get their attention. "LISTEN TO ME, EVERYONE! HELL IS REAL!"

When he looks around and sees the only attention he is getting is negative attention he quickly wipes the tears from his eyes and attempts to get up. He tries to stand up but he's still a little shaken and the onlookers take this as a confirmation that he's a drunk.

All though Ed couldn't understand half of what he was saying, it was the last thing he said that got to him. Ed remembered The Visionary talking about his password being 'theoway' and trying to give Ed advice. "He must've been talking about them," Ed thought as his mind was racing. "Is that what The Visionary meant when he said, 'those two have more abilities and opportunities than any other humans on the planet?'"

Ed tries himself off the street, at first it's hard, the world is still spinning. himself off and clears his head. He needs to think this through. "Is this really happening?" He thinks to himself. The words, "They are planning something big," echo in his head.

Ed's analytical side kicks in. It's what made him so dangerous on the street and the boardroom.

For every decision whether it be business or life, you need as much information as you can get.

So Ed does what every other homeless man does, he goes to the public library.

The Librarian asks Ed if he'd like to sign up for a library card. He's got so much going on in his head that he instantly complies. He gives the name Angelo Gennaro, his cousin. When they were kids they were almost identical until around seven when Angelo started getting heavy. He got fat enough that the other kids called him "Jello." Ed always called him "Ange" and used him as a reminder of what he would look like if he didn't work out all the time. Ed loved him but hadn't kept in touch with him. Ed knew he was living in New Jersey and owned several pizza parlors. "Oh God," Ed remembers that Ange was a customer of Financial Edge. They even design the website and ordering app for his pizza business, "He's probably out of business."

With his new library card, Ed is able to log in to a library computer and do a search for RAINBOW GENNARO but doesn't come up with anything new past the funeral ceremony, of which she got raving reviews. This gives Ed a momentary reprieve from the anguish. "Ok, no news is good news," he rationalizes in his head.

He then takes a deep breath and lets it out in a WHUSH and shakes his clammy hands dry before he types in VIRGIL STANHOPE and hits SEARCH. And there it is.

The headline reads: BODIES FOUND UNDER OLD STANHOPE MANOR

Remains of up to 23 Missing Children Found As Construction Crew Digs Up Driveway

A story in the Rochester Democrat and Chronicle from 1963 with a black and white mug shot photo of Virgil Stanhope. Ed gasps for air. The room is starting to spin. It wasn't a dream, it wasn't a vision, it was real. Ed had died and gone to hell and his guide was a real person. Ed thinks to himself, "I must've heard about him or seen his photo somewhere." But as Ed scans his memory he faces the realization that he had never heard of even this newspaper until this moment.

He continues reading:

The police were called to the Grand Niagara Hotel and Resort when a member of the paving crew tearing up asphalt on the long winding driveway that leads to the resort found what looks like to be the remains of a young girl reported missing thirty years prior. The police sent in a team and requested the entire driveway be torn up to search the bodies. "Though there is no way to further identify the remains all twenty-three families from cold cases have been notified," Chief Murray said.

The scion of the owner, Virgil Stanhope was often a suspect in many of the cases but was never brought to trial. He was arrested for vehicular manslaughter and was soon beaten to death in prison without ever going to trial on any of the cases he was linked to in 1933.

A further search and in IMAGES and he comes across from a publication titled the

ERIE SOCIAL REGISTER with a sepia-colored photo from an event on Labor Day 1926 with a photo of a young Virgil smiling with a group of friends and he's wearing a suit with a bow tie and has a straw boater hat on his head.

There really was a Virgil Stanhope and he looked just the same in 1926 as when Ed saw him days ago. He can hear Virgil when he said, "The road to hell is paved with good intentions."

"Was that a sick joke or was he trying to tell me something?" Ed wondered. But the very next thought in his head was, "Now what?" And the words The Visionary told him about this being a second chance at redemption.

The thought that maybe he didn't "escape" from the hotel enters his head. "Was I allowed to leave? He even said it himself, I wasn't really dead. I was in a coma, thought to be dead, perhaps meant to be dead but Max and the crew brought me back to life. Snatched me from the jaws of death and was able to leave the gates of hell. But why would they save me if they're demonic? Maybe they do need me. There's no question those guys are NOT regular men. They definitely have some kind of power. But what do they need me for?"

YOU'RE NEVER GOING TO
SEE ME AGAIN

———————————•:•———————————

It strikes him as he wanders aimlessly that the streets are getting busier, more crowded, more people are scurrying along, and judging by the sunlight they're heading home. Ed was always a man of action but he was never impulsive until this moment. He was always decisive when he had a plan of action. With a business dilemma, it usually came down to 'yes' or 'no.' If the facts were pointing in a certain direction he went with it no matter how difficult the choice or daunting the task. If the two sides were equal he did nothing and let the problem work itself out. But if he had a "gut" feeling he went with it. He could live with a mistake if it was what he wanted to do, but if the universe, in the form of his own voice, was telling him what to do and he went against it, that would eat him alive.

Sometimes it's the unknown that screams out louder than the facts. He didn't know what, as they called themselves, "The Circle of Friends," or as he labeled them, "The Three Wise Men" were up to but it had something to do with the thirty trillion-dollar coins still sitting in the Federal Reserve Bank.

If he couldn't stop them he could beat them to the punch by stealing them first. Then he could contact the brain trust at Circle L and offer the coins for his daughter. He knew they had to be holding her on that island they bragged about.

The coins were still on display. "They took the dumbest idea in financial history and made a tourist attraction out of it," Ed thought.

And every night they'd have to be put in the vault where they keep all the gold eighty feet below the city street. It ran on a time lock and once it kicked in at five o'clock nothing would open it until the next morning.

He had no other intel aside from the time he went there for lunch. He knew there were at least two guards with machine guns at the front door along with a metal detector and a scanner you had to put your hand under. That's all he knew. That and it was getting close to five. Maybe, just maybe, if he had two weeks he might come up with a feasible plan but desperation was the mother of intention and if he ever wanted to see his daughter again he'd have to commit the greatest, high tech, high stakes smash and grab job in history.

The Financial District was becoming a shanty town as more and more people were living on the streets. The dichotomy of it slapped him in the face. It gave him the opportunity to hide in plain sight. He took off his designer bag threads and put on his tactical suit. He thought about wearing it under his street clothes but it was too loose-fitting, except, of course, for the chest plate. He didn't like it skin tight as Rainbow did. He liked the room to move and for his skin to breathe. He wanted to be comfortable when kicking someone's ass. All of his clothes were custom-tailored and though he lost considerable weight while in a coma he wouldn't be able to wear the tac suit underneath them.

He took a raincoat off a homeless and slipped him a hundred-dollar bill. This allowed him to walk up to the building incognito but it stunk to high heaven. He kept his face down for the camera and pounded on the door with the old SHAVE AND A HAIRCUT-TWO BITS cadence. He then slipped on the mask and clicked on the locking collar, the same one that electrocuted Max when he tried to take it off.

Sure enough, the same two guards came out in a similar fashion as the last time, one followed by the other with rifles out. He pushed down on the muzzle of the rifle, bringing the lead guard down with it, while giving him a hard sidekick into the solar plexus, doubling him over and pushing him into the second guard. When his kicking foot, the right, landed he used the momentum to propel his left foot upward kicking the guard in the face with the same velocity as he would a fifty-yard field goal in football. He gave a slip to the right, hiding behind the lead guard, in case the second guard could get off a shot, and then by pushing off his right foot and torquing his upper body similar to that of Mike Tyson, gave the second guard an uppercut to the exact spot, midway from the chin and the mandible that Ed liked to refer to as either the "sweet spot" or especially in this case the "off button" because that's exactly how it worked. Now, they were both taken out and it would cost them no more than a few days off and an ice pack each. The first guard might have a concussion though. The back of his head hit the floor pretty hard.

This time there was a third guard on the scene. A female reaching for the sidearm on her hip. Ed cocked his arm back to deliver a haymaker when he momentarily froze. He estimated that she was about five-six, maybe a hundred and forty-five pounds, and judging how the uniform fit she put on weight since being a security guard. She was cute and Ed liked women who were a little thick but she would no longer be cute if Ed hit her as hard as he was gearing to. She would probably need reconstructive surgery and it just wouldn't be worth it. So, with his left arm still raised, he reaches with his right hand, pulls out the baton mounted on the inside of his left forearm, and whips it backhanded extending it so it meets her as she's running forward somewhere around her clavicle sending fifty thousand volts through her body and sending her crumbling to the floor. Three members of the Federal Bank Police were down in under three seconds.

He drags their three bodies along with their rifles under the security station desk and presses the button to let him into the building. He takes off the coat and throws it over the sleeping bodies. While he's back there he sees the myriad of video screens and spots two more guards putting the coin display on a cart. From there he enters a ladies' room close enough to hear the ding of the elevator and the doors open and close. While in there he tosses the rifle magazines in the trash.

Once the elevator door closes, he comes out and moves silently, due to his specially soled boots, to the elevator and with the help of his servomechanism in his gloves is able to pry the doors open. A sudden rush of what he would describe as "danger deja vu" but mental healthcare experts would identify as a panic attack comes over him. It almost stops him cold but knowing the stakes are too high and time is limited he pushes through and leaps out to the elevator cables but not before slapping himself in the face and tells himself, "Man up!"

He grips tight to the thick metal cables and with the help of his specially made gloves slides down and lands gently atop the elevator car as it goes to the bottom floor. With those specially made boots, his landing is so soft they never suspect he's there. So, it'll be a total surprise when they wake up in the ambulance mere minutes from now. He reaches into a compartment on his belt and pulls out a canister of pressurized gas he made from a cow anesthetic he bought off a farm veterinarian. He also had a vial of Kolokol 1 that he bought off an ex-Russian military officer. That's the stuff they use in hostage situations to knock out the kidnappers but it's strong enough to kill some of the hostages. The stuff Ed was using was used mainly by psychopaths to rape sleeping women. In the close quarters of an elevator car, it should just do the trick and it acts fast enough so that he can jump down and be out before the doors open on the bottom floor. The sleeping guards will be pulled out and given medical attention before any long-term effects could take hold.

And that's exactly what happens. Ed pops up the escape hatch and drops the canister into the elevator and in less than three floors the two armed guards are out cold. He opens the hatch, jumps down, smashes the glass case, and grabs the coins mounted on a decorative board. Each one is individually encased in a hard plastic shell. He takes a brief moment to admire their beauty until he asks himself how is he going to carry them out. That's when he looks down and sees on the lower shelf of the cart a money bag filled with large bills a coworker asked the guards to take down to the safe for him. "Chance favors the prepared mind," he thinks as he stuffs the coins in the bag and in one leap grabs the roof of the car and pulls himself up and out.

"Damn!" He yells in a whisper after closing the escape door and not hitting the Emergency Stop button in the elevator to buy himself some time. He practically runs up the emergency rescue ladder mounted on the wall and ascends it with lightning speed until he reaches the first floor.

He has both magnets and suction cup attachments for his gloves and he uses both of them to leap from the ladder onto the inside of the elevator door where he pries them open and sees a straight shot from the elevator to the door outside. "This is too easy," he thinks to himself.

By now the doors have open and other members of the team discovered the unconscious men and the smashed case inside the elevator.

"WHAT THE HELL HAPPENED?" One Bank Guard asks thinking the knocked-out guards can hear him.

"SOUND THE ALARM!" The Shift Commander commands. (Isn't that what they do?)

"Spoke too soon," Ed says to himself as he sprints toward the exit.

With a suit made of Kevlar, polymer, hard rubber, and carbon fibers he runs right through the metal detector not making a sound as he slides the money bag across the top of the conveyor belt used to inspect people's belongings. He heads toward the security desk to buzz himself through but sees the female guard coming to her senses.

"Damn," he thinks, "What the hell am I going to do now?"

THE ALARM BLARES THROUGHOUT THE BUILDING.

He hesitates to hurt the woman again but he needs to get back behind the desk to hit the buzzer, "Wait a sec," he thinks.

He takes off his right hand and swipes it under the scanner. The red light turns to green and the electric door lock BUZZES announcing to the world he's free.

He pushes the door open and is out in the street. THE ALARM IS GOING OFF OUTSIDE but no one even cares.

Ed disengages his locking collar and pulls off his mask once he's sure the security cameras don't see him and he's lost in the crowd.

Back inside the bank, Peter Simon is at the security desk looking over Taggert's shoulder as he manipulates a bank of monitors trying to find images of whomever it was that just robbed them.

They show a man dressed head to toe in black running down the halls. "Oh my God," Taggert gasps.

"What? What is it?" Peter asks anxiously.

"I dint know he really existed," Taggert whispers.

"WHO? WHAT?" Peter asks now frantically.

"The guy is like a legend in the security business. He's an international super-criminal!"

"WELL, HOW THE HELL DID HE GET IN AND OUT UNDETECTED?"

Taggert finds the recording of the front entrance and rewinds the tape until he gets to the clip where Ed takes off his glove and passes through the scanner. "Because he's in our system."

"WELL, WHO THE HELL IS HE?"

Taggert taps some keys to see the scanner history before announcing in a soft voice, " Edward D. Gennaro. I thought he was dead."

"OBVIOUSLY NOT!"

"How does this affect the economy?" Taggert asks.

"THERE IS NO MORE ECONOMY!"

Peter steps away and wipes the perspiration off his bald head. "I have to call my brother."

A few blocks away, Ed has retrieved his clothes and is weaving his way through a throng of homeless people until he comes upon an empty camping tent. He looks around before ducking inside and pulling the zipper shut. He opens the money bag and inspects the coins. He has all thirty and they're still in mint condition-literally. He then checks out the cash and learns he has hundred of thousands if not millions in cash. The cash is probably the biggest score in his life and he's not even thinking about it.

He takes off the tac suit and puts it in his bag along with the money bag and zips it up and puts his locking collar around the handles to secure it more. He puts his street clothes back on and as he gets dressed he knocks on the chest plate as a way of acknowledging that it's really helped to support his injured spine. He comes out of the tent surprising the man that lives in it. Ed smiles at him and walks away.

"It's all good, man!" The Homeless Man calls out to him.

The dark couldn't come soon enough for Ed as he succumbs to what fighters call an adrenaline dump. Though he succeeded with ease in his caper he is coming done from the high it gave him and that is more exhausting than the heist itself. Though he feels more comfortable at night he knows he must get off the street. He passes hotels he could easily pay for with his newfound money and walks twenty blocks to the Garden District and the home of his friend Jay Bruce.

He knocks on the door, waits, knocks, knocks, knocks again and then knocks some more until Jay finally opens up wearing only a robe and tying it as he peers out the door with eyebrows raised. His expression goes from angry to elated.

"I heard you were dead," Jay says in a surprised screech.

"Rumors of my death have been greatly exaggerated," Ed says as he steps through without asking.

Jay nonetheless lets him in and cracks a smile when he says," I also heard that you were a bad boy."

"Don't believe everything you hear."

"I also heard that my portfolio is worthless." Jay zings back at him.

Ed reaches in the breast pocket of his jacket and pulls out a stack of a hundred one thousand dollar bills and holds it up for Jay to take, "This ought to cover it."

In disbelief, he takes the was of bills and rolls through it with his thumb fanning it so that it blows his hair. A smile retakes his face as he quotes, " Anyone who lives within their means suffers from a lack of imagination. This will buy me a new thinking cap."

Ed drudges into the living room like a zombie dragging his gym bag along. Jay follows along and says with giddiness, "Have a seat, my good man."

Ed plops down on the sofa and drops the bag between the sofa and the coffee table at his feet. He looks around the room and says, "The place is quaint. I don't know, I expected something with a little more ... character."

"The wallpaper and I are fighting a duel to the death. Either it goes or I do. You should see my studio in the cellar. That's where I spend most of my time. That's where I do my projects. That's where I was when I heard you knocking. There's a lot that happened since we last saw each other. I'm sure you have a good story to tell me."

"Nah, same old same old," Ed says slyly.

Jay bursts out in his insidious laughter and falls back onto a chair. "Laughter is not at all a bad beginning for a friendship and it is by far the best ending for one!"

"You wouldn't happen to have any beer?" Ed asks.

Jay leaps up and grabs his head in embarrassment, "What bad manners! Forgive me!"

He runs into the kitchen as Ed hears the fridge door open and the rattle of bottles. "All I have is imported," Jay calls out from the kitchen apologetically.

"I have the simplest of tastes. I am always satisfied with the best," Jay yells along with the opening and shutting of drawers as well as the POP of a beer top. Jay comes back in with a chilled Pilsner glass full of beer, hands it to Ed, and places the bottle on the table in front of him.

"So please, enlighten," Jay starts as he sits back down, "For research purposes only, how does one disappear, cause a stock market crash and then reappear? I'm asking for a friend."

"Long story. Short answer, I was set up. Somebody tried to kill me and pin this financial meltdown on me. But they failed, as you can see, and I'm going to pay them a visit tomorrow. I just need a place to crash for the night."

"Crash away," Jay says joyously, "You are always welcome! I should be thanking you!"

"Oh?" Ed takes another sip.

"Well, as you're little Ponzi scheme fell apart, something I wished you had let me in on, I decided I needed to cut back on my socializing. It is better to have a permanent income than to be fascinating. That's when I was offered a unique opportunity. One that I never would've entertained had I not lost my nest egg. The local PBS affiliate came to my theater department looking for young talent for a children's show. I laughed in their face at the notion of one of my students teaching little children anything. And they loved the sound of my laughter. And then they asked, 'What about you?' And I told them 'I'm not young enough to know everything and anyone who is incapable of learning gets into teaching.' And they got a bigger kick out of that. And I told them that 'I am an artist and art should never try to be popular. The public should try to make itself artistic.' And that I would never talk down to small children. They loved it so much they immediately wanted to go national. You, my friend, are having a beer with Mr. Giggles."

"Huh," Ed says finishing his beer, "You? Really? You? teaching children? Really?"

"I wouldn't call it teaching. I'm entertaining. Yes, there's an agenda they give me to jam down these little rat bastards' throats but I make it more palatable. The name of the show is Mr. Giggles' Classroom and the premise is the kids are taking my class from home because there's a new pandemic or some such."

"What do you mean 'agenda,'" Ed asks pointedly.

"Oh, they give me these subjects they want me to teach, more like talking points. For instance, they come to me and they say, 'we want the first episode to be called "It's OK to be Gay."' Well, nobody wants to watch that, especially not gay kids. So, I did my first episode on Oscar Wilde. When my parents were killed my uncle took me in and read Wilde to me and I loved it! The rest of my stay with him was a disaster and he died suddenly but that's another story. But it was reading

Oscar Wilde at a young age that got me through it. So I thought, 'Let's do it!' I even used kids from the English Department for research and we got a week's worth of shows out of it!"

"You spent a week teaching little kids about Oscar Wilde?"

"Oh yeah, we get into history, and then I use The Picture of Dorian Gray' to teach how looks aren't everything. Then I did an episode on honesty using Them Importance of Being Earnest." And I did one on 'Salome' and I was getting emails from Right Wing Christian mothers who homeschool their children telling me how much they loved it. Can you believe that? And that's not the best part! I did an episode on the Marquis of Queensberry and boxing and how to defend yourself. Did you know that the man who invented the rules for boxing had a queer son that slept with Wilde?"

"And people are loving this?"

"The public is wonderfully tolerant. It forgives everything except genius. There's always going to be critics but the only thing in life worse than being talked about is not being talked about."

"I'm speechless."

"Let me stop rambling about my good fortune. You look tired. Let me make up the master bed." "The couch is fine."

"Nonsense," Jay insists. "I don't have a lot of guests, so I don't have a guest room, just give me a moment to change the sheets on the king-sized bed. I was already in bed when you knocked. You have to be up early for children's television."

Ed quickly turns his head when he hears something. "What was that?"

"What was what?" Jay asks a little nervously.

"I heard something. It sounded like a ...bump...coming from downstairs."

"It's nothing. It's an old house settling. Come upstairs. I'll take your bag for you."

"When I got here you said you were working on something downstairs," Ed says suspiciously.

"Did I?" Jay getting increasingly more nervous, "I am so clever sometimes I don't understand a single word of what I am saying."

"Is somebody down there?" Ed walks over and turns the doorknob but it's locked.

"Of course not! But if you need me to prove it let me get the key," Jay goes to the breakfront near the front door and reaches into a drawer where he pulls out a pistol and shoots Ed in the chest.

Ed's limp body slams into the far wall and slumps down to the floor.

"And this time STAY DEAD!" Jay yells shaking the gun for emphasis before bursting into laughter. He fires twice more into his chest and the body jolts around before drooping down. "Sorry, buddy. I couldn't help myself. Now, let's see what's in the goody bag."

Jay picks up the gym bag and sees the collar wrapped around the handles preventing him from opening the bag. He puts the gun down on the coffee table and uses both hands to undo the ring when he is zapped by the voltage and falls backward over the coffee table onto the living room floor.

Ed stands up a little gingerly. The Kevlar chest plate stopped the bullets but he's bruised badly from the point-blank shots.

He stands over Jay who is still incapacitated from the shock but can still open his eyes and raise his eyebrows while Ed's eyes swell up with tears.

Ed drops to his knees straddling him. He grabs the lapels of the robe.

"A true friend shoots you in the front," Jay quips apologetically.

Ed lifts him off the floor by his robe, "Shut up! Shut up and listen to me! I did die! I died and went to Hell! Hell is real! It's true!"

"A thing is not necessarily true because a man dies for it."

"I swear to God it's true!" Ed swears.

Jay comes right back with, "The truth is rarely pure and never simple."

"Believe me! It's real! You don't want to go there! You have to change! It's still not too late I know you had a tough childhood! I know what it's like to lose both your parents!"

Jay chuckles, "To lose one parent may be regarded as a misfortune. To lose both parents looks like carelessness."

A frustrated Ed starts raining punches down on his face after each sentence, "Shut the hell up! (Punch) Shut up for once in your life- SHUT UP! (Punch) Please! Listen to me! There is a hell and it's real! I've seen it! I was like you! I was a sinner! But I've been given a second chance! You can still change! I can help you!"

"The only difference between the saint and the sinner is that every saint has a past, and every sinner a future," Jay says spitting up blood.

This sets off three rapid-fire devastating punches to the face. Tears fall from Ed's eyes as he pleads with Jay. "Don't think you can't change!"

"I can resist everything except temptation," Jay smiles and the blood pours out the corners of his mouth.

"GOD DAMN IT! I'm trying to help you! Please let me help you! Just say you love God! Say it with me...Dear God in heaven-"

Jay cuts him off, "I have never given adoration to anybody except myself."

"Listen to me. You're sick. I'm trying to help you. You think you know about the world but you have no idea. You think you're a monster but God loves you. You just have to love him back!"

"I think that God in creating man somewhat overestimated his ability."

Ed tries to reason with him, "You're not giving me much choice here! You're too sick, too dangerous to let live. If I kill without giving you a chance I'm condemning you for eternity."

Ed gets up and tries to open the door leading to the cellar leaving Jay motionless but still alive. When it doesn't open he first tries to look for the keys in the drawer Jay went to when his cell phone rings. He checks to see who it is as he walks over to the kitchen to grab another beer. The cell phone rings and rings and rings and RINGS as he plops back down on the sofa sipping a beer right out of the bottle.

"Hello," he answers while holding the phone with his shoulder as he opens his gym bag.

"What the hell is going on up there?" Virgil Stanhope asks angrily.

"Hello, Virgil," Ed answers, "I figured you call."

"You really got the boss roaring now! What the hell did you do?"

As Ed goes through the contents in his bag he inspects the coins and the money bag he notices something different about Virgil, "What happened to the Katherine Hepburn accent? Why'd you drop the Great Gatsby act?"

"We stopped laughing a while ago. What did you do?"

"I did what you told me to do. I-" Ed tries to explain.

"I didn't tell you to steal anything!" Virgil erupts.

"You wanted me to nab those three demons. Rather than go after them I took what they need. They'll be coming to me and I'll be ready for them. Tell your boss I'm on it." Ed says in a soothing manner.

"Yeah, well, he thinks you're trying to pull a double-cross! He's not even thinking about escapees anymore. He's put the word out that whoever brings him your soul gets a free ticket out of here. So watch your back."

"Thanks, Virgil. Say, why doesn't he send you here? Don't you want a ticket back to the world?"

"I'm hurt, Ed," Virgil says, "Besides, I like it down here. There's a party every night. Besides, my life was no big shakes when I lived it."

"Yeah," Ed sighs, "I read your obit and I read about all the bodies they found. They weren't even sure how many children you killed. They didn't have DNA tests back then. How many was it?"

"Who in hell knows?" Virgil says dismissively.

"Is that what you meant when you said 'the road to hell was paved with good intentions?'"

Virgil gets a little louder as Ed raises his ire, "It doesn't even matter because the coppers through me in the hoosegow for something I really didn't do but they didn't care as long as they got their man! Nobody cared what happened to me! Do you know what happens to a little rich kid in prison, Ed? YOU THINK THIS PLACE IS BAD?"

Ed is taken aback. He's never heard Virgil yell or even show anger. There's a moment of silence where all he hears is Virgil letting out a deep breath.

"You know, Ed," Virgil calms a little to try to explain, "people think you grow up in a resort with a little money and your whole life is peaches and cream. Especially in my day. They didn't talk about the dark side. And when things went bad and you have a few coins in your pocket and there's a target on your back. You can't trust anyone. Not even your uncle! You know, when you're a little kid they teach you about good and evil. They read you these fairy tales, 'Gee, grandma, what big eyes you have!' But they don't tell you where the evil comes from or that it could be coming from the God Damned person reading you the story!"

"Virgil, listen," Ed tries to relate to him, "I know what it's like to be betrayed at a young age."

"A parent has one job! Protect their kids! And hey, if they can't do that, well then, don't blame me when something happens to them. You know, Ed, they called me a monster but they never asked me why or how I became one. You show me a monster and I'll show you someone who was a defenseless child. It's a vicious circle and it keeps going around and around and around."

"I've learned a lot about forgiveness, Virgil. The first person you have to forgive is yourself."

"I tried, Ed. I tried to forget the past. I tried to bury it. But I couldn't!"

Ed is taken aback when Virgil says 'bury it.' It was the same thing Theo said to him.

"But listen, enough about me," Virgil tries to regain his composure. "I just wanted to warn you about the

239

boss wanting your head. Just wanna give you a "heads up."(Virgil tries to laugh at his own joke but returns to being serious) Just watch your back. These demons can take the form of anybody. Be careful of wolves in sheep's clothing. You're about to learn what happens when you cross the boss. You're about to learn how bad your world can get. So, I'll let you run. I'll see you soon."

"Virgil, you're never going to see me again," Ed says before crushing his phone.

I'M NOT GOOD!

T he Breakfast Nook is a small bagel shop on a tree-lined street a few blocks away from Jays's town-house and luckily for Ed, it opens very early in the morning. When Ed enters his hair is still wet from the quick shower he took before leaving Jay's.

He is the first customer of the day and he finds a small table in the corner where he can watch the television that's already on but with the volume off. An adorable young woman with brown curly hair stands behind the counter waiting for him to order but he keeps his eyes on the TV screen. She finally goes over to wait on him. Ed is accustomed to being waited on at expensive restaurants or fine hotels. It's been years since he's been in a neighborhood cafe.

Ed can tell by the way she moves that she is a classically trained dancer and by the name tag pinned on her tee-shirt that her name is HAZEL.

With a bright smile and bubbly personality, she asks, "What can I get for you?"

"Hello, Hazel. A platter of Taylor ham, egg, and cheeses on toasted sesame bagels and a large black hazelnut nut coffee."

"The platter comes with a choice of home fries or hash browns," she declares while writing.

"No," he corrects, "A platter of Taylor ham, egg, and cheese sandwiches on toasted sesame bagels with a large hazelnut coffee. Oh, and make those with fried onions and salt, pepper, ketchup."

She's a little confused by the order. She's never heard someone say 'salt-pepper-ketchup' like it was one word before. But she eventually writes down four sandwiches on her pad before declaring, "Right away."

Ed fixes his gaze back on the TV where the news is replaying the story of the day:
 ROBBERY AT FED BANK scrolls along the bottom third of the screen and the other two-thirds just has a camera fixed outside the building showing cops just killing around. He thinks about asking to have the volume turned up but he already knows what happened and he likes the peace and quiet.

This is until the door opens up and a young woman leads an elderly woman into the shop and guides her to the table right next to Ed. The woman seems to be having trouble with her sight and is wearing wrap-around dark glasses very similar to the ones worn by The Visionary.

"I know the place is small but do they have to sit right next to me," Ed wonders to himself, "There are other tables."

Hazel brings Ed the steaming hot cup of coffee and greets the elderly woman by putting her hand gently on her shoulder and bending down so that her mouth is close to her ear, "HI, NAOMI."

"What is it about being blind that makes people think you're also deaf?" Ed wonders.

"Hazel, this is my granddaughter EMMA, she just back from her first semester at college and she's staying with me while I have a procedure done on my eyes."

Ed returns to watching the TV as Emma asks if they have vegan cream cheese but the only thought in his head is, "Why did they announce the robbery? They could've covered it up and no one would've known. It's not like them to be honest with the public."

Emma looks directly at Ed and hisses. She even shows her teeth. Ed pretends not to notice but says to himself, "HOLY- DID THAT GIRL JUST HISS AT ME?" But he plays it off like he didn't notice.

Emma then says out loud to no one in particular, " I'm so glad that bank got robbed! It's good that the rich learn what it's like to have things taken away!"

"Oh, sweetie," Naomi says, " it's not good to wish bad on anyone.

"You're just as guilty as he is!" Emma fires back but now extending her arm and pointing directly at Ed. He can't play this one-off if he tried.

"Excuse me?" That is the only response he can muster.

"I'm sorry," Naomi tries to apologize, "I've never seen her act like this before. She's usually so sweet.

Just then a ROAR OF MOTORCYCLE ENGINES rattles the glass of the shop as four motorcycle cops park on the curb right outside the window.

The last thing Ed wants to do is engage with this woman and bring attention to himself. He puts his head down and quietly sips his coffee.

The FOUR POLICEMAN enter the shop. One is white, one is African American, one looks Mexican American and one looks Asian American.

Emma says under her breath but loud enough for one of them to hear, "Fucking pigs!"

The smile quickly comes off OFFICER ROJO's face as he turns to OFFICER BLACK, "Did you hear what she just said?"

"Forget it, Rojo," Officer Black (that's his name) says gently pushing him toward the big table under the TV screen, "I'm famished and I just want to eat." "THE USUAL?" Hazel calls out from behind the counter.

OFFICER WHITE responds, "Not for me. I'm not feeling well. Just some hot tea, please."

"You do look pale," Hazel says with a caring tone.

"And give the check to the rookie," Officer Black says pointing at the Asian Officer, "He's still green."

The four of them place their helmets on the table and sit down.

Hazel asks the cops, "Hey, what going on? I heard helicopters flying around earlier."

"Turn up the volume," the Asian cop points to the TV, "They're talking about it now."

"Yeah, some guy robbed a bank last night and they put a tracer on the money and they tracked it to this guy's house. They wanted us to do crowd control but since the Feds ain't paying overtime we all went on break. This is our dinner time." The four cops high five each other.

"Emma, be a dear and get my wool shawl out of my bag," Naomi asks.

Emma complies, taking the shawl out of the bag, going around and draping it over her grandmother's shoulders, and sits back down.

"Thank you, dear," Naomi says sweetly.

Hazel goes to get the TV remote. When she comes back out she turns to Ed. "We're out of Taylor ham but we have pork roll. Is that OK?"

"Sure," Ed answers.

Hazel has the remote and turns up the volume to hear:

YOU'RE WATCHING MORNINGSTAR NEWS AND WE ARE COMING TO YOU LIVE FROM THE

GARDEN DISTRICT AS SWAT TEAMS HAVE
SURROUNDED THE HOME OF PROFESSOR JAY
BRUCE, A COLLEGE PROFESSOR WHO SOME OF
YOU MIGHT KNOW AS "MR. GIGGLES" ON THE
CHILDREN'S TELEVISION SHOW "MR. GIGGLES'
CLASSROOM.

They show a promotional headshot of Jay dressed up
in his persona with a devilish smile.

"God," Hazel blurts out, "he looks downright evil."

WE ARE GOING TO CUT IN LIVE AS WE HAVE JUST
GOTTEN A DIRECT FEED FROM THE BODY CAM
OF THE LEAD OFFICER WITH THE SWAT TEAM
WHO HAVE BEEN OUT HERE ALL MORNING
AND HAVE BEEN WAITING PATIENTLY UNTIL
THE AREA IS LOCKED DOWN AND THERE ARE
NO PEDESTRIANS IN THE AREA.

We see the POV of the officers as they take a battering
ram to the front door to Jay's home and smash it in
two pieces as one goes flying and the other stays par-
tially on the hinges. Another whack and the rest fly
off the hinges.

They enter the living room and see Jay lying on the
floor in the center of the room still incapacitated from
the beating Ed gave him. Laying on his bare chest is

the tracker Ed took off the coins and left to make his escape undetected.

THAT SEEMS TO BE THE BODY OF JAY BRUCE AND HE SEEMS STILL ALIVE BUT BARELY BREATHING.

Two SWAT MEMBERS come back down from the stairs and one of them yells, "UPSTAIRS CLEAR!"

Ed mumbles to himself covering his mouth with his coffee cup, "Check downstairs."

IT SEEMS THERE'S AN ENTRANCE TO THE BASEMENT BUT THE DOOR IS LOCKED.

This time, since it's an inside door, the battering ram splashes it to splinters with one blow.

We see what the SWAT TEAM SEES as they switch to flashlights as there's no light at all in the basement. The flashlight beams converge on a naked blonde college student tied to a chair. When the flashlight goes directly on her face she cowers from the harsh light and can only whisper, "Help me."

The TV cuts back to the studio where the same FEMALE ANCHOR is once again reporting.

FEMALE ANCHOR: I'm sorry, but we felt what was being shown was not suitable for daytime television but we will update you with any new developments. But we do have some breaking news to report at this time. Our research team has just learned that there's a connection between Jay Bruce and Edward Gennaro, the former President of Financial Edge who defrauded six million customers causing the greatest financial collapse in history.

Ed thinks to himself, "Yeah right, six million. If I had six million investors I'd still be in business."

A STOCK PHOTO OF ED APPEARS ON SCREEN.

FEMALE ANCHOR: Gennaro was presumed to be dead but it is now believed that he faked his death and performed the robbery last night and was hiding at his childhood friend's home before attempting to murder him and set him up to take the fall. He is believed to be on the loose and is considered dangerous. Please notify Federal Police if you come in contact or know the whereabouts of this man. Do not engage him yourself.

"You know, I do hate wearing these glasses," Naomi says innocently enough before taking them off and revealing blood-red eyes that look so scary that Emma almost falls back out of her chair.

"GRANDMA, YOUR EYES-" Emma screams getting out of her seat.

Naomi to Ed and says, "Today's Good Friday. You shouldn't be eating meat," and then her demeanor changes and her voice becomes demonic and she growls'" You're just like your mother! She can't keep pork out of her mouth!"

Ed sips his coffee surprisingly unfazed. He expected a demon to attack him but says, "I thought she was the demon from hell," nodding toward Emma.

"NO, SHE'S JUST WOKE!" The Demon snarls.

Ed throws the hot coffee in the old lady's face and leaps out of his chair. He then grabs her by the throat and lifts her over his head.

The cops are stunned by this big guy in the nice suit about to body slam a little old lady until he throws her across the room hitting two of them, knocking them to the floor.

He then picks Emma up over his head and throws her across the room landing on the other two cops.

"IT'S HIM!" Hazel screeches.

Ed smiles at her, "Can I get my order to go?"

He then picks up the table he's sitting at lifts that over his head and throws it through the plate glass window smashing it completely before picking up his bag and jumping through it and running down the street in the opposite direction of Jay's house.

As he's running down the middle of the street, his bag draped over his shoulder he sees a young woman pushing a baby stroller along the sidewalk in the opposite direction. He and this young woman make eye contact and they both hold it. The woman extends her arm and points at him the same way Emma did back inside The Breakfast Nook.

The woman then reaches into the stroller and pulls the baby out by its neck and holds the baby out in front of her, strangling it, just so Ed can see. He knows that a demon has possessed this woman and if he doesn't do something the baby is dead. To make matters worse, the woman flips the baby upside down and is about to drive the baby's head onto the concrete pavement.

Now in striking distance, he kicks the woman in the chest and catches the baby before she can throw him down. Ed cradles the baby in his arms and looks down to make sure he's OK since he's stopped screaming. The baby's eyes turn the same demonic fiery red that

Naomi's were. The demon has transferred itself from mother to baby. The little bastard even tries to claw at him with those adorable little hands.

By now, the woman has recovered and is on the sidewalk in pain from being kicked and unable to get up, "MY BABY! PLEASE DON'T HURT MY BABY!"

Ed HEARS the RUMBLE of the Motorcycle Cops in pursuit. He tosses the baby back in the stroller and takes off running. The demon knew he couldn't stop Ed with the body of a woman or a baby but at least slowed him down. Hopefully, Ed thinks, once he's run away the demon will leave them alone and continue the pursuit for him.

Up ahead is a garbage truck. The loud noise it makes joins the motorcycle engines in a medley before drowning them out. There is only one driver operating the claw that lifts the cans and dumps the contents in the back of the truck.

Ed reaches into the cab, which is on the right side, and yanks the unsuspecting GARBAGE MAN onto the street and climbs into the cab. He pulls out two thousand dollar bills and throws them at him before taking off with the garbage truck. It's been a long time since Ed is happy to learn that they're no longer stick shift since it's been a while since he's driven one, but he's surprised to see how many buttons and knobs there are. It looks like the space shuttle to him. It's odd for him to be driving on the passenger side but soon he has the truck going at top speed.

The Motorcycle Cops try to get past him to cut him off but Ed keeps swerving left and right. He's not trying to hit them but he can't let them get through. The Policeman doesn't appreciate Ed's kindness and pull out their guns and shoot at him. One cop even takes out Ed's driver-side rearview mirror forcing Ed to close his eyes and duck to avoid flying shards of glass.

"That's it," Ed says aloud, "No more Mr. Nice Guy!" He veers to the right pinning Officer Rojo and his bike between the truck and a parked car knocking him off his bike and the chase. He then yanks the steering wheel to the left making a sharp turn, crossing into the opposite lane, clipping the cars parked on the other side of the street, taking out his passenger-side rear-view mirror and giving Officer White nowhere to go and forcing him to skid out of control and in doing so taking out Officer Black who can't avoid him.

At this point, Ed can't see what's behind him and he doesn't hear the cycles anymore. "Are they gone?" He wonders. But something doesn't feel right with how the truck is handling. Ed turns and sticks his head out the window to see The Asian Rookie cop, the one they said was still Green has foregone the motorcycle and is hanging from the side of the truck. Ed turns the wheel back and forth trying to shake the rookie cop off. "How the hell is he still hanging on?" Ed wonders as he sticks his head back out to look. He sees that and Ed says to himself, "Ah, the rookie wants to be a hero! Alright, I got something for his ass."

Ed grabs the joystick that operates the lift arm but he realizes he first has to turn on the power and hit the "pump" switch. A lighted message comes on the dashboard. ENGINE MUST BE BELOW 900 RPM.

"Damn!" Ed says out loud before rethinking the situation.

He slams on the brake coming to a complete halt that almost throws the Green cop off but Ed sees that the cop smartly braced his feet on top of the "grabbers" of the lift arm- the things that grab the garbage can. This is perfect for what Ed wants to do.

With the truck stopped and Ed's foot on the brake, he grabs the control and opens the grabbers just enough so the cop falls straight down putting him within the grabbers. He then closes the grabbers and raises the lift arm sending the cop up into the air like a garbage can.

"HEY! HEY! HEY! PUT ME DOWN!" The cop commands. It's not until the lift arm has him up over the vehicle that the command turns into pleading, "PLEASE! PLEASE! PLEASE!"

Ed releases the grabbers dropping the cop into the hopper of the garbage truck. He then floors it swerving from left to right to scare off oncoming traffic and to piss off the cop. He sees a vacant storefront up ahead and thinks this is his chance to escape. He veers the truck so hard when it turns it stays on only two wheels almost toppling over before bouncing to all four tires and heading straight for the plate glass window. THE TRUCK SMASHES THROUGH THE STOREFRONT.

Once the dust settles on the crash, Ed notices an oily rag on the floor of the cab next to his foot. He then sees a cigarette lighter on the dashboard near the windshield. He grabs both and hops out of the truck. He can't hear the cop in the back, "I hope he's not dead," he thinks to himself.

He unscrews the cap to the gas tank, sticks the rag as far down as he can, and lights it on fire before he runs out the back door of the store.

When the other cops responded to the call all they found was a garbage truck parked inside an old store filled with smoke and the rookie cop outside coughing and the perp gone.

Ed didn't even see which subway station he went into. He just runs down the stairs and when he saw a guy about to go in, he offers him a thousand dollars to have him swipe his card to let Ed in.

By now, the early morning commuters filled the station and Ed was able to lose himself in the crowd. For whatever reason, maybe due to him, the trains were delayed and it felt like forever.

Eventually, ten uniform police officers enter the station pushing their way through the crowd looking for Ed. From a distance, he sees the guy who let him in being questioned by a cop, and though he can't hear what's being said sees the guy shake his head no, and the cop moves on to the next commuter. "Wow," Ed thought to himself, "the guy didn't give me up. That's the power of a thousand bucks." And in being honest with himself Ed wouldn't have been mad at the guy if he did give him up.

The two trains come into the station at the same time, one going uptown and the other going down. Four cops get on each one of them and go from car to car looking for him. By the time both leave the station the only people still on the platform are two cops who just look at each other and shrug.

Ed watches all of this from deep inside the tunnel. He is able to find a place in the wall where he can hide from the cops and the rushing uptown train misses hitting him by mere inches.

By this time, he estimates that the police will shut down the entire subway system and have everyone evacuate all the stations on all the stops on this line. This allows him to take a leisurely stroll uptown unseen.

Ed never considered himself a professional criminal. It was more of a hobby for him. Which means he spent lots of spare time thinking of ways of getting out of trouble like this.

Halfway between stations, he locates the yellow and red emergency exit sign. Beyond that door is a set of steps that dead-ends with an iron plate. It would probably take two regular people to push the door open but not him. Not a guy who does handstand push-ups almost every morning. He does a military press and pushes on the crossbar and the door swings open. It's heavy but it has counterweights so once it's open it's pretty easy. He emerges onto a busy street corner where no one even notices him coming out. Based on what he overheard the Motorcycle Cops say about the

Federal Police not wanting to pay overtime he doubted very highly they'd put someone on the emergency exits and he was right.

He closes the hatch and casually walks up the block. He looks around and sees the security cameras at each light post and the drones flying around scanning people's faces from afar and running the photos through facial recognition software and he knows it's only a matter of time before they pick him up. He looks around for a secure location where he kind hide the coins. When they catch him he'll need some kind of bargaining chip to demand they take him to the island to see his daughter. "Hopefully, she's there," he thinks.

A parade of Armored Personnel Carriers and Riot Control Vehicles cruise along the Main Street with soldiers getting out at every light to maintain crowd control. The vehicles have machine gun turrets mounted on the roof and speakers on both sides blaring a recorded message:

ATTENTION CITIZENS THERE IS A DANGEROUS CRIMINAL ON THE LOOSE. PLEASE REMAIN CALM AND OBEY ANY ORDERS GIVEN TO YOU BY MILITARY PERSONNEL

"They haven't sent out an alert to people's phones yet with my picture on it. What do I do then?"

He keeps his head down and keeps walking. People don't make eye contact when they pass him, not even the women. That never happens. "They must be too scared," he thinks.

He notices the soldiers are practically harassing everyone but him. Old ladies, teenagers, everyone but the white adult male who actually committed the crime.

"It's not about me! It's not even about the coins! It's all just an excuse for them to lock down the city and declare Marshall Law. If they sweep me under the table like that I'll never see Rainbow again and these people will never get out from under the government's thumb. I'll gotta do something."

He sees a public pay toilet across the street. "Oh man, I wish they still had phone booths like back in the day," he thinks as he crosses the street.

There's a skinny BLACK HOMELESS MAN shaking a coffee cup with spare change just outside the pay toilet. As Ed passes by the man spits on him and yells, 'White Devil!"

Ed does his signature move of grabbing the guy by the throat, his Adam's Apple just above Ed's thumb, and lifts the lightweight clear off his feet.

"Get off me mother-" he wants to say more but Ed's grip tightens.

"Wait a minute," Ed says to him, "you're not a demon! You're just a crazy homeless guy! But you have some quarters."

Ed takes the change out of the cup that he needs for the toilet. When the man starts to protest Ed punches him in the chest knocking the wind out of him and bringing him to his knees.

It turns out that he served two purposes. One was to allow Ed to steal his change and not feel guilty about it. The only thing worse than a homeless drug addict in his eyes was a racist one but without him, Ed could never get the fifty cents to go inside the stall and change into "The Edge." The second was he reinforced the notion that Ed didn't want to hurt real people and he would have to devise a quick way of dividing them from the demons sent to hunt him down.

Ed is pleasantly surprised by how clean and well-kept the toilet stall was. He was against the city putting them in and charging the people but charging the fifty cents allowed them to stay clean. "Kudos to you, big gov," he thought to himself. That would be the last time he ever feels that way.

He re-emerges from the pay stall in full "Edge" gear, black from head to toe. But no one notices or cares. There are plenty of people dressed like superheroes posing for photos with tourists in much cooler outfits. The one time he wants to get noticed- he can't!

He looks out into the square and he even sees a woman dressed like Rainbow. "Huh, she was right all along about wearing a flashy outlet.

He turns to the Homeless Man still writhing on the ground in pain, "Sorry man, if I had listened to my daughter I could've made some tips and not had to steal from you."

Ed walks out to the middle of the square and people start to take notice. Even the soldiers know there's something "wrong with this guy" and start to move in. They are reaching for their com sets to notify the others. He looks up and around and doesn't see any snipers. The buildings are too tall in this part of town to place anyone on any roof. He then looks at the people around him, some just stare, some don't even notice him but there are others that creep toward him like animals stalking prey with angry looks on their faces. Those are the demons.

He reaches into the gym bag and pulls out a stack of thousand-dollar bills and tosses it high up in the air so the wind catches it and sends the bills scattering all around the square. There's an insane scramble of people trying to grab as many as they can.

Ed makes sure to run amongst the crowd as to not be a target for the soldiers and anyone he sees who is looking at him and not going for the money he punches in the face as he passes them. He doesn't feel bad because he's hitting them as hard as he can with a running start and they aren't badly hurt. If he did the same thing on a football field against a team in full uniform even the linebackers would be out cold, helmet and all.

Ed grabs another handful of bills and tosses them in the air to cover his tracks and to interfere with the possessed who seem to be getting stronger and more vicious.

A soldier manning a machine gun turret on a Gaia Amir 6x6 APC starts firing into the crowd trying to hit Ed but hitting all the demon-possessed people trying to get him as well as a lot of innocent bystanders.

Now that the military has the order to shoot civilians the game has changed and he has to change tactics. He's the reason these people are getting killed or that's at least how they'd spin it. He never put anything past the government but shooting into crowds like this is beyond even Communist countries and dictators.

He sees an underground parking garage and sprints toward it. As soon as he passes the front gate there's an office directly to the left with two workers inside. The two men are watching him from the news coverage on a little TV on their desk. They're so busy watching they don't notice he's standing in front of them.

"HOW DO YOU CLOSE THE GATE?"

"Huh?" One Car Attendant asks.

"How do you close the main gate?" Ed asks in a more reserved tone.

The Car Attendant points to a button.

"OK, get the hell out of here!" Ed grabs them and pushes them outside before pressing the button and closing the gate behind them.

Ed goes back into the office and sees the live coverage on the TV. He sits down at the desk, puts his feet up, and takes a break to watch what's going on. He sees a mini-fridge and cracks it open to find a treasure trove of snacks and drinks.

From this vantage point, he can still see out into the street where the military immediately cordons off the area around the garage. "What the hell are they up to?" He wonders as he cracks open a can of soda. He raises the volume on the TV.

NEWS ANCHOR: THE MILITARY DOES HAVE THE SUSPECT TRAPPED IN A PARKING GARAGE IN MIDTOWN. THEY HAVE CORDONED OFF THE AREA AND HAVE

CREATED A NOGO ZONE FOR THE ENTIRE CITY. HERE'S A STATEMENT FROM COMMANDANT MILKIE- NEWLY APPOINTED HEAD OF THE FEDERAL POLICE.

We see Commandant MILKIE giving a press conference to a group of reporters.

COMMANDANT MILKIE: We have identified the criminal as Edward M. Gennaro. Many of you know him as the financier who raided the pensions of six million investors but he is also known as "The Bump" or as "The Edge" who is considered number one on the most wanted list and Interpol has identified as the most dangerous criminal in the world. We will not be answering any questions from the press at this time.

"Where the hell do they keep getting this six million number from?" He asks himself aloud.

NEWS ANCHOR: IF YOU WANT TO TRACK THE CULPRIT'S WHEREABOUTS AND KEEP WATCHING ALL THE ACTION DOWNLOAD THE MORNINGSTAR APP.

It takes about two hours for them to do something and Ed appreciates the much-needed rest. It also allowed him time to scope out the garage and to plan an escape route, just in case. He sees the blue Thunder Riot Control Vehicle on television as it speeds toward the gate leading into the garage. It raises the hydraulic shovel in the front as it plows through the gate smashing it and then driving right over it as it crashes through. Ed can hear the echo of screeching tires as they turn down the spiral driveway leading down to the underground parking structure.

They find Ed standing in the center of the garage with his hands up. They stop in front of him with the headlights flashed on him. Three soldiers get out of the vehicle. Their guns trained directly on Ed.

"I surrender!" Ed calls out, "I'd like to make a deal."

The Leader gets out of the driver's seat. He looks and acts like a real badass. Ed sees his rank is Captain and his last name is Adams. "The name of our squad is Kill Team Six, not Deal Team Six." He lights a cigar as he says it.

"Son," Ed warns, "you should've brought teams one through five"

"There are no others. There's six of us," Captain Adams responds blowing smoke.

"I only count fo- OH SHH," Ed dives between two cars as two soldiers come from behind him on either side to outflank and surround him.

The THUNDER from the M-60s RAINING BULLETS is deafening as it echoes through the he cavernous garages shredding parked cars into Swiss cheese. The plan of Ed negotiating trading the coins to see his daughter has just blown up just as some of the cars around him EXPLODE as bullets hit the gas tank of one of the cars.

The soldiers duck back into their armored vehicle as the smoke settles from the explosion and their ears stop ringing. It's not looking good for Ed. There's nowhere to hide.

Adams gets out of the vehicle and calls out, "Find the body, make sure he's dead and then make sure there are no cameras around here."

The men get out of the vehicle and scatter to find him.

"Hold on a sec, fellas!" Ed yells out hiding between two cars. "If you kill me you'll never get the coins."

"You heard the man," Adams calls out, "make sure we have the coins before we kill him."

"WAIT! HE'S MINE!" A female voice echoes throughout the garage.

The soldiers turn to see a tall, black woman wearing bright golden armor standing atop a car.

She's holding a golden staff six feet long sharpened at both ends.

"Who the hell are you?" Adams asks.

Ed, still hiding is able to see my looking at the reflection of the rearview mirror of the car he's hiding behind. He sees the statuesque woman in full body armor complete with a face gauntlet looking like something out of King Arthur's court. He immediately knows who it is and why she's there.

Ed sticks his head out from behind a car. "HER NAME IS BLACK AMAZON!"

"I'VE BEEN TRAINING EVERY DAY FOR THE PAST TWENTY YEARS WAITING, JUST WAITING FOR THE DAY I'D GET MY REVENGE ON HIM AND NO ONE AND I MEAN NO ONE IS GOING TO TAKE IT AWAY FROM ME!"

"All right, boys, " Adams orders, "Light her up!"

"But sir, isn't that politically incorrect?" One of them asks.

"Just do it!" He demands.

They fire at her as she does cartwheels from the top of one car to another avoiding the bullets coming from their service rifles. They held off on using the M-60s. They won't live to regret it. Ed won't stick around to see if they do. He is able to come around from behind them and while they're shooting at her he's able to grab his bag, jump in the vehicle, and floor it in reverse all the way out of the garage. They spray it with bullets but the armor holds up.

The windows of the vehicle are shaded and it's difficult for him to see in the dark garage but he dare not roll down any window. He makes his getaway by flooring it in reverse and heading back up the spiral ramp they came down. He tries to turn back to see if he can look out the back of the vehicle but the torque on his spine sends a bolt of electric pain shooting through his body. He's still not fully recovered. From the elevator shaft fall.

He faces forward, relying totally on his mirrors but sees The Black Amazon walking in the middle of the garage totally unfazed as bullets whiz by her and cars explode to the left and right of her. The BOOMS from the explosions are so loud Ed can't help but wince and blink but she keeps her gaze focused on her target-him. When looking at her you'd swear she doesn't even notice the team of trained assassins trying to kill her. And she, with a staff as her only weapon doesn't seem to mind.

He makes it up to the exit where he stops and lets the engine idle. He sees the mangled fence on the floor and the semicircle of military vehicles holding everyone back and waiting for him to come out. "This is it. You're done," he admits to himself, "If you're gonna go, don't die a coward running away from a fight and leaving a woman alone to die."

He slaps it into drive and floors it back down the ramp. It's cloudier than a London morning but he can see bodies lying on the painted concrete floor. One of them is Black Amazon. He creeps out of the vehicle afraid of getting ambushed but comes to the conclusion that they all shot and killed each other. He can't believe it. But the common-sense voice in his head declares, "You can't have a circular firing squad in an underground garage with cars exploding around you and expect to make it out alive. Except you, big fella." He literally reaches around and pats himself on the back.

He notices her moving. She's barely conscious but writhing in pain. He looks left and right like he's crossing a busy street before running over to her. He takes off his mask and takes off her helmet to check if she's still breathing. He puts his ear to her mouth to listen for breath. She kisses him on the cheek. Picking her up by her armpits he drags her into the passenger seat of the vehicle and gets in to take her to a hospital. He has enough room to swing the large vehicle around and he hits a bump which, at first, he thinks is a dead body but turns out to be the hood of a car whose engine exploded.

He's able to locate the switches for flashing lights and he turns on the PA system to announce,

"THIS IS CAPTAIN ADAMS! I HAVE CASUALTIES AND AM HEADED TO THE NEAREST HOSPITAL! CLEAR A PATH! I REPEAT: CLEAR A PATH! MAKE WAY!"

He does his best to muffle his voice doing the best impression he can of a guy he just met and he doesn't slow down long enough to tell if people can really see through the shaded windows. His BANGING ON THE HORN and the FLASHING LIGHTS AND SIRENS should let the pedestrians know he's not stopping. One EMT gets in front of the vehicle to have him pull over so they can put her into a waiting ambulance, "THAT'S A NEGATIVE!" he squawks over the truck's PA, "NO CAN DO! WE ARE PROCEEDING TO THE NEAREST HOSPITAL!"

And alas, he makes their escape, narrow as it was. But still feels the need once in the clear and there's absolutely no traffic ahead to roll down his driver-side window and give the finger to a traffic cop and a television news crew.

He looks over and she's sobbing, "Just hold on! I'm taking you to the hospital!"

"No!" She punches the side of the door, "I came there to kill you! I've thought of nothing else for the last twenty years."

His first reaction is to stay quiet. It's best just to let a woman talk. Especially when she's so mad at you she's willing to risk her life just to kill and tough enough to take out a team of highly trained soldiers to do so.

"Just keep your mouth shut and nod approvingly," he repeats over and over to himself.

"I've trained every day just waiting for this moment! I was so ready and so stupid! I know now that no matter how hard I can try I just can't beat you."

Against his better judgment, he speaks, albeit encouragingly, "Hey, you did a pretty good job of taking out a team of Black Ops assassins all by yourself and last I checked you were the only one still breathing! They had me dead to rights."

"I know I can kick your ass! It's just when I saw how slippery you are I knew that some people always get away with stuff and some people no matter how hard they try are always gonna get the best of you."

"It got nothing to do with who's better than who, you've devoted your life to helping people and you did. I've devoted my life to hurting people and I did. But you showed me how low I was and you've shown me how good I can be. And for that I thank you."

He reaches back and grabs the gym bag and says to her, "There's some money in here. I want you to have it." He places it between the two seats.

It looks like she's slipping. He nudges her, "Hey, hey, stay with me!" He keeps talking to keep her conscious, "You know, seeing you in that outfit with your curly hair out the back reminds me of a TV show I used to watch with my daughter when she was little. It was called 'Batwoman.' Ever see it?"

He taps her on the shoulder and she nods yes.

"At first they had a skinny white girl," he remembers, "but she got hurt doing a stunt so they brought in this really cute black girl and she was badass. But the show got ridiculous, I mean even for a superhero show, every single woman on the show was a lesbian. I wouldn't let my daughter watch it anymore. I didn't want her to grow up to be a carpet muncher but it turns out they had to cancel the show anyway because it got too PC and no one watched it. But you reminded me of that girl. That's how badass you were today."

"I loved that show," she says smiling as she grabs the bag with her left hand and opens the door with her right, and falls out of the vehicle going eighty-five miles per hour.

He screeches to a halt and spins out almost losing control. He's halfway down the block before he gets out and runs to her.

He cradles her in his arms. She looks up at him and says, "This is how I beat you."

People run over and gather around them. Different voices shout out from the crowd.

"Hey, is that Black Amazon?"

"Yeah, I think it is!"

"Is that the dude they're looking for on TV!"

"Ooh yeah, it is!"

"Did you see how he tossed her outta that car?"

"Hell yeah! He tried to kill her!"

"Is she dead?"

"I think she's dead!"

"He killed Black Amazon!"

"Let's kill his ass!"

That was all he needs to hear. He knows these are innocent people so he doesn't want to hurt them. He lays her head down gently and puts his mask back on without securing the collar because he has the bag in his other hand. He rises nonchalantly while everyone watches his attempt to walk back to the vehicle to make his escape but they surround him and cut him off. No one in the crowd has the guts to actually touch him at first, or he touch them until someone from the back hits him in the head with a beer bottle, and then all hell breaks loose. Pushing people out of his way he runs in one direction but the crowd gets too big and forces in a direction he doesn't want to go. There is a courage that comes to those in a crowd but the men brave enough to hit him get knuckle sandwiches. The woman, emboldened by his sense of chivalry, knowing he won't retaliate lash out at him by cursing, spitting, throwing whatever they can get their hands on at him.

He picks up speed when he sees what he hopes to be an alleyway. He reaches into the bag and pulls out what's left of the cash and throws it up in the air behind him at the women chasing him and they fight over it like a bride throwing a bouquet at a wedding.

With the gym bag, now only holding his clothes and the coins, thrown over his shoulder he runs through the space between two buildings to have his biggest fear confirmed; its a courtyard and there's no way out except the alley he came down which now funnels the mob into a single file of assailants which he can defend against one by one. With each person that runs at him, he is able to punch, kick or toss away.

The madmen who keep coming are now tripping over knocked-out former attackers even tripping over them to get to their quarry. "What keeps them coming?" He asks himself breathlessly. He spent his whole life testing himself; pushing his limits of cardio and endurance always knowing in the back of his mind that a day like this will come.

He no longer kicks. It takes too much energy and leaves his balance erratic. He plants his feet firmly and throws punches that are lightning quick but sound like thunder when he catches you behind the ear with one of them. If the speed by which he throws haymakers slows it's not perceptible by eye but it allows one of the angry mob to grab his arm saving another from receiving a blow and driving their shoulder into his body. This forces him to punch down on the tackler and gives another fighter the chance to grab him by the shoulder. The weight and sheer force of the rushing mob drive him into the brick wall. He stood his ground and has now ceded it. While his arms are still somewhat mobile he grabs the handles of the gym bag and using the mechanic grips of the servo motors to lock the clinch on the bag so that even when he loses consciousness they won't be able to pull it away from him.

He ducks down and gives up his head hoping the shielding and padding in the back of the mask will absorb the blows he's taking. He can feel knuckles breaking and they smash into the crown of his head. With his head down, and the men hurting their hands on his head, one man kicks upward catching him right in the temple sending his head into the air but then falling down on his back.

Now, lying on his back, clutching the bag with both arms and teems of men and women fighting for a spot just to stomp on him he looks up and sees the bright light of the sun. He can no longer see the angry faces or at this point feel the individual blows. The mob has now trans-morphed into one loud, angry monster. After facing demons and demon-possessed people he knows they are neither. They're just angry. But angry at him? Do they know who he even is? Are they angry for Black Amazon? No, he determines. They are just a mob. A man on the ground, close to death and they still keep kicking and screaming. They're fighting each other for a chance to hit him like it's a carnival game. Do they actually think that their blow will hurt more or be more devastating than the one hundred and five before it?

"What is it that turns an individual into a raving pack animal?" He asks himself lying there occupying his mind to ignore the pain. Even when he aligned himself with the mob he felt a need for individuality and when he committed crimes he did so with a flair that was uniquely his own. Is it that these people think they won't get caught? That they can hide in the crowd? Is it in blending into a crowd that one reveals their true self? He thinks of the irony, "If they only knew what was in their bag would solve all their collective problems but they don't care."

The "old" Ed would've gotten out of here, gone back, reviewed footage and tracked down each and every single person, and exacted revenge. He would've bought up every ticket to every sporting event and offered to each person for free just so he could get his hands on the person who kicked him while he was down. As far as Ed was concerned, kicking someone when they were down was subhuman.

But the recent events have changed him. Now, he actually felt sorry for them. He doesn't want anyone to go to the place he came from, especially for the sin they're now committing. So he does something he's never done. He prays for them.

"Dear God in Heaven. Please forgive these people. They are poor and angry and see me as the source of their problems. Please have mercy on them. I know I've failed. I know my time is here and that I'll never see Robin again but please look after her. I know I was given a second chance and that I've failed.

He instinctively looks to the sky as the fists and feet keep raining upon him. Put through the crowd he sees a dark figure standing in the sun. His arms raised in a tee. The shadowy figure leaps from the ledge of the building and dives bombs toward the crowd and at Ed.

He still can't make the figure out and decide whether it's real or not but the hand reaches down for him and instinctively he reaches up toward it. But to do that he has to unlock one hand off the bag while keeping the other one clenched. The people don't even notice the figure diving toward them or care to even wonder why he has his hand up in the air. They keep hitting him.

When the figure arrives Ed sees the face looking at him is familiar but doesn't know who it is. It's a gift horse and he's looking it right in the mouth. The hands meet. The grip of this "descending angel" is like a vise and would've crushed Ed's hand if not for the eco skeleton glove. And some force lifts the two of them off the ground shooting toward the sky.

The weight of the crowd and the world is lifted off of him and he feels light as a feather as the two bodies rocket skyward. When they get toward the top of the building their moment comes to a halt and Ed feels gravity taking back hold. So, the one who grabbed him grabs hold of the bungee cord they're riding and flings Ed straight up into the air flying over the ledge of the building and landing on the asphalt of the roof.

He hits the roof rolling in a mixture of pain and disbelief. His head swirling and close to throwing up, he can hear the clang of the figure springing off from the fire escape and clearing the roof sixteen feet above. Ed falls back on the rooftop and exhales as the mystery man collects the bungee cord before collecting Ed who tries to get to his feet but can only make it to his hands and knees.

The unknown savior grabs Ed by the back of his utility belt and lifts Ed's six foot four two hundred and forty-pound frame like a child picking up a toy from the playroom floor. So, with him clutching Ed and Ed clutching the bag the man gets a running start and leaps from one rooftop across the street to the other.

As Ed looks down he sees the street below screaming past him and can only hear the wind bristle through the earholes in his mask. Through the carrier sticks the landing on the rooftop perfectly, Ed's head gets clipped when going over the ledge.

"You good?" The familiar-sounding voice asks.

"F@#& NO! I'm not good!" Ed yells back while throwing up in his mouth a little.

It's the last thing he remembers before passing out.

MY BROTHER THE DEVIL

What causes deja vu? The feeling that you've been somewhere or have done something before. Scientists say it's a glitch in your memory while psychics say it's a window into the future. In Ed's case, it's neither. He's been in this space before doing exactly what he's doing now. The room is the same, the bed, even the IV drip in his arm. But the man looking over him seems familiar...yet...different. He's just waking up and his vision is still blurry and his mind a little fuzzy but there's a man holding Ed's wrist with his fingers while measuring his pulse against his wristwatch.

The physician attending to him looks likes he's straight out of central casting of one of those old soap operas set in a hospital. The word that popped into his head was "stoic."

When the doctor leans in to listen to the stethoscope Ed gets a closer look and makes the connection, "Max didn't tell me he had a brother who was a doctor."

"I don't," Max answers matter-of-factly.

"Wait! What?" Ed sits up a little in bed. "Oh my God! Is that you?" "Yup."

"What the hell is going on? What the hell did you do? Did you go on a diet? Or lipo?"

"Let's focus on your health right now. What was the last thing you remember?"

"I was getting beaten on by an angry crowd and I remember looking up and seeing this guy, I couldn't make out who it was because the sun was in my eyes but he dropped down from the sky and lifted me out of there. He was carrying me across the rooftops jumping from building to building. But then I hit my head on something and I was out."

"Yeah...sorry about that," Max tries to cover his regret with humor, "Physician, do no harm, right?"

"THAT WAS YOU?" Ed almost rips out the IV.

"Just calm down. I'm going to have your buddy come in to talk to you. That ought to sedate you."

"I heard that," Theo announces as he comes through the door. "How's the patient?"

"The patient wants to know what the hell is going on around here!" Ed demands.

"No, no no, you don't get to do that. When you left here I didn't think I'd ever see you again. Then you're on every channel robbing the Federal Reserve and doing a car chase scene throughout the city until you get beaten by every citizen uptown. It got so bad I had to beg Max to go save you and bring you back here."

"Well, since all my favorite shows were preempted..." Max jokes.

"How the hell did he-"

Theo raises his hand to settle Ed down, "First things first, you said you were going to look for your daughter. What happened?"

Ed is reluctant to get into it but once he starts he just flows, "Do you remember I told you I had a dream and it seemed real?"

"I remember. You said you were in a forest," Theo recalls back to him.

"There was more," Ed restarts the story," I really did die. And I went to hell. There was a guy there- a guide. I thought it was a dream but it was real!"

Ed waits for a reaction but all Theo says is, "Go on."

"Well, when I left here, I went to retrieve my cell phone and the guy I met in hell CALLED ME ON MY PHONE!"

"The guy you saw in your dream, I mean your vision, called you on your cell phone. What did he say?"

"He said that you three were demons with superpowers and you were here to cause chaos on earth and you weren't to be trusted."

"We were demons?" Max jumps in.

Theo gets in front of Max and whispers, "Let me talk to you for a second." They take a few steps back and Theo asks, "You don't believe him?"

"He's taken a lot of shots to the head. Besides, it could be a manifestation of his guilt. Then again, he was technically dead when I found him. When I got him back here I put him under pretty deep. They say going that deep into sleep can change you, change your personality. I'll check his phone. He's probably getting robocalls from a car warranty service and is hearing voices. Listen, his body is OK. My job is done. The rest is up to you."

Max slaps Theo on the shoulder and heads for the door. "Good luck!" He wishes to both.

Theo drags a chair over and sits close to the bed. "Who was this guide?"

"His name was Virgil," Ed answers.

"Virgil? Like the poet?" Theo tries to clarify.

"No, his name was Virgil Stanhope. I looked him up. He was from the 1920s. He molested and killed a lot of children and buried them-"

"Under the driveway of the hotel his parents owned. I was raised upstate. He's infamous in Western New York. But you didn't know that. Did you?"

"Listen," Ed explains, "when I was here I saw things in John's office. Designs on the Fed and information about the coins. And you saw how he turned that spoon to silver. And how does a guy go from weighing five hundred pounds to jumping over city streets? And you said it yourself that you wanted to destroy the economy. It actually makes sense that you'd be demons."

"You thought we were demons?" Theo struggles to process.

"Beware of false prophets which come to you in sheep's clothing, but inwardly they are ravening wolves," Ed fires back.

Theo dismisses it by countering, "A proverb in the mouth of a fool is like a thorny branch brandished by a drunk."

"YOU SEE WHAT I MEAN?"

"You got a point," Theo concedes. "Go on."

"I thought you were going to steal the coins. Virgil said that if I stopped you I would get in good with the big guy-"

"The big guy," Theo repeats.

"I thought if I could get the coins I could use them as leverage to get my daughter back. I know where they have my daughter. Leo Epstein is a billionaire who owns his own island. He's having a party this weekend and he's inviting the world's most powerful people! The President is going to be there! He has a business partner, a woman named Lupe, who kept asking if my daughter was going to be there. My daughter has paparazzi following her around twenty-four seven and none of them know where she is. She has to be on that island! Now, if I can make a few calls I can charter a flight for tomorrow and be there by Sunday. It's my daughter's birthday."

"It's already Saturday," Theo tells him. "You've been asleep for an entire day."

When Ed hears that he looks frantic. He puts both hands to his head in utter frustration.

"Did you happen to see the news coverage on you? The minute you step out that door you'll be arrested, or shot, or worse."

Ed, almost in tears, "I don't care anymore! I can't live another day like this! I need to see my daughter one last time!"

Ed takes a moment to recover and switch gears. He should've never shown that kind of weakness and emotion. He kicks back into salesman mode, "Listen, if you help me, I can get you onto the island. They'll let me in, especially since I have the coins. I can get you in. They'll listen to me. They'll accept you if I say you're with me. Once you're in you can wreak havoc on the place. You'll finally get your chance!"

"Are you trying to bargain with me?" Theo asks incredulously. "I'm not the Loan Manager at the bank. You have no power here. You can't even get out of bed. I can help you but you're going to have to show some humility and you're going to have to ask!"

Ed's lip quivers as he says the words he's never said in his life, "Please help me."

Theo sticks out his hand. Ed reaches over and shakes it. Theo takes hold with his other hand as well. Then Ed does the same. "If you're going to help your daughter you're going to need help. But you're going to have to ask each of us. I can't ask the others for you."

"I thought you were their leader," Ed says legitimately confused.

Theo chuckles at the notion. "You've seen them, you've seen what they can do. They don't need me."

"Yeah, about that," Ed tiptoes through, "Who the hell are you guys?"

"Let me start from the beginning," Theo lets out a deep breath as he collects his memories, "I was given a certain insight at a young age. I can see things other people can't or don't."

Ed interrupts, "What? Like ESP?"

"No, I can't read minds nor do I really want to. Let's just say that my sight had allowed me to become quite wealthy. It afforded me a certain lifestyle that I enjoyed. The wealthier I became and the richer and more powerful the people I was dealing with I started to see that something is not quite with the world. One night, I was in a casino in Macau and some loudmouth at the Baccarat table kept bragging to me how he had the goose that laid golden eggs. He had a young man in his employ that could literally turn lead into gold. At first, I didn't pay attention and then I didn't really care. But this man, fueled by booze kept going on and on to the point where after he lost all his money he took me to his palace to meet this young man. Now, this young man was living a lavish lifestyle, there were women serving him when I got there but he was still a prisoner nonetheless. Now, as wealthy as this man was he was spending the money faster than his charge could create it. So, I challenged him to one hand of poker for ten million dollars. And, of course, I won. I took the young man instead. There were armed guards all over but there was nothing they could do. You see, the rich and powerful have no problem with thieves, crooks, murderers are molesters but nobody likes a welcher. When he sobered up the next day it was a different story but by then it was too late."

"Who was it? Was it a Regal?" Ed pops up at just the chance it was a Regal.

"I'd rather not say," Theo says with a wink.

"If you got over on a Regal-" Ed's imagination races.

"The young man had informed me that he had the ability to change the molecular structure of the objects he touched and that it was genetic and that the men in his family could do it for generations."

"That's why he calls himself John Brady the fourth," Ed concludes aloud.

"By this time I had learned that many legends are based on historical fact and they become fairy tales when they are mistold or told to children over the years to actually conceal the truth."

"Hide in plain sight kind of thing."

"In a manner of speaking," Theo continues, "The young man informed me that he could only do it with lead and gold and coal and diamonds because he didn't know the chemical makeups of anything else. Why should he really? He told me though he lived a lavish lifestyle he hated his life in servitude and resented his family selling him into slavery. I told him his life was his and from that point forward he was free to go and to do whatever he pleased. He knew the dangers that await him and over a glass of wine I told him of the things I had seen and what I saw for the world and he wanted to join me on this journey."

"Can he turn water into wine?" Ed asks.

Theo chuckles, "We don't go there."

"So there's a whole family of people that can do this? How come I never heard this?"

"Because not everyone in his family has this genetic marker. The members of his family that cannot do this are murdered. So, he's seen what man can and will do for greed and he wanted no part of it."

"If you two were that big I would've heard of you!" Ed throws out there.

"We decided to stay under the radar and became Angel investors. We were looking for people who could help us so we started a foundation that would give grants and scholarships to seek out the best and the brightest and offered them the freedom to pursue their goals without corporate or collegiate or government intervention. Now, we had seen thousands of candidates and financed hundreds of projects and have made millions of dollars but the most remarkable person we ever met was a young man who wanted to study the human body so that mankind can reach its maximum potential."

"Max Po," Ed concludes.

"Max Po. He surmised that calories, being a form of energy were a good thing just as higher octane is better gas. Now, you've heard the stories of people in extreme duress having superhuman strength. That was fine and good but he developed a way that a person could control the hormones that control the body so that an overweight person, who has energy reserves can release them in an instant giving him what people might deem superhuman speed and strength."

"My God," is the only response Ed can muster.

"He has trained himself with a trigger word so that in an instant his neurotransmitters release adrenaline and cortisol and redistribute the blood to the muscles burning fat and making him grow instantly. That black suit he wears, similar to yours, is a compression suit. It allows him to do this without sagging his skin. He wears it under his clothes all the time, except for showers and such."

"So he stays fat on purpose?"

"He purposely keeps an energy store reserve at all times. He struggles with weight so that when someone is in need he can instantly jump twenty feet in the air to rescue someone fallen in an elevator shaft or to leap over rooftops to avoid an angry mob. He tells me carrying the extra weight makes him stronger when the time comes but it seems in more ways than one. The very people that mock and ridicule him are the ones he may save."

"Was he a fat kid growing up?"

"When I first interviewed him I asked him why he wanted to study this. He told me that his mother suffered from panic attacks and he wanted to teach people to control their fear. That's why we found him so remarkable."

"He could make a fortune," Ed just imagines the possibilities.

"For the blood and chemicals to go throughout the body so quickly it puts great strain on the cardiovascular system. Remember when you first asked me how he did the things he did do you remember what I said?"

"You said 'because he had a big heart.'"

"He only does it when he has to. It's ironic really, the most powerful human in the world can drop dead at any moment."

"And so your little circle was formed."

"That's right," Theo answers.

"So, what's the plan for tomorrow?"

"Don't worry about tomorrow. Tomorrow will bring its own worries. Let's just see if you can get out of bed. Can you eat? Because John is cooking Lobster Fra Diavolo."

Ed laughs as Theo helps him out of bed.

Theo can't help but laugh along while asking, "What's so funny?"

"It means lobster made by my brother the devil."

YOU'LL NEVER WALK ALONE

E d is able to walk up the stairs without any problems until he gets to the kitchen where he and Theo walk into an argument between Max and John.

"Seafood again? Lent is over."

John corrects him, "It's not over until tomorrow. Besides, I got all this leftover seafood. I made clams casino, fried shrimp, and garlic bread in honor of our Italian guest."

"Can't you make some stuffed filet mignon?"

John loses it, "THIS IS THE LAST SUPPER I COOK FOR YOU!"

Theo turns to Ed and whispers, "He doesn't know the half of it."

They sit and eat without saying a word to each other. Only the sound of classical music drowns out the sound of forks and knives hitting plates.

Ed attempts to break the silence by asking, "Who is this playing?"

John responds, "Beethoven."

Ed uses this as a conversation starter, " Beethoven once said, 'I will take my fate by the throat. It will never bend me completely to its will.'"

Theo looks up from his plate impressed by Ed's knowledge and never being one to miss an opportunity to use a famous quote, "He also said, 'Hope nourishes me, it nourishes half the world and has been my neighbor all my life. Else what would become of me?'"

John takes this time to show that he can sling a quote too, "Anyone who tells a lie has not a pure heart and cannot make a good soup." He chuckles and raises a glass to himself.

Max puts down his knife and fork and looks directly at Ed when he says, "Prince, what you are, you are by accident of birth, what I am I am of myself. There are and there will be thousands of princes. There is only one Beethoven.'"

They can all tell there was something behind that and that Max wasn't just adding another quote to the conversation or trying to impress them with his Beethoven knowledge.

Theo uses this as a good time to make an exit. He stands up and raises his glass. "I am going to go out to the balcony to smoke a cigar. My compliments to the chef." John nods as Theo gulps the last of his white wine before saying, "The soup was a little salty."

His little dig does little to break the tension at the table as he exits.

It's Max who breaks the silence, "Beethoven was the greatest composer who ever lived. And he had his hearing taken away from him. Just think of that. It's not like there were loud amps back then to make him go deaf like these old-time rock stars. It was taken away from him. And you know what? It forced him to perform less and write more. And the world benefitted from it. Don't you think?"

"Yeah," Ed agrees.

Max's tone changes, "You went around Wall Street telling anyone who would listen you couldn't lose money. But you did. And instead of being honest about it and learning from your mistakes you got dressed up at night and stole from people to make up your losses because you refused to lose.

"That's right! I don't lose!" Ed fires back.

"No? Well, you're the only one, then. We lose every day. We accept it. We don't run from it. We even have a name for it," Max says and then looks at John.

"Stacking Ls" John finishes the thought.

"That's right," Max declares, "Stacking Ls. That's what we do here. Because we know that no matter how good you are it's all a house of cards and it's going to come down. And what will you do when everything crashes around you? When you can't cheat or lie your way out of it. What do you do then?

"What are you getting at?" Ed says frustrated and angry.

"Whatever you thought you were or what made you great is gone. Your money is gone. Your status is gone. Your super suit is gone. Now, you come here with nothing! You're a nobody! And you expect us to save your ass a third time and risk our lives to save YOUR DAUGHTER?"

"Yes."

"That's all you have to say," Max returns to his meal.

"That's it?" Ed asks in amazement.

"Yup," John answers for the both of them because Max has food in his mouth.

Ed cracks a smile and sighs in relief. Now, feeling more comfortable he asks them a question in a hushed tone, "What the hell is his story?"

"He never told you about his childhood?" John asks.

"No," Ed answers.

"He told you about us but not about him, right?" John clarifies.

"Figures," Max tosses in.

"He was born in a monastery. His mother was a nun."

That makes no sense to Ed who asks, "What?"

His mother was a nun living in a monastery upstate. She was still a teenager when a bank robber, or something, came to the church where they were living seeking sanctuary from the cops. He was shot up by the cops and needed a place to lay low and heal.

He claimed sanctuary knowing the priests and the nuns would protect him and that the cops wouldn't go after him. I doubt he was seeking redemption but his mother tended to his wounds and tried her best to help him. And one thing led to another and about nine months after he escaped Theodore Way came into the world. Little Teddy, as they called him, was born blind. And I think deaf, too. Right?"

"Probably," is Max's answer.

"So, even though his mother sinned and broke her vows they couldn't kick them out into the cold. So, they raised him there and taught him the best they could. Then one day, he told me, the world came crashing through to him and he could see and hear everything. Now, as you know, our eyes take in the reflection of light waves and send a message to our brains telling our brain what we're seeing. Not Teddy's eyes. Have you ever seen him without his glasses?"

"No," Ed responds.

"Well, one day you will. His eyes take in the whole spectrum. He can see a phone call coming from the cell tower to your phone. And most of all, his eyes were not trained like ours. He doesn't fall for optical illusions. His eyes don't lie to him as ours do."

Max takes this time to jump in, "You know how people say, 'I see what you mean?' Well, he does. He doesn't know a damn thing about physics or chemistry (pointing to John) our medicine or the law (pointing to himself) but if you go to him with a problem he can see something you don't see- literally and figuratively."

"We're the best in the world," John says humbly, "because he makes us better.

"So, if he sees something in you," Max concludes, "then it's there. And if he trusts you then I trust you. But you have to trust us. We know you need our help but we have no idea what's going to happen tomorrow. But know this. You have to trust us completely. No matter what happens you have to have trust and faith in us. From this moment forward we are with you until the very end. From this moment forward you'll never walk alone again."

THE THINGS WE DO TO
OUR CHILDREN

E d was now a member of the team and since he was the new guy it was up to him to do the dishes while everyone went to bed. It was fine by him he wouldn't be able to sleep anyway.

When he did go to bed he laid there devising scenarios in his head of what could happen tomorrow. Needless to say, it will be nothing like he expects.

At six in the morning, Theo came knocking on his door. He walks in with a cup of coffee for Ed and a travel bag.

Ed speaks first, "What are you wearing?"

"Bermuda shorts and an island shirt. I didn't know what to get you so I bought you a bathing suit and a tee shirt. I bought some of those sneakers with the

Velcro strap, size thirteen. I wasn't sure about your size but they were on sale. The only other thing I have is some large sandals.

Ed, sitting up in bed, when hearing about the Velcro sneakers thinks instantly of Jerry Keen and says, "Sandals." But it sounds more like a question coming out of his mouth.

"Suit yourself. I got you the shorts with the built-in underwear. Not the ones with the mesh lining. Those are like razor wire on your junk. What did you think we were going to wear, tactical gear?"

"I just thought a guy called The Visionary would have a better eye for fashion," Ed says punctuating it with a sip of coffee.

"Ironic, isn't it?" Theo then asks rhetorically," You know where we're going, right? Right into the middle of the Bermuda Triangle. Be ready in ten."

As he walks out of the room Ed calls out to him, "How are we getting there?"

Theo sticks his head back into the doorway, "We're taking the car." He leaves not bothering to clarify.

Ed had never been in the garage of the townhouse which was at the other end of the hall. He enters to find Max, wearing a dark navy blue suit preparing a sleek-looking Klein Vision Flying Car for travel. Even with the wings folded and the tail retracted it still takes up most of the garage. The other car is a black Mercedes.

The Klein Vision is metallic silver in color and resembles a low to the ground sports car with doors that open upward at the press of the button allowing the passengers to get in both the front and back seat. The back of the car has a large tail going across like a louver and a large propeller in the back. It's got two long wings that run front to back on both sides of the vehicle.

"This is the biggest Klein Vision I've ever seen," Ed says with a little awe.

"Yeah, this is the Deluxe Four Seater twin-engine Amphibious model. They only made one," Max answers while putting water in the tank.

"Yeah, I heard they shut the company down for unsafe practices," Ed remembers.

"They shut the company down because they couldn't figure out how to regulate drivers- I.e. give them tickets," Max responds.

"How'd you get this one?"

"The same way the company is called Klein- Vision," Max emphasizes the "Vision."

Theo and John come into the garage. Theo now dons a Panama hat while John is sporting a summer fedora with Ray-Bans and expensive shorts and a linen shirt.

"You two are dressed for a beach party and he's dressed for a funeral," Ed points out.

John replies, "Let's just hope it's the former not the latter."

The three of them get in while Ed is hesitant. "You're going to fly this thing to Bermuda?"

"Yeah, it should take a couple of hours but we'll get there." Max answers.

"Don't you need to submit a flight plan?"

"Nah, the only problem is if we crash in the ocean no one is going to come looking for us. The good news is if we do it's an HHOS engine so it runs on water."

"You're the lawyer, doctor, and pilot?" Ed asks. His concern isn't so much in the technology but he's never seen one fly with four guys in it. Luckily, Max isn't at his full weight, or else Ed wouldn't get in. Ed is a fearless daredevil but he's not stupid.

"While we're young!" John yells from the back seat.

"Have faith, Edward," Theo says.

"OK, Teddy." Ed shoots back as he gets in the second back seat.

Theo looks at Max who pretends to be busy starting the car but hiding a snicker before turning behind to look at Ed, "The only people who call me Teddy are all dead."

Once inside it's quite roomy with legroom in the back even for a big guy like Ed. The interior is black with leather seats. It has both a center stick for the drive train and a yoke for the steering wheel. The dashboard is very similar to modern cars with two computer screens. The larger one where a glove box would be. It's even got cup holders.

As Ed straps himself in Theo drops a Manila folder thick with photos and an iPad wrapped in a rubber band on his lap.

"What's this?" Ed asks before opening.

"It's some photos and layouts of the island," Theo answers.

"They're pretty close up. Where'd you get them?"

"The internet," Theo answers, "Leo Epstein paid a local kid to tune the piano while no one was there. The kid made himself at home. He went all around the place. Obviously, Epstein has no security when no one's there so the kid had the whole place to himself."

"What's this blue and white striped building on the hill?" Ed points out.

"The kid shot a video and posted it online. I downloaded it for you. The kid said Leo called it a temple but the kid was too scared to go in. I tried contacting the kid but he's dead."

Those last words linger in the air as the garage door opens up and the sleek car shoots out onto Straight Street. They drive a little until they get out onto the open road. On a stretch of two-lane highway, Max straddles the middle line and presses a few buttons. The tail fin going across the back of the car stretches back and out while the wings extend straight up before opening out to each side. The vehicle is now taking up both lanes of the road. It's early on a Sunday morning so there's no traffic.

"Everyone put on your headsets so we can talk," Max announces, "The sensor on the dashboard display says there are no cars ahead for at least a quarter-mile. That should give us enough lift we need to get up. Buckle up."

Max floors it taking the car to about 150 miles and slowly pulls back on the yoke as Ed feels the air rushing underneath him and lifting them off the ground. Ed just puts his head back and closes his eyes as the car goes up and up and up. Max does a good job of not raising the nose up too much making for a nice and even elevation. He levels off at about eight thousand feet and maintains a speed of about two hundred miles per hour. Ed opens his eyes and looks out only seeing water below. It's loud as the air rushes around them. They need the headsets to communicate.

"SO, WHAT IS THE PLAN WHEN WE GET THERE?" Ed asks through the headset.

"THE PLAN IS THE PLAN," Theo answers somewhat cryptically.

Ed doesn't bother asking for any clarification. Ed has done just fine on his own all these years by calling the shots himself. Relying on these guys and being a part of a team isn't going to stop him from getting what he wants. He just keeps poring over the pictures.

Ed wakes up when they land. It's a smooth landing. Somehow he got all four tires to touch down at once gently jarring Ed awake. He's mad at himself for falling asleep and not studying the pictures more. He's practically memorized as much of the compound as possible and he must've really needed the rest.

The vehicle never stops. By the time they turn off the runway and onto the tarmac the wings are already raised, folded, and put back into place and they are now in driving mode and turning onto the road that leads to the compound. There was no one at the airstrip and there was only one plane in the hangar- Leo's private jet.

There's one road that goes all the way around the island as they pass the pier where the ferry takes workers back and forth from the main island. They pass locals in maid and kitchen uniforms walking from the compound to the ferry.

They come to a large circle where they swing around passing a tall building they call The High Tower and stop in front of what is called The Main House. There are some people milling around but not much going on until the Klein Vision Deluxe pulls up. It's not the car that attracts the attention it's the men getting out. There's one in particular that Leo Epstein comes out to greet with a security detail of four very muscular and very armed men wearing matching uniforms consisting of powder blue polo shirts with navy blue cargo shorts and navy blue baseball caps. His arms held out and open just as the car's doors open up and wide open.

"IS THAT HIM? IS THAT JOHN BRADY?"

John gets out of the car with his arms as wide open as his smile while the others stay seated, "It is I!"

"A real live Alchemist! At my house!" Leo is truly enamored by John's presence. "And I can't wait because later today you're all going to meet the big guy!"

Ed, looking down trying not to be noticed shoots his head up when he hears "the Big Guy."

"And I come bearing gifts," John declares as he nods for the others to get out of the car.

Theo gets out and hands John Ed's gym bag and he, in turn, hands it over to Leo who, when unzips and looks inside is dumbfounded.

"Oh, my- where did-" Leo is unable to finish a sentence he's so amazed.

"He brought them," John says pointing to Ed. "He's my other present to you."

Max comes behind Ed and puts him in a bear hug just as Theo takes thick plastic zip ties and wraps them around Ed's wrists like handcuffs.

Ed is amazed. The men he was told would be with him to the end just gave him up as soon as they get there.

Theo leans in and whispers in his ear as he tightens the restraints, "Have faith," and then kisses him on the cheek. The kiss makes everyone watching focus on that and not what he said to him.

"Did he just kiss him on the cheek?" Leo asks John.

"He's my employee. I'm not allowed to ask him personal questions or else he'll sue me."

"That makes sense," Leo says before turning to his guards. "Take him straight to the temple."

Ed, feeling thoroughly beaten and utterly betrayed simply puts his head down and takes a step forward when John sticks his hand out stopping him like a mother puts her hand out to keep a child from crossing the street before her and in doing so touching his wrist and the zip ties.

"Sorry, man," He says looking him in the eye.

As the guards take him away, Leo slaps his hands together, "Now that that unpleasantness is done there's something I want to show you!"

John introduces the other two to Leo by saying, "Mr. Epstein, I'd like to introduce you to my personal assistant Max Po and my business consultant Theodore Way."

Leo announces to them, "Gentlemen, I'm excited you're here. We have a lot going on today. We are going to have a lovely young lady perform for us tonight and this afternoon we are going to have our annual toga party. But first, there's something I want to show you that we are all really excited about."

Just then, an open-air Jeep pulls up beside them and Leo gestures for them to get in. John turns to Leo, "Where do you want Max to park the car?"

"Over there is fine," Leo waves his hand toward no particular place.

John points at Max, "Stay with the car!"

Max abides dutifully but knowing that John is having a little too much fun acting like the boss. John and Theo get in the back of the Jeep and the driver pulls away as soon as Leo gets in. They pass the four armed guards leading Ed off to the temple. One guard pushes Ed to walk faster and when Ed turns to give him a mean look the guard cracks him in the back of the head with his rifle. This is the last thing they witness as they drive off.

"What did you mean when you said take him to the temple?" Theo asks Epstein.

Leo tilts his head so that Theo in the backseat can hear him but doesn't bother turning around, "It's a joke. It's just a storage unit and we can lock it. We'll just hold him for the big guy."

"I don't think you need to rough him up like that," John adds. "When he came to us he was pretty beaten up. That mob in New York did a number on him. I doubt he's going to try something."

"I hope he does!" Leo says with a certain glee. "My guys are all ex-Israeli Special Forces and Mossad. They'll tear him apart!"

Back at the compound, the four guards surround Ed who is still on his knees and elbows from getting clunked on the back of the head by the rifle butt.

"This is the guy that's been on the 'most wanted list'? He doesn't seem so tough, " One Guard spews out as he spits on him.

"Let's just get him into the temple," The Second Guard suggests.

"Are you kidding," The One Guard scoffs, "What would you do if you were the one that found Hitler while he was still alive?"

The Second Guard gets emotional just thinking about him. He fights off tears as he raises his rifle like a sledge-hammer and brings it down on Ed's back. Without a word, the other two guards get on each side of him and start kicking him in the ribs while the other two watch.

Suddenly, The One Guard drops to his knees. Someone has gotten behind him with them even noticing and kicked him behind his knee crashing him to the ground. While still on his knees the guards see Rainbow slap her hands hard onto his ears causing him pain, disruption, and quite possibly a broken ear-drum. She then throws his head down to the grown by grabbing one of his ear lobes and tugging so hard on it that it almost comes off.

The One Guard now rolls in the dirt cradling his bleeding ear. The other guards train their rifles on the young woman.

She stares them down and says, "If you want to get to my father you have to come through me!"

The Second Guard motions for them to lower their weapons. Not only is she a formidable figure that would put up a good fight but she is also an honored guest of the owner himself. They take a step back and allow her to pick her father off the ground as they do the same for their comrade.

"But Mr. Epstein said-" The Third Guard starts but is cut off by The Second Guard that holds up his hand as if to say 'be quiet."

Robin helps her father walk as he's still a little wobbly. She leads him to the tallest building on the island. What everyone refers to as The High Tower. Without speaking she brings him through the lobby and past the security guards and concierge straight to the elevator that goes only to the penthouse floor.

The Jeep is cruising along the road that circles the island as Epstein makes small talk. "This island is something, isn't it? It's only two thousand years old. Geologists say there was a giant earthquake that ruptured plates and the volcanic pressure caused this island. They say the earthquake was felt all around the world. The epicenter was somewhere in the Middle East or the Mediterranean. Can you believe that?"

"Did you build all of this?" John asks.

"They were building a resort. The High Tower was the hotel and my main house was going to be the country club. But when that guy wrote the book in the seventies about how dangerous the Bermuda Triangle was the money dried up and no one wanted to go. I picked it up about twenty years ago for practically nothing. There used to be a beautiful hotel on the other side of the island built back in the eighteen hundreds and it was a big getaway for the rich up until the Great Depression. You can't do much building on the island. It's got huge pockets of natural gas underneath us. I could make a fortune just from fracking but you know how Simon says fossil fuels are a no-no. But what I'm about to show you is what I'm most proud of.

They turn off the road and come to a large hospital building with a sign that reads:

GILDA   MESH   EPSTEIN   MEDICAL
RESEARCH CENTER.

"Gilda Mesh was my mother's name. Gilda meaning 'woman of sacrifice' and Mesh means 'brass' and let me tell you. Those two names fit my mother well. She sacrificed everything for me and she had some brass let me tell you."

Leo motions for the driver to pull up to the entrance and wait. "Let me show you around. It's really a great place. A lot of the doctors and medical staff live here on the island. Many of them stay at the High Tower. But it's downstairs that's going to interest you most.

They take the elevator to the very bottom floor. Leo needs a key card to access the floor. Once inside they walk down a corridor where both walls are glass windows and they see rows and rows of babies in incubators, older children on respirators while bigger kids are in beds with breathing tubes in their throats.

Leo walks a few paces ahead of them guiding them through this ward. He doesn't detect any emotion on Theo and with his wraparound sunglasses on you wouldn't unless you know him as well as John does, "Just relax. Be cool. Stick with the plan, " he whispers under his breath to Theo hoping Leo doesn't hear.

Leo spins around to face them with a big grin on his face as he goes into his sales pitch, "I was so excited when you called me. We can really use you on the team. We are already the richest and most powerful people in the world but as you know the competition is tough. The Regals still think their shit doesn't stink and the Chinese are nipping at our heels. We had to do something. So we made a deal. A deal with The Devil. He will give us everything we could ever possibly dream of but when we die- well, he gets our asses- forever! So, I figure, if we don't die he can't get us. So, I try to eat right and exercise, but let's face it. Who are we kidding? I tried investing in medicine. You know, curing cancer and all that. But I was just dumping money down the drain. I'm a finance guy, not a doctor. So I started a hedge fund to hedge our bets in the market. We're here growing our body parts. With a new heart, new kidneys, even new lungs every couple of years we can quite possibly live forever. Or at least till modern medicine can catch up and cure some of these diseases. We can beat that son of a bitch! We can BEAT THE DEVIL!"

Leo holds his hands out with a big smile on his face signifying 'Whadda ya say?" He doesn't say another word. He goes by the old notion that the first one to speak in a negotiation loses. It's Theo who breaks the silence, "Where do these children come from?"

"Some of them were bought. Some of them were donated. It turns out that millions of women have unwanted pregnancies every year. We already have their DNA and their blood types in the national database. We take the ones we want and invite them down here for a little vacation while we take the fetus. We call it a 'Leisure Procedure.' We have waiting lists for women wanting to give us their babies! A lot of these girls like to stay, you know, live here. They love days like today when the rich and wealthy come along. They have sex with us, hang out for a few weeks and whadda ya know- we have fetuses with stem cells already implanted with our DNA. It's a win-win. As a matter of fact, you two can make some deposits tonight if you like. I mean, if you're into girls. Otherwise, we can think of something else. Tonight we're having a toga party!

"What about the souls of these children?" Theo asks.

"Huh?" That leaves Leo a little befuddled. He looks at John for clarification but John just shakes his head. "You know," Leo struggles to remember, "You're the second person to ever ask me that. Someone else asked me that not too long ago."

"Who?" John wants to know.

"I can't remember," Leo answers honestly. He gets back to business aiming his question directly at John, "So, we can really use you as a member and membership has its privileges. Now, seeing as your consultant is with you I can probably get him on the program as well. Maybe the lawyer you brought. Unless you have any family you want in on this. Are you in?"

John looks over at Theo who inside is seething. He needs to diffuse the situation without committing to anything. He looks back at Leo with a big smile on his face and says just one word but he says it over and over again, "Toga." But he re-enacts the John Belushi role in 'Animal House' as he raises the volume each time he says it, eventually getting to the point that the character "John "Bluto" Blutarsky" did by jumping up and down with every chant, "TOGA, TOGA, TOGA!"

His sophomoric antic is just what Leo wants and it plays into his sensibilities so well that Leo joins him in the chant as the two of them jump up and down like frat boys while Theo, the lone adult in the room, looks on.

As silly as it looks Theo realizes what John is doing is brilliant. Theo could've easily let his emotions get the better of him and cause a scene but by acting in this way John has Leo believing wholeheartedly that these guys are "his kind of guys" and in doing so, melts away any suspicions Leo may have had as to why the mysterious "Alchemist" come out of hiding after all these years and not only be able to return the stolen coins but deliver the thief himself and somehow convince the most dangerous man in the world to come out for the weekend and visit the same people that he stole from and have his daughter with them. All that from a stupid dance.

When they reach the ninth-floor penthouse suite Rainbow drags him through the threshold with his arm over her shoulders. She helps him across the huge marble floor into the bedroom and drops him on the large circular bed.

"Who are your friends?" She asks heading into the bathroom to wipe his sweat and grime off.

"They're my ride here," he answers in the same everyday tone.

"What are you doing here?" She asks as if he crashed her middle school sleepover.

This attitude finally gets him. He sits up in the bed, albeit very painfully, "I came here for you! I thought whoever tried to kill me took you!"

She hurries out of the bathroom and bends over so that her face is close to his when she says," I tried to kill you!"

The sound of it cuts right through him as she made sure she could see his face when she said it.

His lips pucker to first try to say "What?" but it doesn't come out. He does eventually push out a tear-filled,"W-why?"

"Because you were in my way- DUH!"

He sits on the edge of the bed looking down at the zip ties around his wrists unable to speak while she checks her hair in the mirror. "Oh come on! Don't act all surprised now! You taught me how to shake down drug lords and avoid cops. Don't act all surprised that I'm not daddy's little girl!"

"What did they offer you?"

"Away out of your shadow and out of your grip. You were never going to let me do the things I want to do! I wouldn't want it to be a bad reflection on you! Tonight, they're going to have me perform. I've been here rehearsing for weeks. I have a whole team and a band behind me."

"You can't trust these people! They're not family!"

"I have a family."

Ed is even more bewildered. Only a daughter can make the world's greatest criminal look like a complete idiot including a wide-open mouth when he responds, "What? Who?"

The door leading to the next bedroom opens and Ed's mother Lucia comes out as she's been listening to them the whole time and waiting for the right time, "Hi, Eddie."

Ed stands up and probably for the first time in his adult life stutters,"M-m-mom?"

The two women embrace each other. Lucia, being only a few years older, looks more like a big sister than a grandmother.

Ed uses both hands raised to point at her, "That isn't your grandmother! Look at her! You're the same age!"

"It doesn't matter! We had a blood test done!" Rainbow getting angrier and more aggressive, "You told me you adopted me but Lucia and Ed are my real grand-parents! You used my mother and then told me that I wasn't really yours. What kind of sick game is that?"

"I loved your mother." Ed murmurs.

"YOU RAPED HER! And then ruined her life!" Lucia has to hold her back from attacking him. Ed turns and walks away trying to come to terms that he is the cause of all this. That he had created a monster who hated him and for good reason. He has problems coming up with the next thing to say. He can't really look them in the eye right now so he walks over to the glass doorway leading out to the balcony and while resting his bound forearms on the glass looks out over the beautiful view. He looks out over the lush greenery and from this height can look out over the entire island. He watches as Air Force One touches down on the runway followed shortly by the C-141 Starlifter support plane carrying the President's limo referred to as "The Beast."

As a businessman, he sees it's a good deal. Too good of a deal for his liking. He knows these people. "What do they want in return?"

"You," she says with no warmth or empathy as if this was a run-of-the-mill business deal.

Ed gets lost in the gravity of it all. He's trapped on an island run by real-life Bond villains who are having a party, attended by The President of the United States where the headline attraction is his daughter where his dead mother will be in attendance. But just beyond the runway, over the canopy of trees he can see a meadow, and out past that is a dilapidated building. It looks like a quaint motel that he's seen before, maybe even stayed at. "Oh God," he blurts out when he recognizes The Way Station Hotel.

Just then, his mother puts her hand on his shoulder and whispers, "I can't go back there. They're releasing your father too. He can't take the torture anymore. You'll be saving us and her. It's a good deal. Three souls for the price of one. He must want you pretty badly."

"The things we do for our children, huh?" Ed chuckles as he takes in the enormity of it all. His parents and his daughter conspiring with the devil to send him to Hell for eternity. But now, Ed knows the players and sees their motivations and like in a business deal sees through the lies.

His mother corrects him, "More like the things we do TO our children."

GET THE HELL OUT OF HERE

The toga party was in full swing and both Theo and John are out by the pool sipping on drinks in full Roman regalia (with shorts and tee shirts hidden underneath) like a modern-day "Jan and Dean" amazed that there are "two girls for every boy" though most of the "boys" are dirty old men and some of them don't enjoy the company of girls. There's plenty of eye candy for them, too.

As self-conscious as they might've been about their own dress, neither of them could take their eyes off Thade, the large black man wearing a heavy leather coat over a dark hoodie on a tropical island. He's the only one not drinking. He's the only one not smiling. Actually, he looks like he's crying.

"Who is that guy?" John asks holding his glass up to his lips so the cameras can't pick up what he's saying. John knows they have cameras all over the place to record the dalliances that go on here for future blackmail and he's pretty sure they have professional lip readers on duty watching all the footage.

"I don't know," Theo confesses.

"Do you think he's a player?" John questions.

"Could be," Theo admits.

" I don't know, Viz," John relates, "We figured Ed would take out the security and Max would handle the Secret Service. I don't remember Leo having a personal body-guard. He never stays too far away from him. This guy could be a wild card."

The large man cuts through the crowd like a shark and the guppies get out of his way. Whenever he passes by a group chatting their laughter is cut short as they collectively hold their breath as he walks by. It's only when he's out of earshot do they let out a sigh of relief and resume frivolity.

At the next moment, Leo comes over to check on them, "I just got word that my second esteemed guest, POTUS has just landed and is headed over here. When he gets here we've got some business we have to take care of but we'll all catch up for dinner tonight."

"Say, Leo, who's the big guy walking behind you?"

"Oh, that's Thaddeus Isidor. But he likes to go by Thade." Leo explains as Thade gets close.

Theo sticks out his hand as a friendly gesture, " Hi Thade! I'm Theo. How do you spell that? T-H-A-D-E?"

Thade doesn't answer nor does he shake hands.

"Thade's not big on touching," Leo says apologetically.

"Geez, give the guy a break! This isn't a spelling bee!" John chides.

Leon slides up to Leo's ear and whispers loud enough for them to hear, "The Beast just rolled up."

"Have him come in," Leo responds as if it's obvious.

"He says he doesn't have time and doesn't want to be seen. I'm taking him straight to the temple," Leon recommends.

Leo agrees, "Have the lamb brought down, too."

Leo puts a smile back on his face to address his guests, "Gentlemen, please excuse me. I'll see you later tonight." He quickly makes his leave and Thade follows behind.

"Here we go," John says nervously. "What was that all about with the spelling of the name?"

"I think I know what Thade is," Theo responds softly.

"Will he be a problem?"

"God, I hope not."

John reacts to that answer, "Should I be worried?"

"No. Everything is going to plan. I'll start it, Max is going to do his thing and when they retaliate, that's when you come in. Then it's up to Max." Theo states reassuringly.

"The Beast isn't coming here it's going to the temple. Do you think that will throw Max off?"

"Let's go inside. The show is about to begin."

The same four armed guards that were assigned to Ed before are back to take him away. There are no words spoken and no one looks anyone else in the eye as he leads the group to the elevator without having to be pushed, prodded, or even asked. No words are spoken on the elevator as all five men look straight ahead watching the lit numbers change to L.

But once outside it's a different story. Whether they were ordered or just naturally sadistic they start hitting Ed as he tries to walk to the temple. The first blow was a billy club behind his knee stopping him in his tracks. As he crumbles the men hit him again. But the beating they give him goes beyond orders or even enjoyment but out of frustration. For no matter how hard they hit him they can't get him to react- not even an "OW." "How can this be?" They ask each other through their eyes. When passerbies notice and stop to watch is when the men help the badly beaten man up from the ground and escort him to the temple.

Ed looks out through his quickly swelling eye to see a large black Cadillac with two flags on either side of the front hood. One is the flag of the United States and the other is the Presidential seal. It's parked right where they are walking to. The blue and white striped building sitting on top of a hill that Leo calls "the temple."

There are only two other vehicles parked about forty yards away from each other in the circular driveway that makes up the courtyard. One is the Klein-Vision where Max stands like a statue holding his hands and a grey nondescript passenger van with two very bored-looking men sitting inside both dressed like naval officers.

Ed makes eye contact with Max or at least looks at his sunglasses. Max mouthes some words to him hoping Only Ed can see them. Which he can but not well from this distance. The only word he can make out from the plosives push of his lips and the exaggerated movement of his tongue is "PLAN."

He scoffs and shakes his head and thinks to himself, "Yeah, this was part of your plan, buddy. To sell me out and let me get my ass kicked?"

But, in the moment of clarity allowed to him by the guards not wailing on him, he does let a glimmer of hope in. Though it would be quite convenient to think that Max gave him that powerful speech the night before as a way of "selling in" on the concept that they wouldn't turn on him as soon as they got there. It wouldn't be like Max, in the limited interactions he's had with him, to be supportive in Ed's most dire moment of need unless there was some sort of a "plan." And that whole line about "the plan being the plan" was a little too glib for The Visionary especially with the stakes so high. It's not like one of Ed's "goomba" buddies from New Jersey telling him "it is what it is" like that was some kind of sage observation. But he could no longer rely on that or nor should he. He got himself into this mess and it was up to him to see it through.

While inside the main house, Theo and John were entering the living room where Lupe was holding court around a huge sectional sofa for all of those attendees not invited to the ceremony in the temple. As big as the house is it still seems crowded with people coming out to and fro.

The room was littered with attractive teenage men and women scantily dressed being chased and fondled by older, much wealthier men. Some of the men are quite recognizable to them.

John points to a man in his forties grabbing a young boy's ass as they pass by, "Hey, isn't that the director of those comic book movies?"

As Theo turns to look, a young girl reaches out to touch the back of his toga. He spins in the other direction as he asks, "Who touched me?"

He catches a glimpse of an adorable blonde girl being dragged and led away by an angry older man. She looks back at Theo in a silent desperate plea she silently mouthes the words "Help me" through her bleeding lips. It's apparent to anyone watching and he's the only one watching that she didn't show much enthusiasm to his advance and he made her pay for it physically.

The two of them sit on one of two modular couches each shaped like horseshoes with two gaps for people to come and go with a glass coffee table in the center. On the opposite couch is Lupe having drinks and entertaining the crowd.

"So," Theo says directed at Lupe but loud enough for all to hear, "do you live here as well? I can't imagine Mr. Epstein to have the artistic flair to purchase an original Diego Rivera," pointing to the painting on the far wall.

Lupe sits up intrigued by this stranger, "So, are you a fan of Diego Rivera?"

"Nooo," the word trails off as Theo searches for the right words to say, "I consider him more of a pleasure-seeking racist who was no better than the cavemen who drew on walls a hundred thousand years before him."

"A racist?" She reacts angered and insulted, "Those are strong words coming from a gringo!"

John gets up off the sofa announcing, "I'm going to get another drink."

"You must admit that someone who followed the philosophy of Vasconcelos and his "La Raza Cosmica" and lobbied for the implementation of eugenics is no better than the NAZIs that hunted down the forefathers of your business partners. You see, Diego didn't believe in God. But you and I and your business partners know better. Why else would you have a building called the temple? Tell me, what goes on in there? Is it similar to what went on in Templo Mayor?"

"What are you talking about?" Lupe asks equal parts defensive and confused.

"Tell me," Theo starts calmly but going in for the philosophical kill, "what do you do with the tears?"

"What?" She asks angry and lost.

"When the Aztecs sacrificed children they made them suffer for hours just to collect their tears offer up to the Rain God. I was wondering if you collected these young girl's tears."

"How dare you!" Is her only response.

John returns with a drink in each hand just as she yells out. He then gulps down both drinks.

"What is it you do for Circle L Investments besides luring teenagers to these parties? Do you import the fentanyl from the Chinese to distribute to the cartels or do you provide the caravans to the coyotes? Or maybe you're the Dark Priestess to the Narco saints."

She shoots up in a rage," SHUT YOUR FAT WHITE MOUTH! WHO ARE YOU TO JUDGE ME?"

Everyone in the room cowers back in hushed silence except Theo who shoots up to shut her down, "Don't forget, Mamacita, you are a descendant of the white Spaniards that came here. Perhaps the women in your lineage provided young girls for them like you are doing now.

Spaniards didn't just bring bloodshed to the new world, they brought God and you hate them for that to this day!"

"THAT'S RIGHT," she fires back not thinking about the fact that everyone in the room hears her and not really caring, " YOUR PRECIOUS GOD HAS LEFT YOU! WHY DOESN'T HE COME HERE TO PROTECT THESE CHILDREN?"

Theo actually chuckles at the thought, "God, to come here? He's not going to waste his time coming here. That's why he sent us!"

"Here we go," John says to himself preparing for what is about to happen.

Max watches as the guards lead Ed into the temple. Unbeknownst to the guards, Ed looks back at him one more time. Max signals him by tapping the bottom of his chin with the back of his hand. His message is to simply "keep your chin up."

It's not until the doors close behind them that Max says to himself aloud in an exhales, "Here we go." He then takes off his glasses and in a full sprint runs toward that nondescript van parked in front of the main house at full speed picking up enough momentum where he launches himself at the side of the van with so much force that it tips the vehicle over on its side.

The force of the hit and the ensuing landing on its side is so jarring that it knocks the driver, whose side the vehicle lands on, out cold. The passenger, who in a stroke of luck for Max and for some unknown reason, kept his seat belt on making it easier for Max to grab his arm that's handcuffed to a leather satchel.

"Sorry, kid," Max says apologetically as he punches down hitting the Naval Officer in that sweet spot on the jaw Ed loves so much sending the young sailor who was already reeling into a deep sleep, unable to defend himself or the package he's sworn to protect. And Max, with his maximized reflexes, moves too quickly for him to react if he could. Max stands on top of the passenger side of the van as he pulls upward on the van door like it's a hatch to get into a submarine and grabs the case and out of the vehicle stretching the chain holding it on the wrist.

He slams the door down on the chain snapping it in half. He then jumps down from the overturned van and runs into the house.

The occupants in the living room are stunned silent from the BOOM coming from outside when he bursts into the house. The crowd that was once focused on the fight between Lupe and Theo has turned all eyes toward this large man carrying a leather case. The look on his face at seeing the crowd standing around in togas is more confused than the expressions on theirs.

He then quietly makes his way to Theo and John and hands Theo the case, "What the hell are you wearing?"

"WHAT THE HELL IS GOING ON HERE? WHAT GAME ARE YOU PLAYING?" Lupe demands.

Theo holds up the leather case in his possession, "Football."

Theo places the case on the glass coffee table and opens it to go through the contents while the party-goers look on with mouths agape.

Theo pulls out a black binder and opens the cover reading the title aloud, "Classified Strike Sites...nope!" He tosses it in the air. He digs into the bag and pulls out another binder about the same size and reads that aloud, "Presidential Emergency Sites...nope." He then pulls out a Manila file folder and thumbs through the stapled pages inside of it, "Emergency Broadcast System Procedures...nope," as he tosses it in the air with the pages fluttering around behind him. He finally pulls out a laminated three-by-five card and announces with glee, "Launch Codes! Got 'em!" He holds them up in the air facetiously as if everyone is happy he found them.

He then pulls out a metallic briefcase and cracks it open," Wow, I thought that would be more difficult."

"WHAT ARE YOU DOING?" Lupe screams.

"Did you think you could escape God's wrath?" Theo asks angrily.

"Give that to me NOW OR DIE!" She demands with her voice getting eerily guttural.

He holds the case out in front of him and taunts her by saying, "COME DEMON, FETCH!!"

Two of her Security Guard Detail burst into the room from the back with guns drawn.

"KILL HIM!" She commands.

What happens next will be the most talked-about part of the whole confrontation and solidifies John's reputation among the jet set. He reaches out and grabs Theo's arm and Max's hand and when the bullets strike them, piercing through their clothing and instantly changing their composition as soon as touching their skin and becoming harmlessly soft. The Alchemist was able to transfer his ability to change the compounds of matter to his cohorts by simply touching them and willing it.

The whole room, including the shooters, stare in shock at what they just saw. All except Max who leaps into action and with his superhuman speed disarms the two guards and knocks them silly, totally eliminating any threat they once held. While they are still reeling he goes through their pockets taking away mace sprayers and handcuffs he uses to bind them together.

"Come, Demon! Show them you're true self and come attack me!" Theo invites her threateningly.

Now called out for who she really is and unable to scare them tries reasoning, "What are you going to do? You can't launch missiles by yourself."

"So you won't mind if I hit a few switches," he taunts as he presses a few buttons and activates something causing lights to come on. He looks around the room and everyone holds their breath.

He then turns to his friends and ponders aloud, "Do you think other countries are alerted when this thing is activated?"

"I hope not," Max answers, "What do you think they'll do?"

They practically have to drag Ed into the temple. It turns out the white and blue striped construct we see from the outside is just the lobby. The lobby is brightly lit with gold marble and a baby grand piano. There are four Secret Service men in the room all standing around looking at each other when the four guards lead him in. The Secret Service members have surely seen odd things over the years but a man, wrists tied and badly beaten being led in by a private security team into a building called "the temple" where their boss, the President of these United States, who against protocol told them not to enter, is quite disturbing.

Even JIM MERRYMAN who's been in for fifteen years wonders what the hell is going on and whether he should call this in, ask for a transfer as soon as he gets back, or just outright quit. He can't take his eyes off the bloody and beaten captive.

Ed just smiles as he goes by and greets them with a "fellas." All they can do is nod as he's led down some stone steps and gone from sight.

One of the detail shrugs his shoulders at Jim and is about to say something when they hear a loud

BOOM. One of them even looks up thinking it's thunder. But when they hear a secondary CRASH they realize something is wrong. They run outside to find their van laying on its side.

They rush over to find both Navy men out cold.

"CHECK ON THE FOOTBALL!" Merryman commands.

A voice comes over the comlink, "Football is negative. Let's sweep out to recover!"

"NEGATIVE, Belay that order! First secure POTUS!" Merryman orders.

The three other agents run back to the temple. Merryman points at one of them, stopping him in his tracks, "Give them medical attention! You two come with me!"

Once downstairs Ed is brought to a subterranean room with stone walls and floors and lit only by torches. There are fifty or so figures in hooded robes standing in a semicircle around a stone table on an elevated altar.

"Well, well, the gang's all here! Thanks for having me over for dinner, fellas! You are having me for dinner, right?"

Leon is the first one to pull down his hood to reveal himself, "No, Edward but the ritual does call for you to still be living when we cut your heart out, or else it doesn't work," he says with glee.

Ed's face curls up not in fear but in disgust, "Jesus Christ!"

Leon grabs a rifle from one of the soldiers and hits Ed with it. "How dare you say that name!"

Ed falls to the floor on his knees and elbows. He tries to catch his breath.

"You know, Ed," Leo pulls down his mask revealing himself to Ed, "it couldn't be working out better if we planned it. The one Goyim who always got the better of us. Who we could never beat no matter how many times we tried to destroy his business. The one, who it turns out, was more of an evil son of a bitch than evil Leon here. The one who was always too good to come to one of my parties is now here in front of us as helpless as a lamb."

"WHERE'S YOUR JESUS CHRIST NOW?" Leon screams at him.

Ed raises himself off the floor to this knees, his hands still bound together but his fingers are pressed together as if he just said a prayer, he snaps the zip ties off like they were paper and takes his right hand and does the sign of the cross before saying, "I just spoke to him. You're not going to like what he said."

Ed jumps up and in one smooth motion snatches the rifle out of Leon's grasp and shoots all four guards before the first one can lift up his rifle. He takes three of the rifles and tosses them onto the stone table.

There's banging on the other side of the large, thick metal door that is their only way in or out of the room. Merryman calls out to the President, "MR. PRESIDENT, ARE YOU IN THERE?"

President Joe Simon pulls down his hood, "YES! YES! I'M IN HERE! PLEASE GET ME OUT! THERE'S A MADMAN WITH A GUN!"

Ed fires a couple of rounds at the stone wall above the door that ricochet through the room freaking out all the hooded occupants, "Just relax, fellas. Everything is A-O-K."

"I'm going to have to call this into the director, " Merryman reports.

"NO! Don't call it in!" Peter Simon, the president's brother yells out.

Theo, Max, and John walk outside to an eerie quiet. Max looks over to see if the Naval officers in the van are still breathing and checks their pulse. He gives them a thumbs up.

"You think Ed's OK?" John asks.

"I don't know. Let's go get him and get out of here.

A low flying drone comes swooping down out of nowhere and blares out of its speakers in a robotic voice repeating: THIS IS THE PEOPLE'S LIBERATION ARMY NAVY. WE WILL COMMENCE BOMBING OPERATIONS IMMEDIATELY UNLESS ALL AGGRESSION IS CEASED. THIS IS THE PEOPLE'S LIBERATION ARMY NAVY. WE WILL COMMENCE BOMBING OPERATIONS IMMEDIATELY UNLESS ALL AGGRESSION IS CEASED.

Merryman bangs on the door, "SIR, DO YOU HAVE THE FOOTBALL?"

The President replies, "No, I don't have it!"

"Sir, someone has the football and activated it" Merryman reports. "Sir, there's a drone flying around outside from the People's Liberation Army Navy stating they are going to commence bombing. What shall I do?"

"FIND THE GOD DAMN BUTTON AND SHUT IT OFF!" The President screams.

"Sir, we're getting reports that there are some Chinese ships in the area. They were doing joint maneuvers with the Russian navy near Cuba. Hold for more info," Merryman relays back.

Ed thinks to himself, "People's Liberation Army Navy... the plan." Then he says out loud laughing and shaking his head, "The plan is the PLAN."

We can tell by his on again off again cadence that someone is feeding Merryman info through his com-link and he's repeating it back as soon as he hears it, "Sir, I'm getting reports of a Type 055 Cruiser with 112 cell VLS, a Type 075 Amphibious Assault Ship, a Type 071 Amphibious Transport Dock and a Type 096

Jin Class nuclear sub all within striking range and closing in."

"All that firepower just happens to be in the neighborhood doing maneuvers?" Ed asks loudly to the President. "I think they're upset they weren't invited to the party."

The President yells at Ed, "You've got to let us out of here!"

"Let me think about it," Ed replies.

"KNOCK THE DAMN DOOR DOWN! GET US OUT OF HERE!" The President calls out.

Silence.

The men get closer to listen if someone is still out there. They creep too close to the door when it BLOWS OPEN WITH A BOOM blowing the hooded men back on their asses. Then the room fills with smoke...but it's not smoke...it's residual gas. When it clears, the only one who walks through the door is Max.

"Hey Ed, the government has more weapons and knockout gas in that van than you ever had," Max says holding a rifle of his own. He's followed by Theo and John both wearing gas masks.

"He's got the football!" The President yells
pointing at Theo.

Theo approaches Ed as he pulls off the gas mask.
"Yeah, we had to knock out those Secret Service guys.
I hope they're OK. So let's get out of here."

President Simon steps up and commands, "I am the
President of the United States and I order you to give
me that device! NOW!"

"SHUT UP, DUMMY!" Theo fires back so forcibly and
with such venom that everyone including Ed takes a
step back, "You had one job! Protect the nuclear codes!
You fluffed the economy on your idiot brother but this
is the one thing you had to protect!"

"He's right," Ed says, "You've got to shut that thing off.
The Chinese military is homing in on it. They are
going to rain hell on us any minute now."

"I know. Everyone is evacuating. The islanders are
heading for the boats and the workers are heading for
the plane."

Leon and Leo step up. Ed takes a step between them.
Leon, being the bigger and ballsier of the two pipes up,
"Get out of our way! This man came as an outsider and

now he wants to play judge? When Thade gets here he's gonna fuck you in the ass!"

"Look at these animals," Theo motions to Ed, "You used to be one of them. Now, you're one of us. And we're leaving. So let's go."

"But there are innocent-"

"Innocent?" Theo cuts him off, "Have you seen all the children trapped in that hospital? There are embryos, fetuses, developing children trapped in incubators just to be body parts and you want to talk of innocents? How many of them are there in this room? Fifty?" Theo motions toward the crowd of hooded men. "How many of them are righteous? Forty? Thirty? How about one? Which one of these Godless pagans is worth saving?"

"What about my daughter?"

"She's one of them now. I'm sorry. It all goes."

"Listen to me! I've seen the future! Remember, the vision I had- I thought it was a dream. It was real! I see now that it was real! I told you it was like a nuclear bomb had dropped and all the trees were dead and all the wildlife was mutated and the place stunk of death. It was here! I recognized the old hotel! I was shown what this place will turn into if we go to war and nukes are dropped. I was sent here to stop it! Everything I've gone through was to prepare me for this moment! Your hate for these people has blinded you and you've been so hell-bent on destroying this world that you don't realize that the Devil might be using you to his means to bring Hell here to Earth by causing a nuclear war!" We're playing right into his hand! He's playing both sides against each other! He's hedging his bet! It's what I would do!

Theo takes in what Ed has just said and looks around the room for reaction. Max is focused on anyone moving and John shrugs his shoulders as if to say, "he may have a point."

"I'll leave it to you. You will be the arbiter. You know both sides- there's and ours- and if what you're saying is true then you were sent here to make the choice on whether they live or die."

"Tick tock, gentlemen," John says reminding them that bombs are coming."

Theo hands Ed the football. Max comes over to remind Ed, "We kept up our end of the agreement." He reaches out and shakes Ed's hand.

The three of them make their way to the door. The men in robes back away cutting a clear path for them, first the Visionary then the Alchemist followed by Max Po.

The three of them exit the temple and make their way down the hill. The drones have stopped buzzing around making alerts and whoever was free to leave has now fled the island. Max presses a button on a keychain and we hear TWO BEEPS before the sound of the engine kick over. The car, run on water, is much quieter than a gas engine but Max likes to rev it up as the car races toward them and screeches to a stop.

After the doors raise open but before they get in a LOUD SCREAMING WHISTLE from an incoming missile comes screeching down from above and shoots straight into the side of the hill only about ninety feet behind them. The missile shoots into the ground like a dart shooting up dirt and leaving a hole only as wide as the missile itself. But a low murmur can be heard of the projectile burrowing deeper into the ground.

"LET'S GET THE HELL OUT OF HERE!" John yells.

"I told you the Chinese had a tracker on that thing!" Theo says as they dive in the moving car.

Ed places the suitcase on the ground and President Simon and he kneels down to deactivate it.

They HEAR A DULL THUD when the missile hits the ground somewhere above them.

It loosens some stones in the ceiling and dirt falls upon their heads when BA-BOOM!

It's not a nuclear bomb but having the device implanted fifteen meters into the earth makes the devastation increase by a factor of twenty.

The ceiling above them as well as the floor below them crumbles causing a giant crater. The earth below them is hollow and the natural gas trapped underneath ignites sending a fireball up all the way through the stone staircase and out the temple entrance.

A seemingly bottomless pit has formed below them as a lake of fire is created by the burning natural gas. Ed is the only one strong enough and with quick enough reflexes to grab hold of something before he falls into the inferno.

One by one, hooded men fall into the fire, each of them screaming in fear and agony. Some of them scratch to hold onto something but slide helplessly into the fiery abyss. The ones that were able to grab onto a ledge or something cannot hold on for long as the heat overcomes them.

Ed, hanging from his perch created by a jagged stone has to watch as each man falls into the flames and each one of their screams is embedded in his brain. The heat is becoming too much for him and it soaks the energy out of his body and he slowly loses consciousness.

Rather than face his fiery death, he looks up to find a hand reaching down to him. It's Max who is reaching down from the edge of the crater created by the blast. He himself is in a precarious position and it takes all his strength just to keep Ed from falling. Max's suit catching on fire and starts burning off his body. With his left hand, he tears his burning clothes off while holding onto Ed with his right. If not for his special black compression suit, Max would be burned alive.

EPILOGUE

For some reason, Theo decided to stretch his legs and go for a walk to buy a cup of coffee rather than make it at home. He was in the mood for something different. Once inside he took his place in a line that snaked around the cramped shop. With all those bodies in there and the coffee, brewing made the place hotter than...well...you know.

The BARISTA calls out to the crowd over the WHOOSH of the coffee brewer, " I HAVE AN ORDER FOR THE O? I'M SORRY! THE WAY? I HAVE AN ODER FOR THE O WAY? O WAY? A LARGE BLUEBERRY COFFEE!"

Ed looks at the other people in front of him. It couldn't have been for him since he hadn't even gotten to the counter. Not only were people looking at each other wondering who's it was but some were questioning out loud, "Who the hell drinks blueberry coffee?"

The Barista put that one off to the side and announced the next one, "LUCY FERN! LUCY FERN! I mean FORD! I HAVE A HOT TEA FOR LUCY FORD!"

Theo bursts into laughter and has to gain his composure while giving an embarrassed smile to the people ahead of him in line as the adorable Lucy Ford that worked for Circle L Investments grabs her hot tea and informs the Barista, "I have four more orders. I'll be back here waiting. I'll take this one too."

"Yes, ma'am" The Barista responds already in the weeds.

Theo greets the young woman with a big smile as he happily accepts the free coffee.

"Lucy Ford, Huh?"

"I hear you and I have a mutual acquaintance," she says with a smile.

"How is dear old dad?"

"I was referring to Edward Gennaro. How's he doing?"

"Last I heard they stuck him in a Super Max."

"That's not like him to give in so quickly."

"We offered him a place to stay but he wanted to come clean. He said he wanted to break the cycle. He called it the vicious circle."

"And he didn't turn you in?" She asks.

"Well, you heard the news reports. A surprise party for the President, a freak accident, blah, blah, blah. Nobody even questions it anymore. They were so happy he turned himself in that part of the deal was he'd go straight to prison without the death penalty if he forgoes a trial."

"He thinks he can hide from me in there." She scowls. "Well, it looks like you got your wish. They immediately gave a vote of no confidence to the veep and the secretary taking over and put in the speaker who immediately got rid of the Fed.

"Imagine that, impeached before you're even sworn in. What's next for you?"

"I think we're going to skew to a younger demographic. Trying to control the older generation with money and power didn't work out. We're going to go in a new direction and seduce the masses with fame, fortune, and glamor."

"LUCY FORD, YOUR ORDER IS UP!"

"I just wanted to congratulate you on your victory and reward you with a free cup of coffee."

She turns away and grabs the cup holder from The Barista holding four more cups.

"I was hoping you'd buy me lunch, " Theo says with a sly smile.

"You should know by now that there's no such thing as a free lunch." She says with a wink as he holds the door open for her as she walks out carrying her coffee and purse in one hand and four other coffees in the other.

She walks toward a parked limo where Thade comes around and opens the door for her where he sees Rainbow in the back along with her young grand-mother Lucia and her grandfather Edward.

He leans down to look into the limo, "Hi, I'm friends with your father," he says waving to Rainbow who ignores him as Lucy shuts the door. Thade sticks his hand out to keep him back but Theo knows better than to let Thade touch him. He backs away and waves as they drive off.

Even in prison, Ed uses his time wisely. He challenges himself to see how many burpees he can do nonstop. He was at eight hundred and eighty when someone pulls the lever on the door to the tray slot where he gets his food every day. He's given three meals a day in that cell and is supposed to be allowed out once a day for a shower and some time outdoors, but that doesn't always happen.

He stops his workout to examine what was left behind. A small flip phone is waiting for him. He tries looking out the small window to see who left it. "It must've been a guard," he reasons to himself as he flips it open to see if any names or numbers were programmed into it.

That's when it rings. He's not surprised when it does. He looks to see the number and of course, this is none. "Hello."

"Hiya sport! How goes it in the hoosegow?"

Ed's annoyance is not well hidden in his reply, "Hello, Virgil. How did you get a phone in here?"

"Oh, I've got my ways. Besides, you didn't expect me to let you go up the river without a kiss-off, did ya? They're all sayin' down here that you took the rap rather than take your chances on the outside. I say that you're trying to redeem yourself so hopefully, you don't come down here."

"Well, one man's purgatory is another man's paradise. Isn't that right?" Ed says as he gets comfortable on his hard bed.

"You said a mouthful!"

THE END

CPSIA information can be obtained
at www.ICGtesting.com
Printed in the USA
LVHW050006231121
704141LV00015B/473